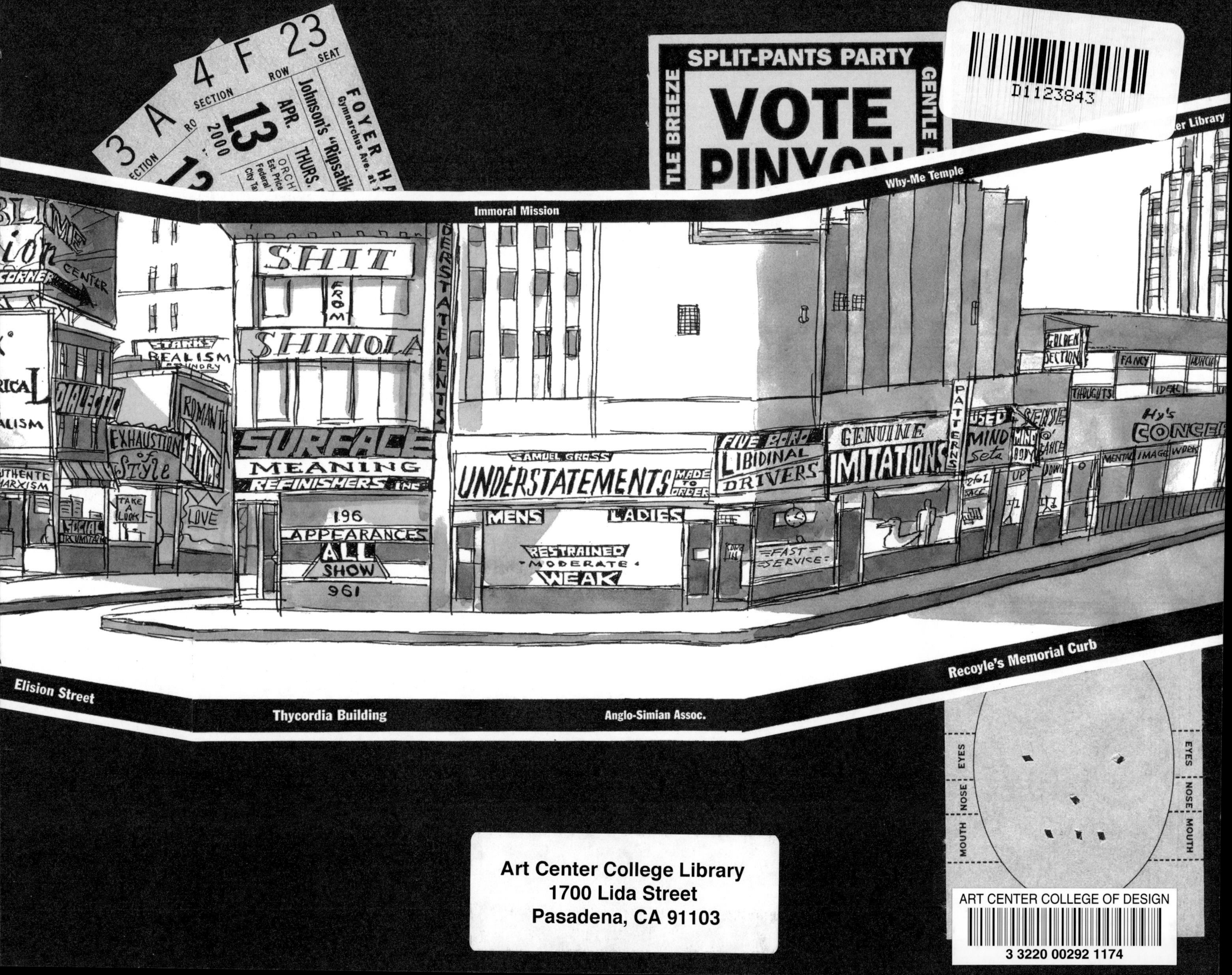
3 A
SECTION
4 F 23
SECTION ROW SEAT
FOYER
Johnson's "Ripsatik
APR. 13 2000
THURS.
SPLIT-PANTS PARTY
VOTE
PINYON
GENTLE BREEZE
Why-Me Temple
Immoral Mission
SHIT FROM SHINOLA
UNDERSTATEMENTS
STARK'S REALISM FOUNDRY
EXHAUSTION of Style
AUTHENTIC MARXISM
TAKE A LOOK
LOVE
SURFACE MEANING REFINISHERS INC
196 APPEARANCES ALL SHOW 961
SAMUEL GROSS
UNDERSTATEMENTS MADE TO ORDER
MENS
LADIES
RESTRAINED MODERATE WEAK
FIVE BORO LIBIDINAL DRIVERS
FAST SERVICE
GENUINE IMITATIONS
PATTERNS
USED MIND SETS
MIND BODY
UP
DOWN
SENSE O' CHANCE
GOLDEN SECTION
FANCY
THOUGHTS
IDEAL
Hy's CONCEP
MENTAL IMAGE WORK
Recoyle's Memorial Curb
Elision Street
Thycordia Building
Anglo-Simian Assoc.
EYES
NOSE
MOUTH

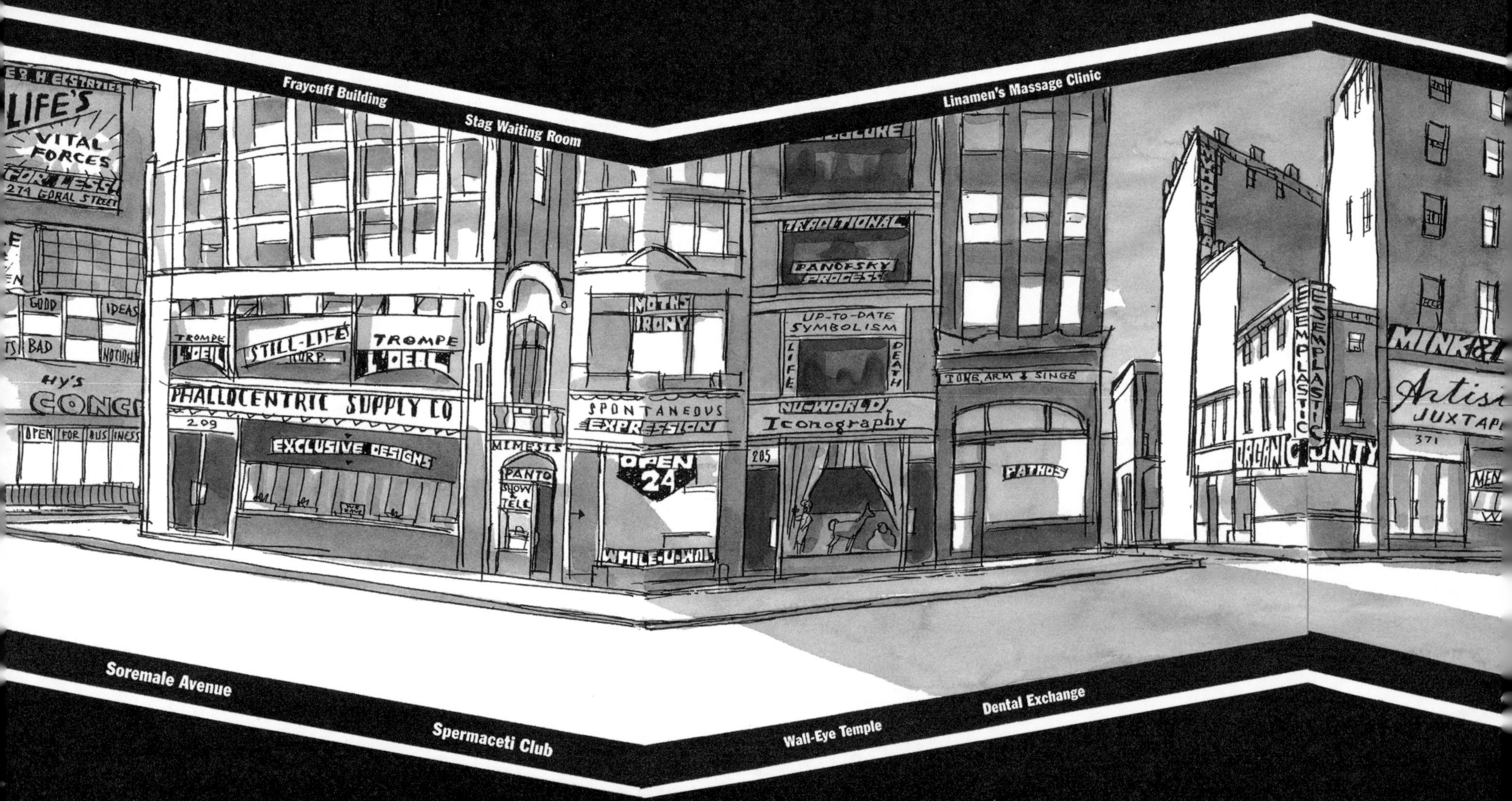
Fraycuff Building
Stag Waiting Room
Linamen's Massage Clinic
Soremale Avenue
Spermaceti Club
Wall-Eye Temple
Dental Exchange
LIFE'S
VITAL FORCES
274 GORAL STREET
GOOD
IDEAS
BAD
OPEN FOR BUSINESS
TROMPE L'OEIL
STILL-LIFE CORP.
PHALLOCENTRIC SUPPLY CO
209
EXCLUSIVE DESIGNS
MIMESIS
PANTO
SHOW & TELL
MOTHS
IRONY
SPONTANEOUS
EXPRESSION
OPEN 24
TRADITIONAL
PANOFSKY PROCESS
UP-TO-DATE SYMBOLISM
LIFE
DEATH
NU-WORLD
Iconography
205
TONE ARM & SINGS
PATHOS
ESEMPLASTIC
ORGANIC UNITY
371

Coin Bath

Outlet Avenue

JULIUS KNIPL, REAL ESTATE PHOTOGRAPHER:

THE
BEAUTY
SUPPLY
DISTRICT

BY

BEN KATCHOR

PANTHEON BOOKS
NEW YORK

SEE-THRU PRINTING CO., 37 Trepidarium Street. Endless Fold-Outs, Hard-to-Handle Brochures, Typo-graphic Force-Fits, Low-Visibility Flyers, Special Occasion Counterfeiting, Dept. of Health Toe-Tags, Loose Leaf Fall-Outs, Papercut Novelties, "Touch-Me-Not" Forms. Call for FREE Estimates.

Gumba Club

Tamper Street

Published in the United States by Pantheon Books, a division of Random House, Inc., New York, and in Canada by Random House of Canada Limited, Toronto.

Pantheon Books and colophon are registered trademarks of Random House, Inc.

The strips on pages 1–83 were originally published in *The Forward* and other newspapers from 1994 through 1997.

LIBRARY OF CONGRESS CATALOGING-IN-PUBLICATION DATA

Katchor, Ben.
[Julius Knipl, real estate photographer. Selections]
Julius Knipl, real estate photographer: the beauty supply district / Ben Katchor.
Selections from the author's comic strip, Julius Knipl, real estate photographer.
ISBN 0-375-40105-9 I. Title.
PN6727.K28 J84 2000 741.5973—dc21 99-055528

www.pantheonbooks.com

Designed by Ben Katchor

Printed in the United States of America
First Edition
2 4 6 8 9 7 5 3 1

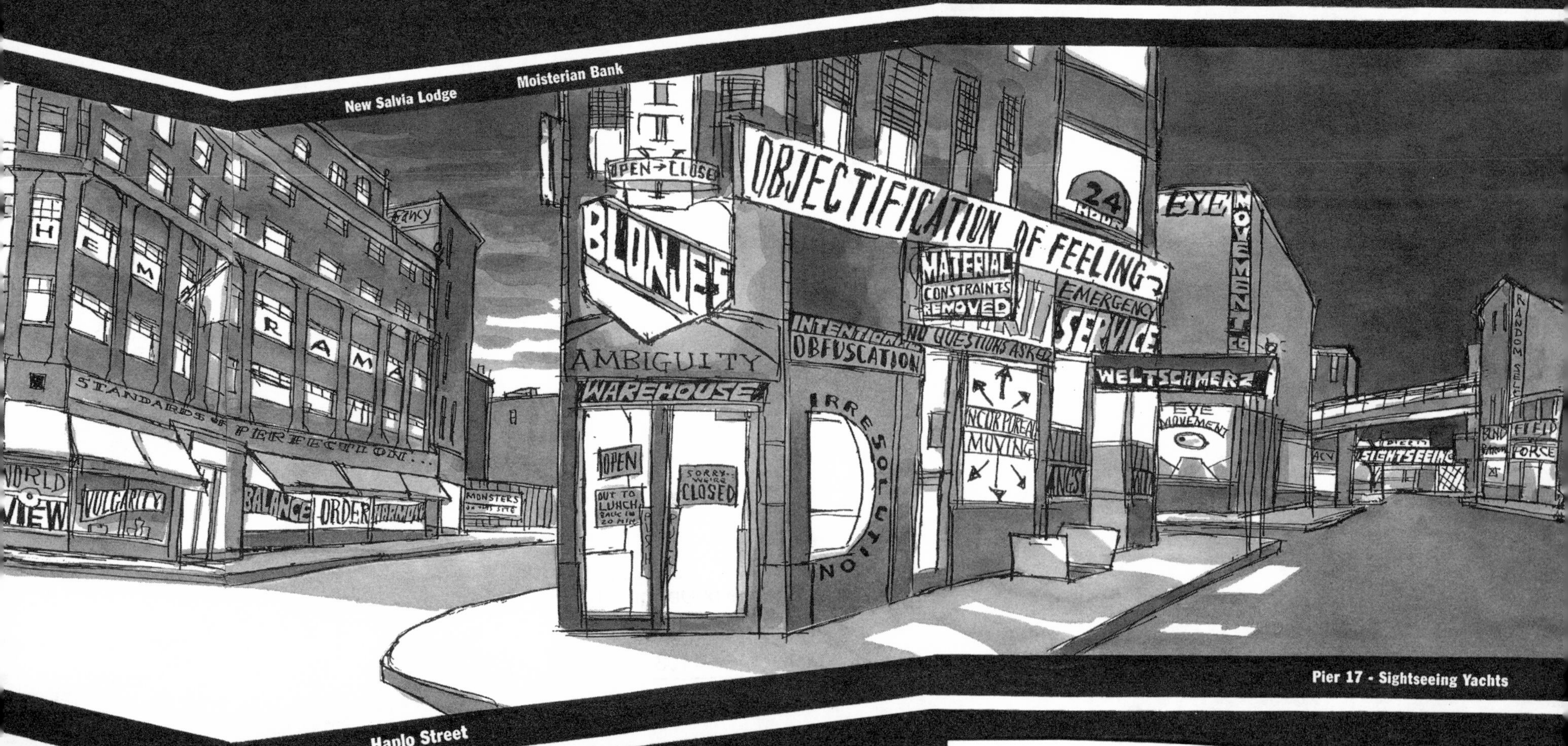
New Salvia Lodge
Moisterian Bank
HEMMORAMA
STANDARDS OF PERFECTION
WORLD VIEW
VULGARITY
BALANCE
ORDER
MONSTERS
OPEN→CLOSE
BLONJES
AMBIGUITY
WAREHOUSE
OPEN
SORRY WE'RE CLOSED
OBJECTIFICATION OF FEELING
MATERIAL CONSTRAINTS REMOVED
INTENTIONAL OBFUSCATION
NO QUESTIONS ASKED
EMERGENCY SERVICE
IRRESOLUTION
INCORPOREAL MOVING
ANGST
WELTSCHMERZ
EYE MOVEMENT
EYE MOVEMENT CO
24 HOUR
SIGHTSEEING
FIELD FORCE
RANDOM SELECT
Pier 17 - Sightseeing Yachts
Haplo Street

In Memory of
Harry Taube, M.D.

Nerve Quarry

Contents

Tomb of The Homely Man

ON ORNAMENTAL AVENUE,

THOUSANDS OF PEOPLE PASS BY EACH DAY...

THAT BROAD, TREE-LINED THOROUGHFARE ORIGINATING AT BEUKELSON CIRCLE

A MONUMENT TO THE INVENTOR OF PICKLED HERRING.

AND EXTENDING EASTWARD FOR TWENTY-FIVE LONG BLOCKS,

ARTERIAL HALL, A LEGITIMATE SURGICAL THEATER.

THERE STAND A NUMBER OF VENERABLE QUASI-PUBLIC INSTITUTIONS.

THE SHOESHINE PAVILION.

MOST, HAVING BEEN WELL-ENDOWED IN THE EARLY PART OF THIS CENTURY, CONTINUE TO OPERATE WITH LITTLE REGARD FOR COMMERCIAL OR POPULAR INTERESTS.

THE INSTITUTE FOR SOUP-NUT RESEARCH.

SOME OPEN THEIR DOORS FOR A FEW HOURS ON RAINY THURSDAY AFTERNOONS

THE HALITOSIS SOCIETY AND THE MUSEUM OF INSECT ART.

WHILE OTHERS HAVE LONG AGO DECIDED TO ELIMINATE THE WEAR AND TEAR CAUSED BY CASUAL VISITORS.

THE MUNICIPAL LAXATIVE GARDEN AND THE KATSIGH COLLECTION OF WORN SHOES AND BROKEN LACES.

IN THIS SITUATION, ONE FORESIGHTED PUBLISHER OF SOUVENIR POST-CARDS SEES A GOLDEN OPPORTUNITY.

...AND LEAVE WITH NOTHING TO REMIND THEM OF WHAT THEY'VE SEEN.

EARLY THAT SUNDAY MORNING, A TRUCK STOPS BEFORE THE MAIN ENTRANCE TO THE NATIONAL RECTAL THERMOMETER OBSERVATORY.

WHILE TWO MEN SWEEP THE SIDEWALK

A THIRD MAN ADJUSTS THE POSITION OF STRAY BRANCHES

ONE INCH TO MY RIGHT.

AND CHASES AWAY THE LESS PHOTOGENIC PIGEONS.

SHOO!

AN EXPOSURE IS MADE, AND THE TRUCK MOVES ON A DOZEN YARDS

TO A POSITION DIRECTLY ACROSS FROM THE MUNICIPAL BIRTHMARK REGISTRY,

MOLE   NEVUS · FRECKLE.   BEAUT

THEY PROCEED, IN THIS WAY, TO PHOTOGRAPH THE OUTSTANDING BUILDINGS AND MONUMENTS ALONG ORNAMENTAL AVENUE.

GUM BOIL PARK, THE ASSOCIATION FOR THE PROMOTION OF WIRE HANGERS, THE PAJAMA MISSION SOCIETY...

THE PUBLISHER OF THE FORTHCOMING POSTCARD SERIES, "25 VIEWS OF ORNAMENTAL AVENUE," SLEEPS LATE THAT MORNING.

A CORNER OF A WAREHOUSE FILLED WITH THE UNSOLD COPIES OF AN ILL-CONCEIVED SET OF POSTCARDS.

"TWENTY-FIVE VIEWS OF ORNAMENTAL AVENUE"

THE PUBLISHER CHEERFULLY ADMITS HIS MISTAKE.

I OVER-ESTIMATED THE PICTURESQUE QUALITY OF THE LOCATION.

WHAT GOES ON BEHIND THE WALLS OF THE HEATING PAD INSTITUTE IS OF NO CONCERN TO THE CASUAL TOURIST

AND IF A VISITING SCHOLAR HAD WANTED TO SEND A POSTCARD HOME TO HIS WIFE,

WHY WOULD HE CHOOSE THIS SAD VIEW, PHOTOGRAPHED ON AN OVERCAST SUNDAY IN FEBRUARY?

The Heating Pad Institute

A FEW WORN SETS REMAIN ON A WIRE RACK NEXT TO THE CLOAKROOM OF THE WETSPOT FOUNDATION—

SOMETHING TO LOOK AT WHILE YOUR COAT IS BEING RETRIEVED—

BUT FOR MOST PEOPLE, ONE VIEW OF ORNAMENTAL AVENUE IS ENOUGH.

IN THE TIME OF A VAST PUBLIC WORKS PROJECT

THE STENCILING OF IDENTIFICATION NUMBERS ONTO IMMOVABLE CITY PROPERTY.

ONE TELEVISION STATION DECIDES TO FILL ITS AIR-TIME, 24 HOURS A DAY, WITH THE ANNOUNCEMENT OF ALL THE LOSING NUMBERS IN THAT WEEK'S LOTTERY.

17, 8, 11, 2, 4, 31... 9, 15, 3, 25, 6...

THAT WAS MY LUCKY NUMBER.

IT'S HOPELESS.

YOU'D HAVE MORE OF A CHANCE TO MAKE A FORTUNE IMPORTING HOT TOWELS FROM TURKEY...

OR BREEDING CODFISH FOR PASSOVER IN YOUR BATHTUB ...ANYTHING!

THE PUBLIC RELATIONS MAN FOR A FAMOUS MANUFACTURER OF NON-SKID BATHMATS ROUTINELY BRIBES A CITY CLERK TO SKIP CERTAIN NUMBERS.

YOU SHOULD LOOK INTO AN EARLY RETIREMENT.

YOU MUST KNOW ALL SIX DIGITS!

THESE NUMBERS ARE SOLD, IN TURN, TO VARIOUS PRIVATE CAR SERVICES TO BE SILK-SCREENED ONTO WINDOW CARDS.

CAR 831649, A BLUE SPORTULA, WILL BE THERE IN FIFTEEN MINUTES.

OCEAN FLOOR INDUSTRIES

AH, THAT'S MY NUMBER!

PECCAVI 831649

THE LIFE OF AN INSTITUTIONAL BLANKET CAN NOW BE PROLONGED INDEFINITELY.

OH, HIM... PUT HIM IN ROOM 417.

THE DAMAGE AND WEAR CAUSED BY A MULTITUDE OF RESTLESS SLEEPERS PASSING THROUGH A SINGLE HOTEL BED IN ONE YEAR

GNAWED BINDINGS, CIGARETTE BURNS AND SODA STAINS...

CAN BE REVERSED, OVERNIGHT, AT THE DE LEÓN BLANKET REJUVENATION PLANT ON AURAPON AVENUE.

REPLACED, REWOVEN AND REMOVED!

THE VERY NAP OF A WOOLEN BLANKET IS RESTORED TO ITS FORMER GLORY BY MEANS OF A HIGH-SPEED, CENTRIFUGAL BRUSH.

JUST A TOUCH OF RED LIPSTICK...

THE BLANKETS WHICH LEAVE THE PLANT IN THE MORNING ARE, IN EFFECT, NEW.

ONLY ONE THIRTY-SECOND OF AN INCH LOST IN LENGTH AND WIDTH.

A TRAVELING SALESMAN WOULD HAVE TO BE GIVEN THE SAME BED AND BLANKET

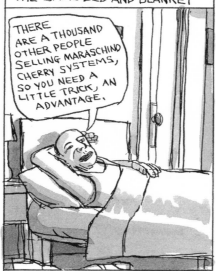

THERE ARE A THOUSAND OTHER PEOPLE SELLING MARASCHINO CHERRY SYSTEMS, SO YOU NEED A LITTLE TRICK, AN ADVANTAGE.

EACH TIME HE PASSED THROUGH TOWN, OVER THE COURSE OF A FORTY-YEAR CAREER,

WHEN IT COMES TIME TO PLACE AN ORDER, THEY MAY HAVE FORGOTTEN ME, BUT NOT MY LIPS!

IN ORDER TO NOTICE THIS SLIGHT SHRINKAGE.

SEE YOU NEXT SPRING!

FROM UPSTAIRS, COMES THE SOUND OF A MARITAL QUARREL.

YOU BASTARD! NOW I SEE WHAT YOU ARE!

WHERE'S MY CAMERA?! LET A JUDGE SEE WHAT YOU DO TO ME!

A RUBBER TUBE, STRETCHED ACROSS THE QUIET STREET, COUNTS PASSING CARS.

YOU BASTARD! NOW YOU'RE FINISHED WITH ME! NOW YOU WANT A FREE LIFE!

I WAS A COWARD, AND NOW MY LIFE IS A MISERY!

WHERE, FOR THIRTY YEARS, A FAMOUS DISCOUNT MATTRESS SHOWROOM STOOD, THERE IS NOW AN EMPTY LOT

THREE HUNDRED PER HOUR WASN'T ENOUGH.

WITH A PORTABLE TOILET, LOCKED FOR THE NIGHT,

TOO BAD.

CALL 807-2243

A FADED SIGN ANNOUNCES THE FUTURE SITE OF A YEAR-ROUND, INDOOR LOVER'S LANE.

THEY HAD EVERYTHING ELSE FIGURED OUT...

1988

HYMEN PLAZA

A LUXURY ROMANCE FACILITY

STAY OUT

PIECES OF HEAVY EQUIPMENT, CAPABLE OF BURROWING TO THE BOTTOM OF A DRAWER OF LINGERIE, RUST IN THE MOONLIGHT.

HEATED BENCHES, ELECTRIC ZEPHYRS, STEREOPHONIC CRICKETS...

AMOR

A NIGHT WATCHMAN, GROWN LAX IN THE SECURITY OF HIS JOB, EATS CHOCOLATE FROM A HEART-SHAPED BOX.

I WAS THERE AT THE GROUND-BREAKING CEREMONY, SAINT VALENTINE'S DAY 1987.

THE DEVELOPER, JOSEPH POTCH, ASSURED OF THE NUMERICAL ODDS OF FAILURE, KISSES HIS THIRD WIFE GOODNIGHT.

TWO YOUNG MEN WAIT IN THE LOBBY.

I DIDN'T KNOW HE HAD CHILDREN.

THEY TOOK A TAXI FROM THE AIRPORT.

DURING THESE HEAVY LUNCHES, PATROAST, THE HIGHWAY ENGINEER, WOULD REMINISCE ABOUT THE FAMILY HE LEFT BEHIND—

IN A WAY I'M GLAD THE BOYS KEPT MY NAME.

HOW HE WORKED HIS WAY THROUGH SCHOOL AS A MASSEUR,

"...THE WIDTH TAKEN BY EACH SIDEWALK IS FROM ONE-FOURTH TO ONE-FIFTH THE TOTAL DISTANCE BETWEEN PROPERTY LINES..."

"ALTHOUGH THIS MAY BE REDUCED IN SOME INSTANCES."

HOW HE RAN AWAY WITH A CIVIL ENGINEER

SHE BUILT THE FIRST ROAD ACROSS THE WET PART OF OUR HOMELAND.

AND CAME TO THIS COUNTRY WHILE THE CLOVERLEAF WAS IN ITS FIRST BLOOM.

CHILD SUPPORT? LET HER BOY-FRIENDS PICK UP THE TAB!

IN THEIR BED AT NIGHT IT SMELLED OF ASPHALT AND FRENCH PERFUME.

TWO BOYS WHO LOOK LIKE YOU.

CALL THE POLICE!

TOGETHER, THEY DEVISED THE GUTTER SYSTEM FOR A MAJOR TOLL PLAZA LEADING INTO THE CITY.

THESE BOYS CONSTRUE MY HARD WORK AS AN INSULT TO THE MEMORY OF THEIR MOTHER.

INTERSTATE 27

MASSAGE REMAINED HIS HOBBY.

IMAGINE IF THEY KNEW I JUST HAD LUNCH WITH A WOMAN WHO DESIGNS AIRPORT SNACK-BARS.

RESTAURANT

FOR A MOMENT, HE WONDERED HOW THEY GOT THERE.

CALL THE POLICE!

2.14

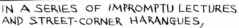

IN A SERIES OF IMPROMPTU LECTURES AND STREET-CORNER HARANGUES,

IT WAS AS A CHILD THAT I FIRST NOTICED THE RUBBER GARNISH GREENS IN THE REFRIGERATED SHOWCASE OF OUR NEIGHBORHOOD BUTCHER SHOP. A PRIMAL EXPRESSION OF LIFE IN THE FACE OF DEATH!

ISIDORE TASY, A SELF-STYLED VISIONARY PLANNER, HOLDS OUT ONE LAST HOPE FOR THE REFORMATION OF CITY LIFE.

I SAW, READY-MADE, IN THAT HUMBLE NEIGHBORHOOD BUTCHER SHOP, THE PERFECT UNION OF THE RURAL AND URBAN LIFE — A PROTO-TYPE FOR MY CITY OF THE FUTURE — "ILEUM"!

IMAGINE, IF YOU CAN, VAST REFRIGERATED PUBLIC SPACES, FESTOONED YEAR-ROUND WITH PLASTIC GREENERY — EVERYTHING FRESH, AS THOUGH JUST PUT OUT THAT MORNING!

THE BEST AND WORST OF HUMAN NATURE CUT INTO MANAGE-ABLE PORTIONS, A CLEAR PRICE PLACED ON THE ACTIONS OF EACH INDIVIDUAL.

ON ALTERNATE MONTHS, HALF THE POPULATION WOULD ASSUME THE ROLE OF "CUSTOMER," THE OTHER HALF, OF "MEAT"...

GET OUTTA HERE.

I'M SPEAKING IN METAPHORS! OF COURSE AN ACTUAL BUTCHER SHOP WAS FULL OF INEQUITIES; INNOCENT ANIMALS HAD TO BE SLAUGHTERED, REGULAR CUSTOMERS WERE GIVEN THE BEST CUTS OF MEAT, ETC.

HE LET HIS MOTHER DRAG HIM SHOPPING ONCE TOO OFTEN.

AT SOME POINT, HIS LISTENERS TURN AWAY

BUT WHAT BETTER MODEL DO WE HAVE TO LOOK BACK UPON? THE TOWNS OF THE HANSEATIC LEAGUE? HAUSSMANN'S PARIS? LE CORBUSIER'S RADIANT CITY?

DECORATED HIS BEDROOM WITH POSTERS FROM THE VEAL COUNCIL.

IN DESPAIR OVER A CHILDHOOD ENTHUSIASM THEY DID NOT SHARE.

IT WAS AS A CHILD THAT I FIRST NOTICED THE RUBBER GARNISH GREENS IN THE REFRIGERATED SHOWCASE OF OUR NEIGHBORHOOD BUTCHER SHOP.

THE SIDEWALK IN FRONT OF A FASHIONABLE RESTAURANT BECOMES SMEARED WITH A FAMILIAR UNCTUOUS COMPOUND.

RENDERED FAT, PATENT LEATHER, HUMAN SPUTUM, SARDINE OIL, SEWER GAS, TESTOSTERONE, PROCESS CHEESE, URIC ACID AND ORANGEADE.

A WOMAN, ON HER WAY TO WORK, SLIPS ON A THICK PATCH.

FORTUNATELY, THERE'S A FIFTY PERCENT CHANCE OF RAIN TONIGHT.

THE VERRUCA GRILL!

THAT EVENING, HER BOYFRIEND, A SANITATION HOBBYIST—ONE OF THOSE YOUNG MEN ENAMORED OF THE GOLDEN AGE OF URBAN STREET-CLEANING (1961–1963)—

EVERYWHERE YOU LOOK, THERE ARE CARTERS AND HAULERS OF TRASH BUT NOBODY TO CLEAN THE STREET.

PICKS HER UP IN A RESTORED 1962 "MOTO-SWEEPER."

I DIDN'T BOTHER TO FILL MY WATER TANK; THERE'S A FIFTY PERCENT CHANCE OF RAIN TONIGHT.

THEY DRIVE TOWARD A DINER FREQUENTED BY THE CREWS OF COMMERCIAL GARBAGE TRUCKS.

PLEASE, JUST TONIGHT, FOR A CHANGE, SOMEWHERE DIFFERENT LIKE THE VERRUCA GRILL.

WHERE'S THAT?

LET'S PARK AROUND THE CORNER.

THE SOONER THEY COVER THEIR ROUTE, THE SOONER THEY CAN GO HOME. NOBODY'LL STOP TO PICK UP A BROKEN BOTTLE OF KETCHUP OR A PIECE OF CHICKEN.

IT'S EXPENSIVE.

WE'LL SPLIT SOMETHING.

LOOK AT THE SIDEWALK— IT'S GLISTENING! EVERYTHING LOOKS SO CLEAN TONIGHT.

THAT'S JUST LUCK.

A POOR TURN-OUT FOR THE FUNERAL OF THE INTERNATIONALLY RENOWNED HAIR TAMER, PROFESSOR DOMBY FECOL.

AN ELECTROLOGIST FROM SAN REMO, TWO RETIRED BOBBY-PIN SALESMEN FROM CINCINNATI... WHERE IS EVERYONE?

INCORPOREAL funeral home, Inc.

THE WHOLE WORLD WAS HIS SCALP. JUST LIKE THAT, WITH A HARD RUBBER COMB AND A LITTLE WATER, HE WOULD APPROACH TAXI DRIVERS IN BORNEO, MALE PROSTITUTES IN PICCADILLY CIRCUS, CATERERS IN BOROUGH PARK — HE HAD NO FEAR.

DOMBY FECOL — 1994

MOST PEOPLE GIVE UP ON A BOY AFTER THE AGE OF TEN, BUT TO DOMBY FECOL IT WAS AN IRRESISTIBLE CHALLENGE TO BEGIN THE PROCESS IN MIDDLE AGE, EVEN IF IT TOOK SIX MONTHS

CAN WE SPEAK? I BELIEVE I CAN HELP YOU.

TO TRAIN A FORELOCK TO FALL JUST SO; TO ESTABLISH A PART IN ACCORDANCE WITH THE LAWS OF ART AND NATURE; TO RESOLVE THE DICHOTOMY BETWEEN HAIR AND MIND... WHERE IS EVERYONE?

INCORPOREAL

Dignified Ser.

MY FATHER SUBSCRIBED TO HIS HOME-STUDY COURSE FOR MANY YEARS.

I MET HIM DURING A SUBWAY TOUR IN 1959 AND THEN YESTERDAY SAW HIS OBITUARY IN THE PAPER.

INCORPOREAL funeral h...

SIX MONTHS AGO, HE CAME UPON A WAITER, HERE, IN SOME LOUSY COFFEE SHOP, WHO MISCONSTRUED HIS SCIENTIFIC ATTENTIONS FOR FRIENDSHIP.

EMPYREAL LUNCHEONETTE

YOU KNOW DR. FECOL HAD ONLY ONE ARM, AND SO WAS INCAPABLE OF DEFENDING HIM-SELF AGAINST AN UNWILLING SUBJECT?

NO, I DIDN'T.

THE HAIR, ABOVE, HE FOUGHT TILL THE BITTER END; BUT THE MAN, BELOW, WAS TOO MUCH FOR HIM.

HAIR REMEMBERS MAN FORGETS

WHAT IS THE LIKELIHOOD OF A MAN DRESSING FOR THE DAY IN AN OUTFIT COMPOSED SOLELY OF GIFTS?

CEREAL OR TOAST?

FOR SOMEONE TO HAVE RECEIVED AT LEAST ONE SWEATER, SHIRT, TIE AND PAIR OF SOCKS IS VERY LIKELY.

WEAR IT IN GOOD HEALTH.

SEXUAL PROGRESS LEAGUE 25th ANNIVER...

GIFTS OF HATS, JACKETS, PANTS, SHOES AND UNDERWEAR ARE RARE.

HE DISAPPEARED, NEVER WORN, TEN AND A HALVES, IT'S A SHAME.

IF, OVER TEN YEARS, ENOUGH CLOTHING WERE ACCUMULATED TO MAKE UP ONE COMPLETE OUTFIT,

DO ME A FAVOR, TAKE ONE, THEY'RE MANUFACTURERS' SAMPLES FROM LAST YEAR.

WHAT ARE THE CHANCES THAT THE RECIPIENT OF THESE GIFTS WOULD APPROVE OF THEM ALL OR CONSIDER WEARING ANY OF THEM IN PUBLIC?

EVENTUALLY I'LL THROW THEM OUT.

FIRST NAT

HERE, WE MUST POSTULATE AN INDIVIDUAL EAGER TO RELIEVE HIMSELF OF THE BURDEN OF DISCRIMINATION,

CEREAL OR TOAST?

OR, A MAN WITHOUT THE MEANS TO REPLACE HIS OWN WARDROBE AS IT WEARS OUT.

I WOULD NEVER BUY SUCH SHOES, BUT MINE NEED NEW HEELS.

LUNCH

DONU

SANITARY

AND THEN, ONE MORNING, NO OTHER CHOICE WILL EXIST.

SORRY, THE OATMEAL IS FINISHED.

BETWEEN ISSUES OF "MOVING MAN MONTHLY," EMMANUEL KALB WORKS AS AN ACCOUNT-ANT FOR THE MAKER OF A WELL-KNOWN NON-DAIRY CREAMER.

ALTHOUGH HE ENJOYS READING ABOUT, AND LOOKING AT PHOTOGRAPHS OF, MOVERS, VANS AND PACKING SUPPLIES,

"THE DANGERS AND THRILLS OF HIGH-RISE PIANO RIGGING."... (ABOVE) A FOURTEEN-WHEELER JACKKNIFED ON ROUTE 17, OUTSIDE CHALAZA, OK."

THE SIGHT OF AN ACTUAL CREW, AT WORK IN THE STREET, SICKENS HIM.

MIDDLE-AGED MEN KILLING THEMSELVES HAULING WORTHLESS CHIPBOARD FURNITURE.

HE RELISHES THE SMALL DISPLAY ADS IN THE BACK OF EACH ISSUE

BUT IS HORRIFIED BY THE PROSPECT OF ONE DAY HAVING TO GO THROUGH THE ORDEAL OF MOVING HIS OWN POSSESSIONS THROUGH THE STREET.

I HAVE A TEN-YEAR LEASE WITH AN OPTION TO RENEW.

HE WON'T SUBSCRIBE FOR FEAR OF BEING PLACED ON A MAILING LIST, LUMPED TOGETHER WITH REAL MOVING MEN.

"LIFT 'EM AND LEAVE 'EM: 1994 DOLLIES AND HANDTRUCKS."... "MY BACK WENT OUT AT 70 M.P.H.!"

THE NEWSSTAND DEALERS REALIZE THAT THEIR CUSTOMERS' INTEREST IN A SUBJECT DOES NOT NECESSAR-ILY EXTEND BEYOND THE PAGES OF A MAGAZINE:

"TANGO TODAY"

"AMATEUR LIPSTICK SPOTTER"

SOMETHING THEY CAN LEAVE BEHIND WHEN THEY'RE FINISHED.

THE NEWS OF A SACRIFICIAL SALE PERCOLATES THROUGH THE INNERMOST HALLWAYS OF A PLAYTZER AVENUE APARTMENT BUILDING.

"YOU MADE US DO IT! ONE DAY ONLY! DRASTIC REDUCTIONS ON ALL MERCHANDISE"

LAST YEAR'S WONDER APPLIANCES ARE OFFERED AT A FRACTION OF THEIR ORIGINAL PRICES.

"FOUR-SPEED, LUCKY LOST-TOOTH POLISHER, $17.95"

AORTA BROTHERS APPLIANCES INC ELECTRONICS

YOU MADE US DO IT! ONE DAY ONLY

MR. KNIPL'S THOUGHTS TURN TO HIS NEIGHBORS WHO'VE LIVED TILL NOW WITHOUT THE BENEFIT OF THESE STRANGE DEVICES,

"PERSONAL POCKET ASPIRATOR, $12.95"

COUGH COUGH COUGH

TENANTS WHOSE ELECTRICAL OUTLETS WERE PAINTED SHUT YEARS AGO AND NEVER OPENED,

"SELF-WINDING BEDROOM SEISMOGRAPH, $8.95"

IT WENT DOWN THE WRONG PIPE.

WHO, IF THEY COULD LIVE AGAIN, WOULD GLADLY PAY THE SUGGESTED RETAIL PRICE.

"ORIGINALLY $29.95"

THAT'S FOR KIDS.

THIS TIME, NO ONE COULD CONVINCE THEM TO WAIT,

THEY TOOK IN MORE THAN THEY COULD EVER SELL.

TO ENDURE, ONCE AGAIN, THOSE TERRIBLE TRIBULATIONS ON A DAILY BASIS

NOW IT'S TIME TO CUT THEIR LOSSES; STOP PAYING RENT ON FIFTEEN HUNDRED DUSTY BOXES...

IN THE HOPE THAT PRICES MIGHT DROP.

AND CLEAR THE SHELVES FOR SOMETHING NEW!

COUGH COUGH COUGH

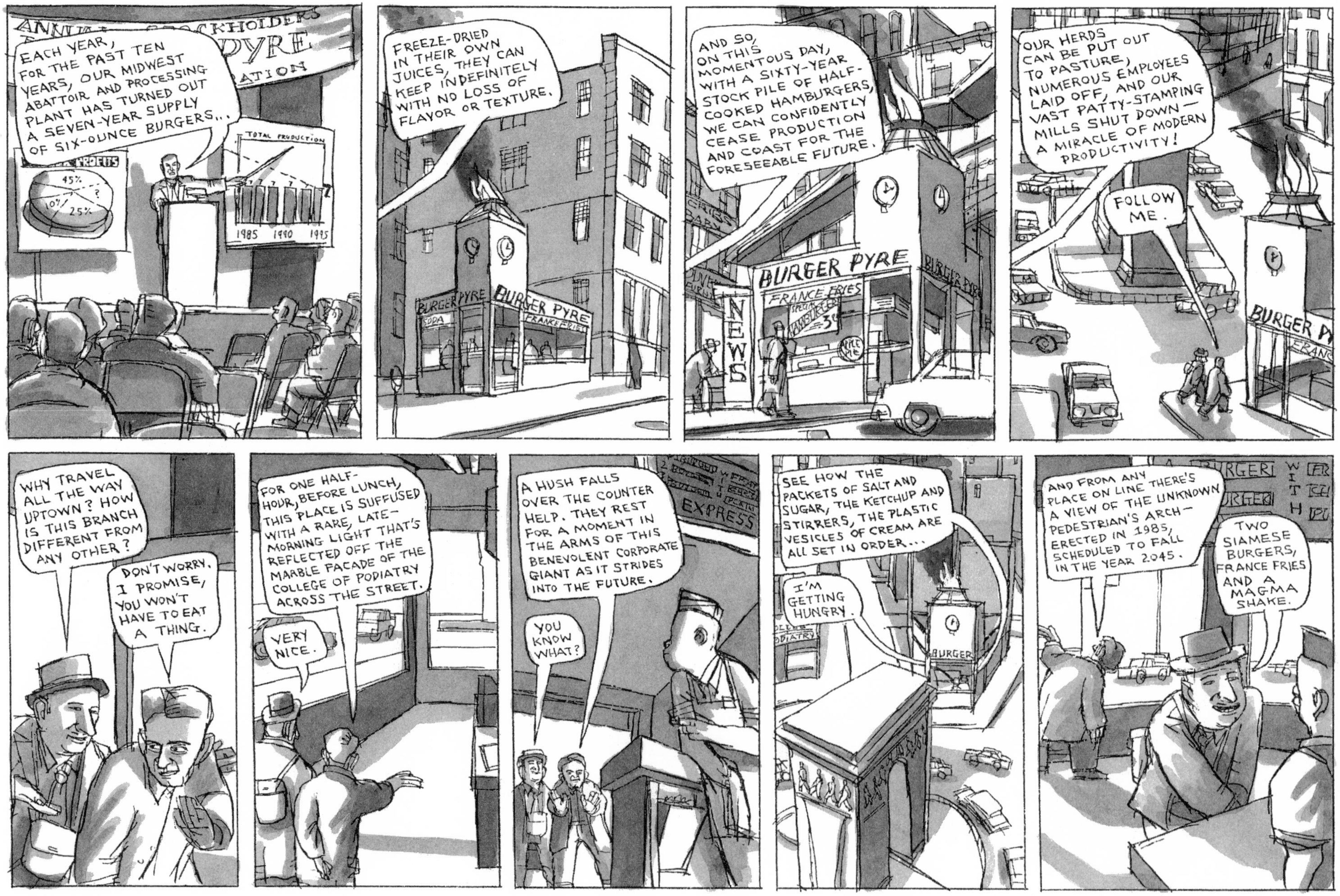
EACH YEAR, FOR THE PAST TEN YEARS, OUR MIDWEST ABATTOIR AND PROCESSING PLANT HAS TURNED OUT A SEVEN-YEAR SUPPLY OF SIX-OUNCE BURGERS...
TOTAL PRODUCTION
45%
10%
25%
?
1985 1990 1995
FREEZE-DRIED IN THEIR OWN JUICES, THEY CAN KEEP INDEFINITELY WITH NO LOSS OF FLAVOR OR TEXTURE.
BURGER PYRE
BURGER PYRE
SODA
AND SO, ON THIS MOMENTOUS DAY, WITH A SIXTY-YEAR STOCK PILE OF HALF-COOKED HAMBURGERS, WE CAN CONFIDENTLY CEASE PRODUCTION AND COAST FOR THE FORESEEABLE FUTURE.
BURGER PYRE
FRANCE FRYES
NEWS
OUR HERDS CAN BE PUT OUT TO PASTURE, NUMEROUS EMPLOYEES LAID OFF, AND OUR VAST PATTY-STAMPING MILLS SHUT DOWN — A MIRACLE OF MODERN PRODUCTIVITY!
FOLLOW ME.
BURGER PYRE
WHY TRAVEL ALL THE WAY UPTOWN? HOW IS THIS BRANCH DIFFERENT FROM ANY OTHER?
DON'T WORRY, I PROMISE, YOU WON'T HAVE TO EAT A THING.
FOR ONE HALF-HOUR, BEFORE LUNCH, THIS PLACE IS SUFFUSED WITH A RARE, LATE-MORNING LIGHT THAT'S REFLECTED OFF THE MARBLE FACADE OF THE COLLEGE OF PODIATRY ACROSS THE STREET.
VERY NICE.
A HUSH FALLS OVER THE COUNTER HELP. THEY REST FOR A MOMENT IN THE ARMS OF THIS BENEVOLENT CORPORATE GIANT AS IT STRIDES INTO THE FUTURE.
EXPRESS
YOU KNOW WHAT?
SEE HOW THE PACKETS OF SALT AND SUGAR, THE KETCHUP AND STIRRERS, THE PLASTIC VESICLES OF CREAM ARE ALL SET IN ORDER...
I'M GETTING HUNGRY.
BURGER
AND FROM ANY PLACE ON LINE THERE'S A VIEW OF THE UNKNOWN PEDESTRIAN'S ARCH — ERECTED IN 1985, SCHEDULED TO FALL IN THE YEAR 2045.
TWO SIAMESE BURGERS, FRANCE FRIES AND A MAGMA SHAKE.

STANDING OUTSIDE OF THESE DISCOUNT DEPARTMENT STORES AND OTHER CUT-RATE RETAIL ESTABLISHMENTS,

A $75. NEGLIGEE FOR $37.50!

THIS COCKSCOMB IS REGULARLY $100. I GOT IT FOR $85.

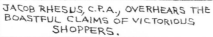

JACOB RHESUS, C.P.A., OVERHEARS THE BOASTFUL CLAIMS OF VICTORIOUS SHOPPERS.

THESE HULA SKIRTS LIST FOR $200. I PAID $165.

SAVED THIRTY-FIVE DOLLARS.

WHO KNOWS WHAT THE "REAL" PRICE IS? AND IF ANY MONEY IS ACTUALLY SAVED, IT'S SOON SQUANDERED ON SOME OVER-PRICED IMPULSE PURCHASE SOMEWHERE ELSE.

A $50. BOTTLE OF TOILET WATER FOR $12.95.

THESE SAVINGS EXIST ONLY FOR A MOMENT IN THE MIND OF THE BUYER AND ARE THEN GONE...

A $10. RAT TRAP FOR $4.25.

UNLESS THEY'RE RECORDED IN LEDGER FORM, ON THE SPOT, BY A CERTIFIED PUBLIC ACCOUNTANT.

A $2. BOTTLE OF SPERM OIL FOR .75¢.

THE DOCUMENTATION OF THIS INTANGIBLE FORTUNE IS STORED EACH NIGHT, FOR SAFEKEEPING, UNDER A PARKED CAR.

1.6 MILLION JUST TODAY.

THERE, IT ACCUMULATES FOR THE EVENTUAL PURPOSE OF FINANCING A GREAT PROJECT OR UNDERTAKING— YET TO BE DECIDED UPON.

AN IMAGINARY BANQUET FOR THE NOW-DECEASED LIBRARIANS OF MY CHILDHOOD, OR, THE TOLLING OF A BELL, EACH EVENING AT FIVE, TO MARK THE REAPPEARANCE OF A SHADOW ACROSS THE FACE OF THE CITY,

OR, THE WEEKLY EXHIBITION OF AN OBSCURE COMIC STRIP IN THE WINDOW OF A LATE-NIGHT TROPICAL DRINK STAND.

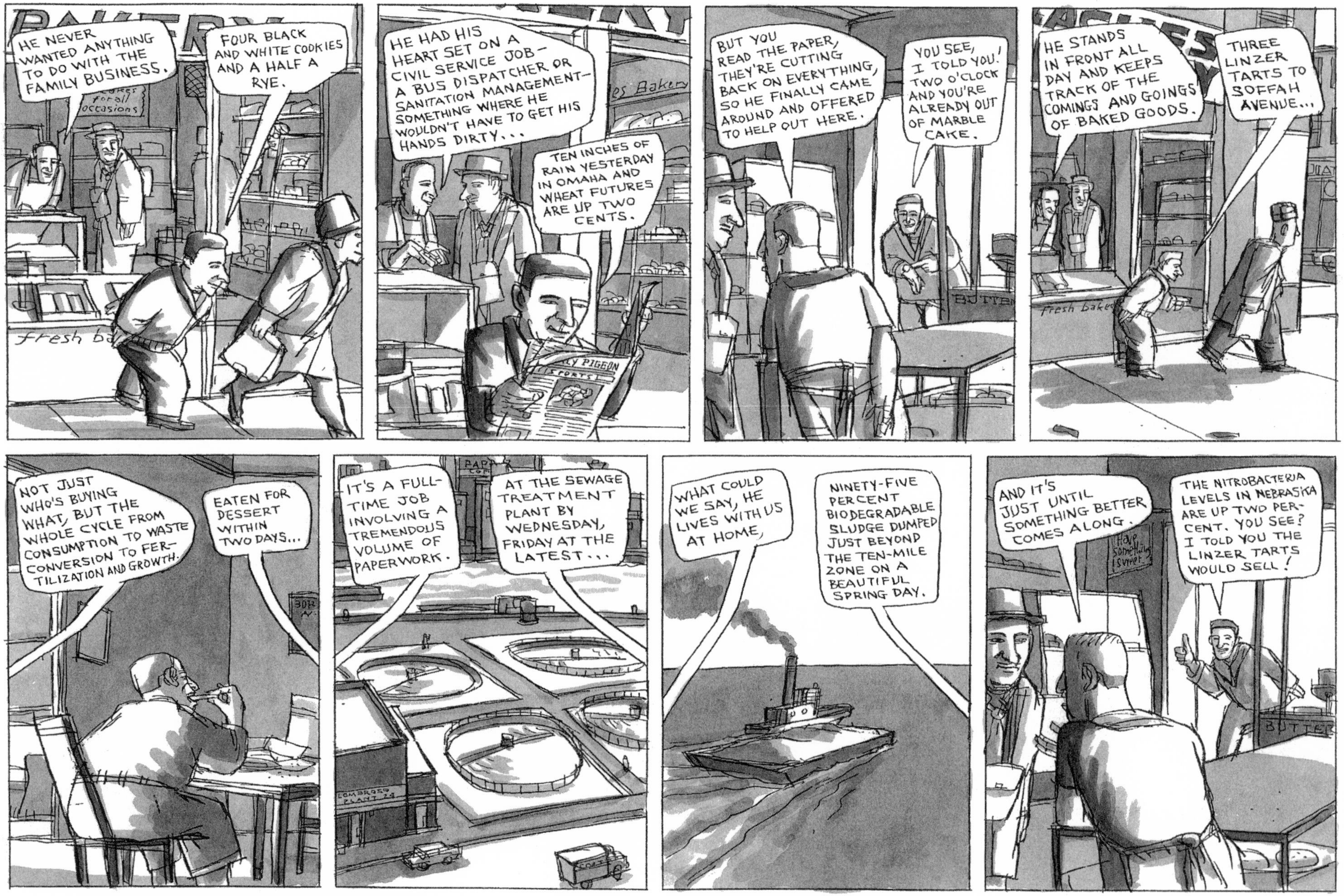
HE NEVER WANTED ANYTHING TO DO WITH THE FAMILY BUSINESS.
FOUR BLACK AND WHITE COOKIES AND A HALF A RYE.
fresh ba
HE HAD HIS HEART SET ON A CIVIL SERVICE JOB - A BUS DISPATCHER OR SANITATION MANAGEMENT - SOMETHING WHERE HE WOULDN'T HAVE TO GET HIS HANDS DIRTY...
TEN INCHES OF RAIN YESTERDAY IN OMAHA AND WHEAT FUTURES ARE UP TWO CENTS.
SPORTS
BUT YOU READ THE PAPER, THEY'RE CUTTING BACK ON EVERYTHING, SO HE FINALLY CAME AROUND AND OFFERED TO HELP OUT HERE.
YOU SEE, I TOLD YOU! TWO O'CLOCK AND YOU'RE ALREADY OUT OF MARBLE CAKE.
HE STANDS IN FRONT ALL DAY AND KEEPS TRACK OF THE COMINGS AND GOINGS OF BAKED GOODS.
THREE LINZER TARTS TO SOFFAH AVENUE...
NOT JUST WHO'S BUYING WHAT, BUT THE WHOLE CYCLE FROM CONSUMPTION TO WASTE CONVERSION TO FERTILIZATION AND GROWTH.
EATEN FOR DESSERT WITHIN TWO DAYS...
IT'S A FULL-TIME JOB INVOLVING A TREMENDOUS VOLUME OF PAPERWORK.
AT THE SEWAGE TREATMENT PLANT BY WEDNESDAY, FRIDAY AT THE LATEST...
WHAT COULD WE SAY, HE LIVES WITH US AT HOME.
NINETY-FIVE PERCENT BIODEGRADABLE SLUDGE DUMPED JUST BEYOND THE TEN-MILE ZONE ON A BEAUTIFUL SPRING DAY.
AND IT'S JUST UNTIL SOMETHING BETTER COMES ALONG.
THE NITROBACTERIA LEVELS IN NEBRASKA ARE UP TWO PERCENT. YOU SEE? I TOLD YOU THE LINZER TARTS WOULD SELL!

AS FAR AS HE KNEW, NO ONE HAD YET MADE A COMPREHENSIVE STUDY OF THE PSYCHOLOGICAL EFFECTS OF HAIR CUTTING UPON THE ADULT MALE.

NOW WE KNOW WHAT THE WILD MAN OF BORNEO LOOKED LIKE.

PLEASE, I'M GOING.

IT WAS TIME TO CORRECT THE FALLACIES AND OLD WIVES' TALES WHICH HAD GROWN UP AROUND THE SUBJECT.

IT'LL GROW BACK IN THREE WEEKS, AND, IN THIS WEATHER IT'S COOLER.

AND SO, ALL THAT MORNING, HE GAVE UP HIS "NEXT" IN THE NAME OF SCIENCE.

NO, NO, AFTER YOU.

HE WAS NOT INTERESTED IN THE REPERCUSSIONS OF BOTCH JOBS OR RADICAL ALTERATIONS OF STYLE.

HIS INTENTION WAS TO ANALYZE THAT COOL BREEZE WHICH PLAYS AROUND THE EARS OF AN OTHERWISE SATISFACTORY HAIRCUT.

THE PSYCHOLOGICAL IMPACT OF HAVING TO LOOK AT THE BACK OF ONE'S OWN HEAD!

AN EXAMINATION OF THE HEAD FRESHLY EXPOSED TO THE STIMULI OF EVERYDAY LIFE.

THE TRAUMA OF WATCHING BITS OF YOURSELF SWEPT INTO A COMMON PILE ON THE FLOOR!

AND THEN, LATE THAT AFTERNOON, IN A MOMENT OF RECKLESS CURIOSITY,

WHO'S NEXT?

HOW ELSE CAN I REALLY KNOW...

HE ASKS TO HAVE A TRIM.

ALL DONE!

WHAT TO GIVE FOR A TIP?

ONE MAN WALKS THE STREET PREPARED TO ANSWER THE CHANCE RINGING OF ANY PAY PHONE HE ENCOUNTERS.

WE'RE TAUGHT FROM CHILDHOOD NOT TO — THAT NO GOOD CAN COME OF IT.

RING! RING! RING!

NO, DR. TARMOOTI IS NOT HERE AT THE MOMENT. THIS IS EUGENE GUMTROP, CAN I HELP YOU?

WITH A PRACTICED FINGER, HE FEELS EACH COIN RETURN,

THE SOILED RECEIVERS, THE UNBATHED STRANGERS ON THE OTHER END OF THE LINE ARE NOT PLEASANT.

BUT HIS TRUE COMPENSATION COMES FROM THE PHILANTHROPIC WORK ACCOMPLISHED.

I DO MY BEST TO HELP THEM OUT — ONLY A SMALL PERCENTAGE ARE UP TO NO GOOD.

RING! RING! RING!

HELLO VICO, YOU STILL THERE? THEY NEED A FRESH SPLEEN AND'LL PAY CASH IF YOU CAN GET ONE TONIGHT. HELLO VICO?

FIVE DAYS A WEEK, DURING A CASUAL STROLL TO AND FROM A FAVORITE SANDWICH SHOP.

MOST ARE JUST INNOCENT SOULS TRYING TO GET IN TOUCH WITH SOMEONE. THEY'LL LET IT RING TWENTY OR THIRTY TIMES BEFORE THEY GIVE UP.

RING! RING! RING!

WHAT MOVIE TONIGHT? HOW SHOULD I KNOW? LOOK IN THE PAPER!

THERE IS NO SUCH THING AS A WRONG NUMBER.

I'M SORRY. I LOST MY TEMPER.

SONNY SEZSUM, HEIR TO THE TURBAN HALVAH FORTUNE, HAS A PRIVATE, ANTIQUE CITY BUS AND DRIVER TO TAKE HIM WHEREVER HE WANTS TO GO.

IT'S A 1972 "HY-FLEXOR." SEATS 45 WITH 15 STANDEES.

YET OVER THE YEARS, THROUGH HABIT, A ROUTE HAS BEEN ESTABLISHED: FROM HOME TO INVESTMENT COUNSELOR,

THEY'RE THE ORIGINAL UNTINTED GLASS WINDOWS...

TO OPERA HOUSE, TO FAVORITE RESTAURANT AND BACK TO HOME.

AND VANDAL-PROOF SEATS.

SOMETIMES, LATE AT NIGHT, AFTER A PARTY, FOR THE AMUSEMENT OF HIS FRIENDS, HE'LL ORDER HIS DRIVER TO FOLLOW AN ACTUAL PUBLIC BUS ROUTE,

FROM HERE, STRAIGHT UP ORFHANAGE AVENUE.

PICK UP ONE RIDER AND LET HIM OFF WHEN HE RINGS THE BELL.

BETWEEN STOPS, DURING THE DAY, THE DRIVER IDLY CRUISES THE NEIGHBORING STREETS AWAITING A CALL FROM HIS BOSS.

YES LAWRENCE, I'M READY.

OUT OF SERVICE

WHERE'D THIS TRAFFIC COME FROM?

OUT OF SERVICE

HALVAH

I'VE BEEN WAITING FIVE MINUTES—WHERE ARE YOU?

TAKE IT EASY. I'VE BEEN HERE FOR TWENTY MINUTES!

BUS STOP

UPON ENTERING A FAMILIAR MACEDONIAN COFFEE SHOP, MR. KNIPL GRAVITATES TOWARD THE REFRIGERATED SHOWCASE.

UNDER THE PRETENSE OF CHOOSING A DESSERT, HE EXAMINES THE STATUS OF THE TRAY OF CHERRY GELATIN,

CANNED PEACH GARNISH, SEVEN-SIXTEENTHS GONE, SLOTTED SPOON AT FIVE O'CLOCK.

HE THEN SCANS THE ROOM TO SEE IF ANYONE'S EATING A PORTION AT THAT MOMENT.

YOU CAN'T MISS IT, THAT SHIMMERING RED BEACON... THERE!

TONIGHT, AT A TABLE IN THE FAR CORNER, ONE MAN STRUGGLES WITH HIS FAVORITE DESSERT.

LIKE THAT TIME LAST SPRING IN THE IONIAN COFFEE SHOP, JUST BEFORE MAYOR ORPHREY WAS ELECTED, BACK WHEN I TOOK A THIRTY-EIGHT WAIST, BEFORE THE RIOT ON BÉCHAMEL AVENUE ---THE CALM BEFORE THE STORM ...

BE STILL.

A BUS-BOY WATCHES FROM THE KITCHEN,

WHAT'S HIS PROBLEM?

THERE IS A PATTERN, BUT I LACK THE MENTAL EQUIPMENT TO DISCERN IT. IT'S HOPELESS... WHERE'S THE MENU?

AND THEN, AT DAWN, IN THE ARMS OF HIS GIRLFRIEND, EXPRESSES HIS ANXIETY.

WHAT CAN HE TELL BY LOOKING AT THIS ONE PAN OF GELATIN? WE GO THROUGH SIX OR SEVEN IN A DAY. WHAT CAN HE SEE AT THAT MOMENT: A SKIMPY PORTION SERVED WITH A DIRTY SPOON?

ALL THE CUSTOMER HAS TO GO BY IS WHAT HE SEES. WHO CARES ABOUT THE REST OF THE WEEK? NOBODY REMEMBERS FROM ONE DAY TO THE NEXT. "YOU GOT JELLOW? HOW'S THE JELLOW TODAY? GOOD? GIVE ME SOME WITH WHIPPED CREAM." I HAVE TO GET DRESSED.

THE NEXT DAY, AT WORK, SHE ANNOUNCES HER OWN DISCONTENT.

HOW LONG HAVE YOU KNOWN HIM?

TOO LONG.

At an airport on the outskirts of Argol City, a businessman waits for an evening flight to Kyanesia.

Ah, the smell of freshly printed matter!

His eyes roam across that section of the candy rack stocked with a multitude of miniaturized snack-kits.

Cheese and crackers, caviar and toast, salami and rye bread squares, pigs in their own blankets, herring in cream sauce with pumpernickel snaps...

Your choice - 65¢

Ingeniously packed into each one-by-three-inch plastic vessel are tiny portions of artificially flavored and chemically preserved foodstuffs.

A paper napkin and small plastic knife are fitted into the pull-top lid.

Across the way, a man desperately scrapes the last globules of sturgeon roe from the bottom of a one-inch-deep plastic well.

For sixty-five cents, you get just enough to trigger a gustatory memory of the real thing eaten under happier circumstances.

A cool summer evening, thirty years ago, on the screened dining room porch of Pollack and Kestir's experimental hotel and bungalow colony — they brought each table a platter of the most beautiful red caviar.

"Direct from the Bald Sea. Take a spoonful, brother, and pass it on."

The poor guy's gone through six snack-kits. He can't help himself.

At this hotel, everyone's their own bellhop — so don't bring more than you can carry! Fresh air and caviar are communally pooled; rooms are assigned for the night, by committee, based upon need and mah-jong is strictly prohibited!

Flight 107 to Kyanesia is now boarding at Gate 11.

Where we're going, he'll be lucky to get a bowl of salted peanuts.

IN PREPARATION FOR THE LIKELIHOOD THAT HE WILL, AT SOME TIME IN THE NEAR FUTURE, BUMP HIS HEAD ON AN OPEN KITCHEN-CABINET DOOR,

"THAT I AM STILL ABLE TO COMMENT UPON THE EVENTS OF THE LAST MINUTE IS A HOPEFUL SIGN."

MARCUS BLAUBOK MEMORIZES A SHORT SPEECH TO BE DELIVERED ON THAT OCCASION—

"I WILL, IN A LITTLE WHILE, EXAMINE THE DAMAGE DONE TO MY SCALP, BUT FIRST, AND MORE IMPORTANTLY, I MUST EXAMINE THE CHAIN OF EVENTS WHICH LED UP TO THIS UNFORTUNATE INCIDENT."

AN ALTERNATIVE TO THE INCOHERENT CURSING OR UTTER LOSS FOR WORDS WHICH USUALLY FOLLOWS SUCH AN ACCIDENT.

"I HAD JUST COME HOME FROM WORK AND WAS IN THE MIDST OF PREPARING THE EVENING MEAL —A TASK I WILL RESUME AT THE CONCLUSION OF THIS SPEECH—"

THESE SMALL PRIVATE MISHAPS GO UNNOTICED BY THE NATION'S PRESS.

"I BENT DOWN TO LOOK FOR SOMETHING— UNDER THE SINK— AN EXTRA ICE-CUBE TRAY OR A GARBAGE-BAG TIE— AND UPON RISING, ENCOUNTERED THE BOTTOM EDGE OF AN OPEN CABINET DOOR."

THEY CAN, SO THEY CLAIM, BARELY KEEP UP WITH THE LARGE-SCALE CATASTROPHES OF MODERN LIFE.

"HAD I OPENED THIS CABINET, MYSELF, JUST A MOMENT EARLIER, LOOKING FOR A CAN OF CREAMED CORN, OR WAS IT MY WIFE HUNTING FOR A JAR OF COCKTAIL ONIONS, OR MY DAUGHTER, HOURS EARLIER AT LUNCHTIME, GETTING A CAN OF TUNA, WHO LEFT THE DOOR AJAR?"

SHOULD THE INDIVIDUAL FAIL TO MAKE SENSE OF WHAT'S BEFALLEN HIM, NO ONE ELSE WILL; CARELESSNESS COUPLED WITH BAD LUCK EXPLAINS EVERYTHING.

"IN THE FIRST CASE, I AM WHOLLY TO BLAME—A SUB-CONSCIOUS ACT OF SABOTAGE WITH THE INTENTION OF SELF-MUTILATION, OR A TASTE THEREOF."

THE BRUISE WILL HEAL, BUT THE UNDERLYING CAUSE OF THE ACCIDENT WILL CONTINUE TO FESTER, IN OBSCURITY, UNRESOLVED.

"IN THE SECOND AND THIRD CASES, WE HAVE A FAR MORE HEARTBREAKING COURSE OF INVESTIGATION TO FOLLOW. FALSE LOVE, PATRICIDE AND MERCY KILLING MUST FIRST BE RULED OUT—AND THEN WHAT DO WE HAVE LEFT? NEGLIGENCE AND COLD INDIFFERENCE TO ANOTHER'S WELL-BEING. LOOK IN ANY THESAURUS UNDER CATEGORY SIX-HUNDRED AND THIRTY-FOUR."

"HERE, THE MOTIVES BECOME SHADOWY AND UNCERTAIN, LIKE A GLIMPSE INTO THE DEPTHS OF A KITCHEN CABINET FILLED WITH THE CLUTTER OF A THOUSAND TRIPS TO THE SUPERMARKET."

HERE WE ARE— THE OLDEST CONTINUALLY VACANT STOREFRONT IN AMERICA!

EXCEPT FOR THE "FOR RENT" SIGN, WHICH FELL DOWN TEN YEARS AGO AND HAD TO BE RE-TAPED TO THE WINDOW, EVERYTHING IS EXACTLY THE SAME AS IT WAS WHEN THE LAST TENANT MOVED OUT IN 1964.

IT WAS A FLORIST'S SHOP— YOU CAN STILL SEE A FEW DRIED BLOSSOMS ON THE FLOOR.

THEY LEFT THE REFRIGERATOR DOOR OPEN.

RENTAL AGENTS AND REAL-ESTATE BROKERS MAKE A POINT OF STOPPING HERE WHEN THEY'RE IN TOWN JUST TO TAKE A LOOK — TO WONDER WHAT WENT WRONG. IT'S THE GRAND CANYON OF COMMERCIAL UNDESIRABILITY — A RARE COMBINATION OF POOR LOCATION AND HIGH RENT.

FIVE YEARS AGO, I STARTED A GUIDED TOUR OF THE PREMISES— EVERY HOUR ON THE HOUR FROM NOON TILL DUSK—THERE'S NO ELECTRICITY.

I MUST ASK YOU TO KEEP TO THE NEWSPAPER-COVERED FOOT-PATH. THE 600 SQ. FEET YOU SEE BEFORE YOU HAVE LAIN FALLOW SINCE THE YEAR 1964.

AND AT THIS POINT, I WOULDN'T RENT IT FOR TEN TIMES ITS MARKET VALUE — IT'S WORTH MORE TO ME EMPTY, AS A TOURIST ATTRACTION.

AS YOU CAN SEE, THE LAST TENANT HASTILY REMOVED THEIR NAME FROM THE AWNING— LITTLE DID THEY KNOW THAT ONE DAY THOUSANDS OF VISITORS WOULD PASS BENEATH IT IN AWE.

A COUPLE OF JOHNNY-COME-LATELIES, FROM OARLOCK, UTAH, CLAIM THEY HAVE A WHOLE TOWN THAT'S BEEN VACANT SINCE 1854 — BUT THAT'S A GHOST TOWN — IT'S A WHOLE DIFFERENT THING—NO ONE LIVES THERE.

HERE, YOU GOT KIDS? TAKE HOME A SOUVENIR UNSIGNED LEASE AND KEY-CHAIN SET.

IF YOU LOOK TO YOUR RIGHT, ON THE FLOOR JUST BELOW THE OPEN REFRIGERATOR DOOR, YOU CAN STILL SEE A FEW DRIED BLOSSOMS — THE SOLE REMAINING EVIDENCE OF THIS FAILED BUSINESS'S STOCK-IN-TRADE.

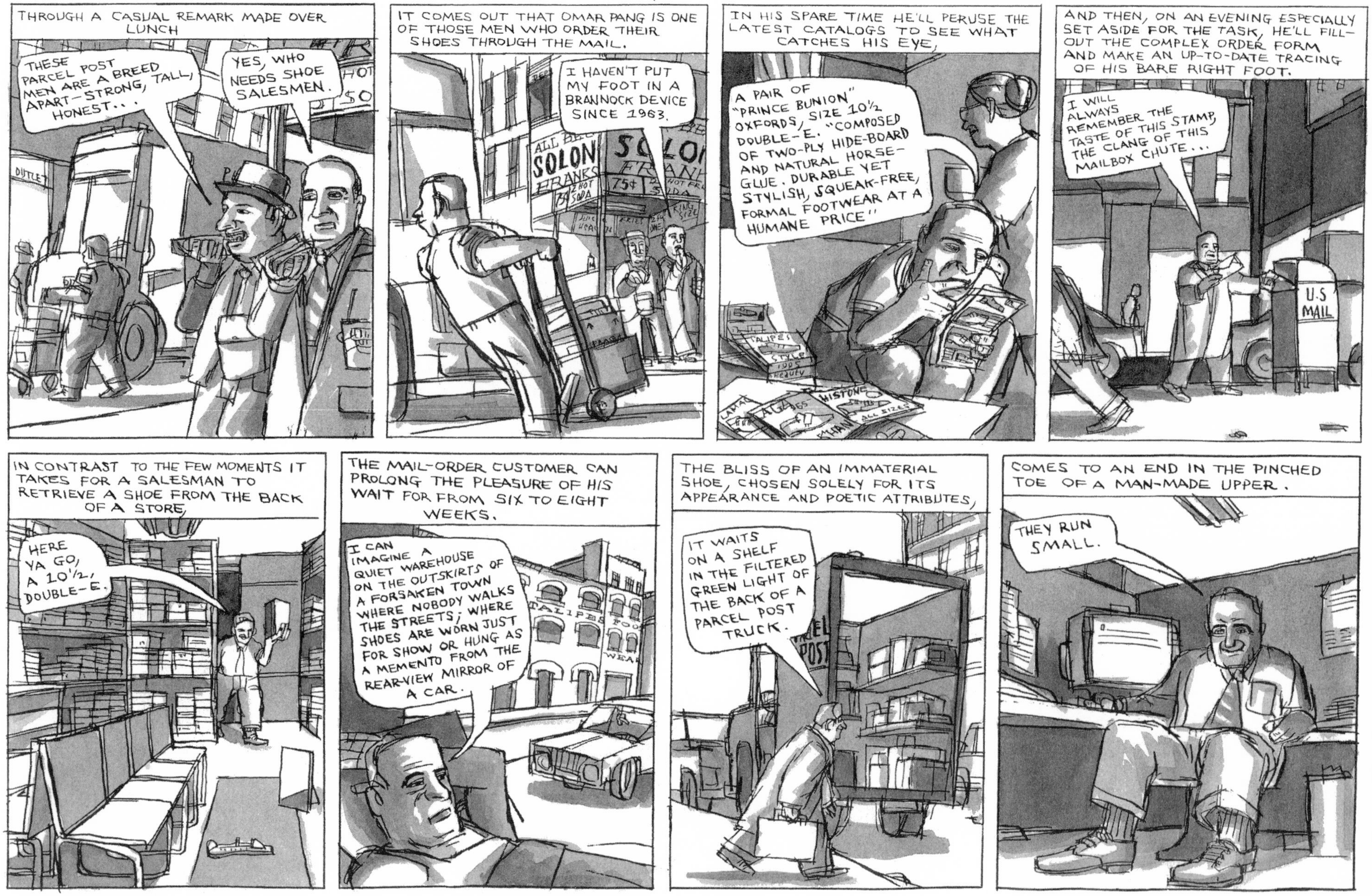
THROUGH A CASUAL REMARK MADE OVER LUNCH
THESE PARCEL POST MEN ARE A BREED APART—STRONG, TALL, HONEST...
YES, WHO NEEDS SHOE SALESMEN.
IT COMES OUT THAT OMAR PANG IS ONE OF THOSE MEN WHO ORDER THEIR SHOES THROUGH THE MAIL.
I HAVEN'T PUT MY FOOT IN A BRANNOCK DEVICE SINCE 1963.
IN HIS SPARE TIME HE'LL PERUSE THE LATEST CATALOGS TO SEE WHAT CATCHES HIS EYE,
A PAIR OF "PRINCE BUNION" OXFORDS, SIZE 10½ DOUBLE-E. "COMPOSED OF TWO-PLY HIDE-BOARD AND NATURAL HORSE-GLUE. DURABLE YET STYLISH, SQUEAK-FREE, FORMAL FOOTWEAR AT A HUMANE PRICE"
AND THEN, ON AN EVENING ESPECIALLY SET ASIDE FOR THE TASK, HE'LL FILL-OUT THE COMPLEX ORDER FORM AND MAKE AN UP-TO-DATE TRACING OF HIS BARE RIGHT FOOT.
I WILL ALWAYS REMEMBER THE TASTE OF THIS STAMP, THE CLANG OF THIS MAILBOX CHUTE...
U.S MAIL
IN CONTRAST TO THE FEW MOMENTS IT TAKES FOR A SALESMAN TO RETRIEVE A SHOE FROM THE BACK OF A STORE,
HERE YA GO, A 10½, DOUBLE-E.
THE MAIL-ORDER CUSTOMER CAN PROLONG THE PLEASURE OF HIS WAIT FOR FROM SIX TO EIGHT WEEKS.
I CAN IMAGINE A QUIET WAREHOUSE ON THE OUTSKIRTS OF A FORSAKEN TOWN WHERE NOBODY WALKS THE STREETS; WHERE SHOES ARE WORN JUST FOR SHOW OR HUNG AS A MEMENTO FROM THE REAR-VIEW MIRROR OF A CAR.
THE BLISS OF AN IMMATERIAL SHOE, CHOSEN SOLELY FOR ITS APPEARANCE AND POETIC ATTRIBUTES,
IT WAITS ON A SHELF IN THE FILTERED GREEN LIGHT OF THE BACK OF A PARCEL POST TRUCK.
COMES TO AN END IN THE PINCHED TOE OF A MAN-MADE UPPER.
THEY RUN SMALL.

MR. KNIPL DISCOVERS A MISSPELLING CARVED INTO THE STONE FASCIA OF A LARGE PUBLIC BUILDING.

AN "I" WHERE THERE SHOULD BE AN "E."

DEPARTMINT OF CORRECTION

IT WAS ON THE SHADY SIDE OF THE BUILDING AND SO THEY LET IT GO — A LEGACY FROM MAYOR HYBAUL'S ADMINISTRATION — 1947–1950.

I WAS STILL JUST A GLINT OF STATIC ELECTRICITY ON MY MOTHER'S RAYON SLIP...

THOSE WERE THE YEARS OF THE HULA SKIRT CRAZE; THEY HAD TROPICAL BREEZE FANS IN ALL THE BANKS AND OFFICE BUILDINGS — NOBODY LOOKED AT WHAT THEY WERE DOING!

... A MUSTARD STAIN ON MY FATHER'S NECKTIE.

IN 1950, THE WHOLE LENGTH OF HUSSERL AVENUE WAS ACCIDENTALLY REPAVED WITH BLACK LICORICE CANDY — IT WAS A TIME OF TREMENDOUS DISTRACTION.

I WAS BORN THE NEXT YEAR.

TEN THOUSAND GARBAGE CANS, BOTH PRIVATE AND PUBLIC, WERE THROWN OUT ALONG WITH THE TRASH; TODAY'S TAX-PAYERS ARE STILL PAYING FOR THEIR REPLACEMENT. PEOPLE BEGAN TO WASH OUT THEIR POCKET CHANGE EACH NIGHT ALONG WITH THEIR UNDERWEAR — OR AT LEAST CONVERT AS MUCH AS POSSIBLE INTO PAPER MONEY — THOSE WERE DARK DAYS.

IT WAS A TIME OF THE LAST GREAT SPELLING REFORM MOVEMENT. MEN SACRIFICED THEIR CAREERS AND BROKE THEIR HEALTH IN AN EFFORT TO EXPOSE THE SECRET RELATIONSHIPS BETWEEN EVEN VAGUELY HOMONYMOUS WORDS.

I FORGOT MY BIRTH CERTIFICATE IN THE SLEEPING COMPARTMENT.

IF YOU'RE CAUGHT, I'LL SEE YOU IN CRIMINAL COURT.

WHICH BERTH, UPPER OR LOWER?

WELL-MEANING HEALTH DEPARTMENT OFFICIALS LOOKED THE OTHER WAY AS MALTED MILKSHAKES WERE BEING SOLD AT CORNER STANDS ALL OVER THE CITY. IN THOSE DAYS, THE WORKING MAN KILLED HIS APPETITE AT 5 P.M. ONLY TO HAVE IT RESURRECTED IN THE MIDDLE OF THE NIGHT.

YOU'RE OLD ENOUGH TO HAVE HEARD OF "MIDNIGHT SNACKS."

YOUR FATHER WOULD BE ALONE IN THE KITCHEN WITH A LOAF OF RYE BREAD AND SOME SWISS CHEESE, WHILE YOUR MOTHER LAY AWAKE IN BED TRYING TO REMEMBER WHICH HULA SKIRT WAS AT THE CLEANERS — MAN'S CAPACITY FOR RETROSPECTION HAD SHRUNKEN IN THE WASH.

WERE THEY MADE OF REAL GRASS OR JUST GREEN PLASTIC?

IN THE WANING YEARS OF THIS CENTURY, THERE HAS COALESCED AROUND THE COMMON HALLWAY FIRE EXTINGUISHER, AN INFORMAL CULT COMPOSED MAINLY OF YOUNG UNMARRIED MEN.

MY BAD LUCK—THREE EMPLOYEES ON MATERNITY LEAVE AT THE SAME TIME.

RELAX, THE PERPETUATION OF THE SPECIES IS GOOD FOR BUSINESS.

IN THESE SOLEMN BRASS TOTEMS, WITH THEIR SINGLE HOSE-LIKE APPENDAGES HANGING LIMPLY AT THEIR SIDE, THESE YOUNG MEN FIND SOLACE.

NO ONE EVER SEES THEM BEING REFILLED, AND YET THEY'RE ALWAYS FULL.

PASSING BACK AND FORTH THROUGH THE HALLWAY OVER THE YEARS OF THEIR EMPLOYMENT, EACH INITIATE COMMITS TO MEMORY THE INFORMATION ENGRAVED ON THE MANUFACTURER'S ESCUTCHEON.

"N. THEWS AND COMPANY, FIRE PROTECTION EQUIPMENT, 1185 MORALS AVENUE."

BUSINESSES COME AND GO, OFFICE PARTITIONS ARE REARRANGED—YET THESE STYLIZED TORSOS REMAIN WHERE THEY ARE, UNDISTURBED THROUGH THE LIFE OF A BUILDING.

MOST ARE NEVER DISCHARGED.

WAITING FOR AN ELEVATOR, OR ON A COFFEE BREAK, THESE YOUNG OFFICE WORKERS WILL STAND IN SILENT EMULATION—

I NEED TEMPORARY HELP...

THEIR BACKS AGAINST SOME HALLWAY CORNER WALL—

MALE, FEMALE—WHATEVER YOU GOT—SOMEONE TO ANSWER THE PHONE...

AS THOUGH FILLED WITH A MYSTERIOUS CHEMICAL SUBSTANCE, UNDER TREMENDOUS PRESSURE—

A WARM BODY AT THE RECEPTION DESK—WHO CARES WHAT HAIR COLOR!

GUARANTEED TO QUENCH A SMALL OFFICE FIRE.

TUNG IMPORTS, ROOM 801!

FROM THE SLEEPING PALLET OF *HIS* MODERN PRISON CELL, HECTOR FRENUM RECALLS WITH AFFECTION

PERFUME BOTTLES FILLED WITH TINTED WATER, HOLLOW TELEVISION SETS...

THE QUARTER-INCH-WIDE METALLIC FOIL TAPE WHICH FRAMED THE STOREFRONT WINDOWS OF HIS YOUTH.

MY GIRLFRIEND WAS AN INSATIABLE WINDOW SHOPPER.

BACKLESS MEN'S SUITS, FIBERGLASS SALAMIS...

THESE EFFULGENT BANDS OF SILVER ON THE PERIPHERY OF EACH CONSUMER'S CONSCIOUS MIND

IN THE DAYS BEFORE STEEL GATES AND SUCTION-CUP MOTION DETECTORS, ALL YOU NEEDED WAS A WOOLEN BLANKET AND A HEAVY CONCRETE BLOCK.

PLASTER OF PARIS WEDDING CAKES...

IMBUED THE MOST ORDINARY OF WINDOW DISPLAYS WITH AN AURA OF WONDER AND MONETARY WORTH.

IT WAS CHRISTMAS THREE HUNDRED AND FIFTY-SEVEN DAYS A YEAR AND CHANUKAH THE OTHER EIGHT.

WHAT CHANCE DID YOU HAVE?

EACH WEEK, HIS REVERIES ARE INTERRUPTED BY A VISITING SOCIAL WORKER.

WITH A SMALL PAPER CUP FILLED WITH THE COLD WATER OF REASON, I TRY TO SLAKE A LIFETIME'S WORTH OF COMMERCIAL TITILLATION.

LET'S GO.

EMPTY RECORD JACKETS...

THE FLESHY LIGAMENT CONNECTING "LURE" TO "DETERRENT" IS METHODICALLY SEVERED.

LET ME EXPLAIN THE NATURE OF "DISPLAY MERCHANDISE" ...YOU SEE, NOT EVERY THING HAS A RESALE VALUE...

WHAT ABOUT CARDBOARD LIVING ROOM SETS?

ONLY THROUGH THE SHARDS OF BROKEN GLASS AND THE CLANGOR OF AN ELECTRIC ALARM BELL

HIS MIND IS WANDERING.

POCKET BOOKS STUFFED WITH YESTERDAY'S NEWSPAPER, TWO-DIMENSIONAL BRASSIERES, SIZE FOURTEEN SHOES, WAX CHOCOLATES...

CAN ONE FULLY APPRECIATE THE QUALITY OF MERCHANDISE ON DISPLAY.

A STUNTED MATTRESS AND BOX-SPRING.

MORTAL CO! BR SPECIAL 2 for 1 EXTRA FIRM

ON ELECTION DAY, MR. KNIPL HAS A LATE SUPPER.

I LIKE TO WAIT AND SEE HOW THE POLITICAL SITUATION SHAPES UP BEFORE I THROW MY VOTE AWAY.

SURE, RELAX, THE POLLS ARE OPEN TILL NINE.

A HUNDRED FEET AWAY FROM THE DOORS OF A PUBLIC SCHOOL GYMNASIUM, A SPLIT-PANTS PARTY MEMBER HANDS OUT SOILED PALMCARDS.

THIS YEAR, THEY DUG UP A CANDIDATE WITH THE SAME NAME AS OUR MAN — JUST TO CONFUSE THE ISSUE.

VOTE PINYON SPLIT-PANTS

A CAMPAIGN WORKER FOR THE GENTLE BREEZE PARTY SOLICITS VOTES BEFORE A BUSY RESTAURANT.

FEELS GOOD IN THERE, DOESN'T IT? A GENTLE BREEZE IS WHAT THIS CITY NEEDS!

THE MAIN COURSE IS SERVED.

WHICH MAN CAN BEST FILL THE AISLE SEAT LEFT EMPTY BY THE SUDDEN DEPARTURE OF THE HONORABLE BACKSIDER OF THE LOWER 79th DISTRICT AND CO-CHAIR-MAN OF THE SEDENTARY FLANNEL COCCYX: JOE NECHO?

A YOUNG MAN AT THE NEXT TABLE DELIVERS AN IMPASSIONED SPEECH.

THEY FIND A SMALL, ALMOST UNNOTICEABLE RENT IN THE FABRIC OF SOCIETY; THEY POKE THEIR FINGER IN AND TEAR IT WIDE OPEN, EXPOSING THE WORKINGMAN TO NEEDLESS HUMILIATION —ALL IN THE NAME OF SOCIAL VENTILATION!

HE'S ONLY HALF-SITTING, BALANCING HIMSELF WITH THE OTHER FOOT.

MEANWHILE, THEY GO BACK TO THEIR STEAM-HEATED OFFICES TO PERUSE THOSE SMALL ADS FOR THERMAL UNDERWEAR IN THE BACK PAGES OF SOME FANCY MAGAZINE!

AND THE OTHER PARTY IS NO BETTER— THEY GIVE US A NEEDLE AND THREAD AND SAY, "GO AHEAD, HELP YOURSELF, YOU'RE GOOD WITH YOUR HANDS!"

WAIT, WAIT, HE'S LEADING UP TO SOME-THING.

I JUST WANT TO GET INTO A NICE, WARM VOTING BOOTH.

AND STILL LATER THAT NIGHT AT THE PUBLIC SCHOOL GYMNASIUM.

SOMEONE SHOULD TAKE A LOOK.

WHAT IS HE DOING IN THERE, STUDYING POLITICAL SCIENCE?

RELAX, WE'RE HERE UNTIL NINE O'CLOCK.

231

79 A. 81 E.

ON A VACANT LOT, IN A SPARSELY POPULATED CORNER OF THE CITY,

THERE STANDS THE BATTERED SHELL OF A FULL-SIZED APARTMENT HOUSE MOCK-UP USED FOR INSTRUCTIONAL PURPOSES.

NEWCOMERS, FROM SMALL TOWNS AND SUBURBAN TRACTS, SPEND A DAY HERE TRAINING TO MEET THE EVENTUALITIES OF HIGH-DENSITY LIVING:

THE NOISE OF UPSTAIRS NEIGHBORS,

THE SMELL OF UNFAMILIAR COOKING,

THE LEAKAGE OF OLD PIPES,

CONFINEMENT WITHIN CLOSE QUARTERS,

AND THE MONOTONY OF A REAR-BEDROOM-WINDOW VIEW.

A FAMILIAR NOTICE TAPED TO THE DOOR OF A RETAIL TROPHY SUPPLY STORE

"CLOSED DUE TO DEATH IN FAMILY."

THAT'S THE FOURTH TIME THIS YEAR.

HAS PROFOUND REPERCUSSIONS AMONG THE LIVING.

I CAME TO PICK UP AN ORDER.

THEY USUALLY SAY WHEN THEY'LL RE-OPEN. NO, THIS MUST BE A CLOSE RELATIVE OR MAYBE EVEN ONE OF THE VIVIFELD BROTHERS— LOOK AT THAT HANDWRITING.

Closed due to DEATH in family

THREE WEEKS AGO, WHEN I LEFT A DEPOSIT, THEY BOTH LOOKED PERFECTLY HEALTHY.

CONGRATULATIONS, CONGRATULATIONS. WHAT CAN WE DO FOR YOU?

THAT EVENING, AT THE TWENTY-FIFTH ANNUAL "EIGHT-BALLS-FOR-A-DOLLAR INVITATIONAL SKI-BALL TOURNAMENT" DINNER, AN ANNOUNCEMENT IS MADE.

WE ARE FORCED, DUE TO CIRCUMSTANCES BEYOND OUR CONTROL, TO POSTPONE TONIGHT'S AWARDS PRESENTATION. THIS YEAR'S WINNERS MUST MAKE DO WITH A SIMPLE VERBAL ACKNOWLEDGEMENT.

FELLOW PLAYERS, THIS IS MADNESS! I KNOW HOW THE VIVIFELD BROTHERS WORK. THEIR FILE CABINET IS THE BACK POCKET OF A PAIR OF GREEN WORK-PANTS; THE AFTERNOON'S LUNCH ORDER BLOTS OUT THE DETAILS OF A COMPLEX ENGRAVING JOB— NOTHING'S DONE UNTIL THE LAST MINUTE, AND THEN, ONLY WHEN A POOR STOCKBOY IS FRIGHTENED INTO ACTION BY THREATS OF BODILY HARM.

I'M TELLING YOU, THE OLDER VIVIFELD BROTHER HAS TAKEN OUR TROPHY ORDER WITH HIM TO THE GRAVE. WE CAN FORGET ABOUT IT, BUT WE CAN'T ASK FOUR HEALTHY YOUNG MEN TO WAIT TILL RESURRECTION DAY TO RECEIVE THEIR AWARDS.

EXIT

LIFE MUST GO ON! SOMEONE GET A YELLOW PAGES— WE'LL FIND ANOTHER GODDAMN TROPHY MANUFACTURER TONIGHT AND PUT IN A RUSH ORDER!

HOTEL ROQUET

A FEW OLDER PLAYERS ARE LEFT TO ENJOY THE DESSERT COURSE.

WHAT'S SIX OR SEVEN WEEKS? ...A DECENT PERIOD OF MOURNING.

WAITER! ROLL ANOTHER ICE CREAM BALL OVER HERE.

THE VIVIFELD BROTHERS SIT WRAPPED IN WOOLEN BLANKETS ON THE FOURTH TIER OF A GRANDSTAND ERECTED FOR THE DAY ON THE GROUNDS OF THE CEMETERY OF THE EXPIRED COUPON REDEEMER.

I HOPE YOU REMEMBERED TO PUT THE SIGN UP.

THROUGH A HAZE OF AIR-BORNE SOIL, THE CROWD CHEERS ON TWO CHAMPIONSHIP GRAVE-DIGGERS.

WHAT BUSINESS IS IT OF THEIRS WHY WE TAKE THE DAY OFF?

THREE TROPHIES WAIT ON A SMALL STONE BENCH.

"FIRST PLACE IN OPENING, CLOSING AND DISINTERMENT, COURTESY OF VIVIFELD BROS. MANUFACTURING COMPANY."

A MECHANICAL HOE STANDS BY IN CASE OF A CAVE-IN.

BUT THERE'S NO GUARANTEE WE'LL GET TO YOU IN TIME.

EVERYONE PUTS UP A SIGN; IT'S A COMMON COURTESY.

IT'S A LIE.

Closed due to DEATH in family

THERE WAS A DEATH IN OUR FAMILY—THREE YEARS AGO—THAT'S WHEN WE FIRST LEARNED ABOUT SEMI-PROFESSIONAL, COMPETITIVE GRAVE-DIGGING.

THAT'S NOTHING. I SAW JOHNNY JOLSON CLOSE A GRAVE IN 10 MINUTES FLAT.

VIVIFELD
MARTIN
1910-1996

THE SMELL OF EARTH, THE FRESH AIR, THE INEVITABILITY— IT'S LIKE NO OTHER SPORT!

THAT'S GOLLICHEK. HE DOES THE SIX-FOOT FREE-STYLE IN 29 MINUTES.

ON THE SIDELINES, SPECTATORS PLACE BETS UPON THEIR OWN MORTALITY.

10 TO 1 I MAKE IT TILL NEXT CHRISTMAS.

DOUBLE OR NOTHING YOUR WIFE GOES FIRST.

A FUNERAL PROCESSION PASSES IN THE NEAR DISTANCE.

GOLLICHEK'S DIGGING TODAY.

I KNOW, I KNOW... I'LL WATCH IT TONIGHT ON T.V.

VINKLE
1905-1995

MORAL
1910—1990

By chance, the existence of a small "social vacuum" is discovered on the sidewalk in front of Shikar's wine and liquor store.

START THE CAMERA! TAKE NOTES! WE MAY NOT SEE ONE AGAIN IN OUR LIFETIME.

A rare confluence of neon light; the hypnotic motion of a motorized window display...

LOOK, THE POOR GUY DOESN'T KNOW WHAT TO DO WITH HIS HANDS.

FOR THE ROAD!

The faint smell of cherry schnapps and the sound of "light music" from a transistor radio behind the sales counter

HE'S DISCOVERED HIS WALLET, BUT NOW MUST LEARN, FROM SCRATCH, THE MEANING OF MONEY.

"YOU'RE A DELIGHTFUL INDIVIDUAL, INDIVIDUAL, DIVIDINDUAL..."

Has, over the past twenty-five years, completely eroded the influence of social norms and values within the immediate vicinity of this storefront.

BUSINESS IS NOT WHAT IT USED TO BE, AND SO MY GRANDSON SUGGESTED THAT I CALL SOMEONE FROM THE DEPARTMENT OF SOCIAL ANTHROPOLOGY.

THANK YOU FOR YOUR PATRONAGE

WE'LL CAMP HERE ALL NIGHT IF NECESSARY — OR AT LEAST UNTIL ANOTHER PASSERBY WANDERS INTO THE "VACUUM."

JUST THINK! AN OPPORTUNITY TO WITNESS HUMAN INTERACTION IN THE ABSENCE OF ALL SOCIAL MORES AND TABOOS.

20TH CENTURY MAN REDUCED TO A FERAL STATE — WHO KNOWS WHAT HE'LL DO? STAND BACK, BUT KEEP THE CAMERA RUNNING! I'VE ALREADY BOOKED A 45-MINUTE FILM PROGRAM AND LECTURE SERIES FOR NEXT YEAR AT THE MUSEUM OF NATURAL HISTORY.

At two o'clock in the morning, another man is attracted by the liquor store's red neon light.

IMPORTED VODKA'S ALMOST TWICE THE PRICE OF DOMESTIC.

THAT'S THE ONLY DIFFERENCE.

THE SECOND MAN'S FLY HAS WORKED ITSELF OPEN. GIVE ME A CLOSE-UP, PLEASE.

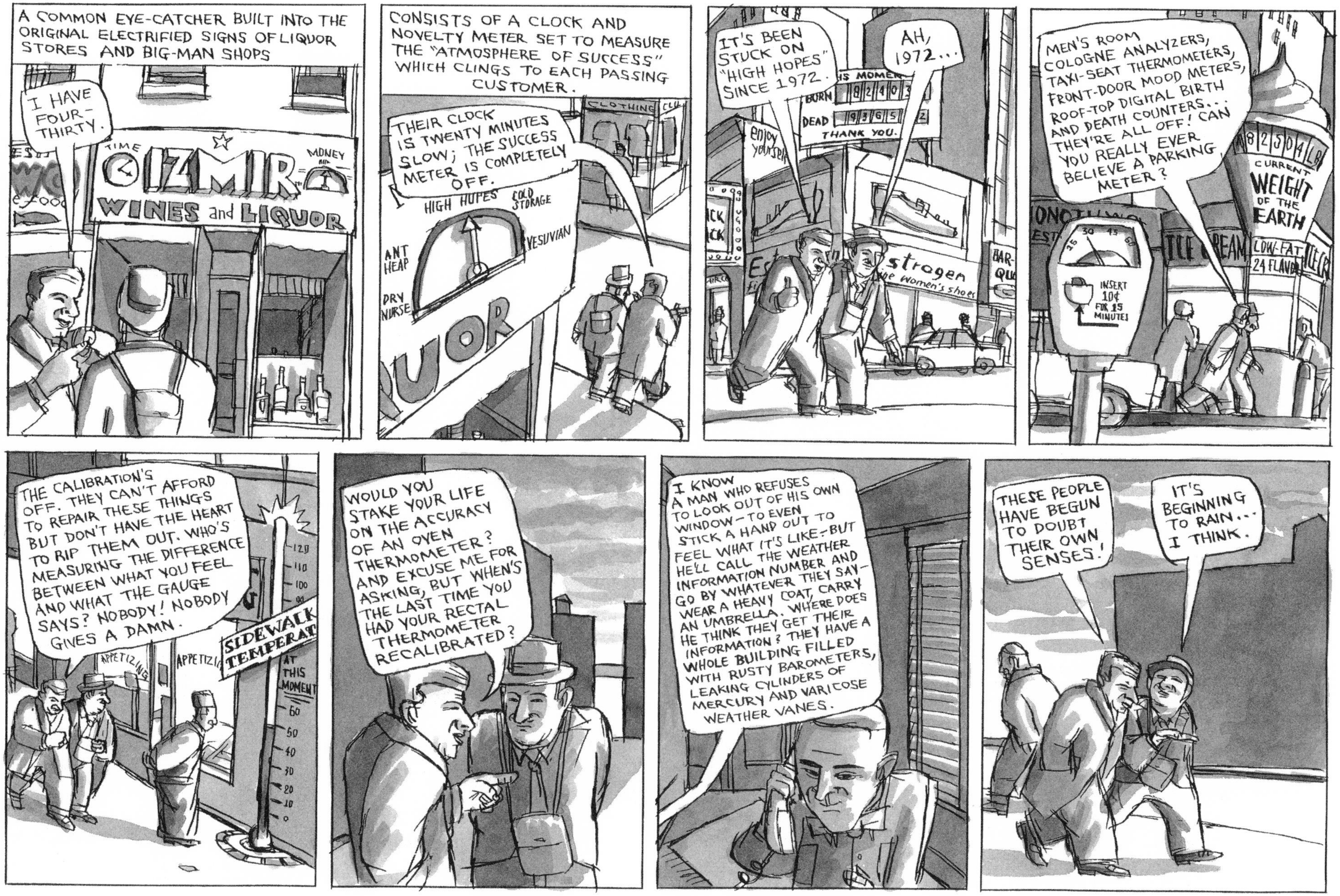
A COMMON EYE-CATCHER BUILT INTO THE ORIGINAL ELECTRIFIED SIGNS OF LIQUOR STORES AND BIG-MAN SHOPS
I HAVE FOUR-THIRTY.
TIME
IZMIR
MONEY
WINES and LIQUOR
CONSISTS OF A CLOCK AND NOVELTY METER SET TO MEASURE THE "ATMOSPHERE OF SUCCESS" WHICH CLINGS TO EACH PASSING CUSTOMER.
THEIR CLOCK IS TWENTY MINUTES SLOW; THE SUCCESS METER IS COMPLETELY OFF.
HIGH HOPES
COLD STORAGE
VESUVIAN
ANT HEAP
DRY NURSE
IT'S BEEN STUCK ON "HIGH HOPES" SINCE 1972.
AH, 1972...
BORN
DEAD
THANK YOU.
MEN'S ROOM COLOGNE ANALYZERS, TAXI-SEAT THERMOMETERS, FRONT-DOOR MOOD METERS, ROOF-TOP DIGITAL BIRTH AND DEATH COUNTERS... THEY'RE ALL OFF! CAN YOU REALLY EVER BELIEVE A PARKING METER?
CURRENT WEIGHT OF THE EARTH
INSERT 10¢ FOR 15 MINUTES
THE CALIBRATION'S OFF. THEY CAN'T AFFORD TO REPAIR THESE THINGS BUT DON'T HAVE THE HEART TO RIP THEM OUT. WHO'S MEASURING THE DIFFERENCE BETWEEN WHAT YOU FEEL AND WHAT THE GAUGE SAYS? NOBODY! NOBODY GIVES A DAMN.
AT THIS MOMENT
WOULD YOU STAKE YOUR LIFE ON THE ACCURACY OF AN OVEN THERMOMETER? AND EXCUSE ME FOR ASKING, BUT WHEN'S THE LAST TIME YOU HAD YOUR RECTAL THERMOMETER RECALIBRATED?
I KNOW A MAN WHO REFUSES TO LOOK OUT OF HIS OWN WINDOW—TO EVEN STICK A HAND OUT TO FEEL WHAT IT'S LIKE—BUT HE'LL CALL THE WEATHER INFORMATION NUMBER AND GO BY WHATEVER THEY SAY—WEAR A HEAVY COAT, CARRY AN UMBRELLA. WHERE DOES HE THINK THEY GET THEIR INFORMATION? THEY HAVE A WHOLE BUILDING FILLED WITH RUSTY BAROMETERS, LEAKING CYLINDERS OF MERCURY AND VARICOSE WEATHER VANES.
THESE PEOPLE HAVE BEGUN TO DOUBT THEIR OWN SENSES!
IT'S BEGINNING TO RAIN... I THINK.

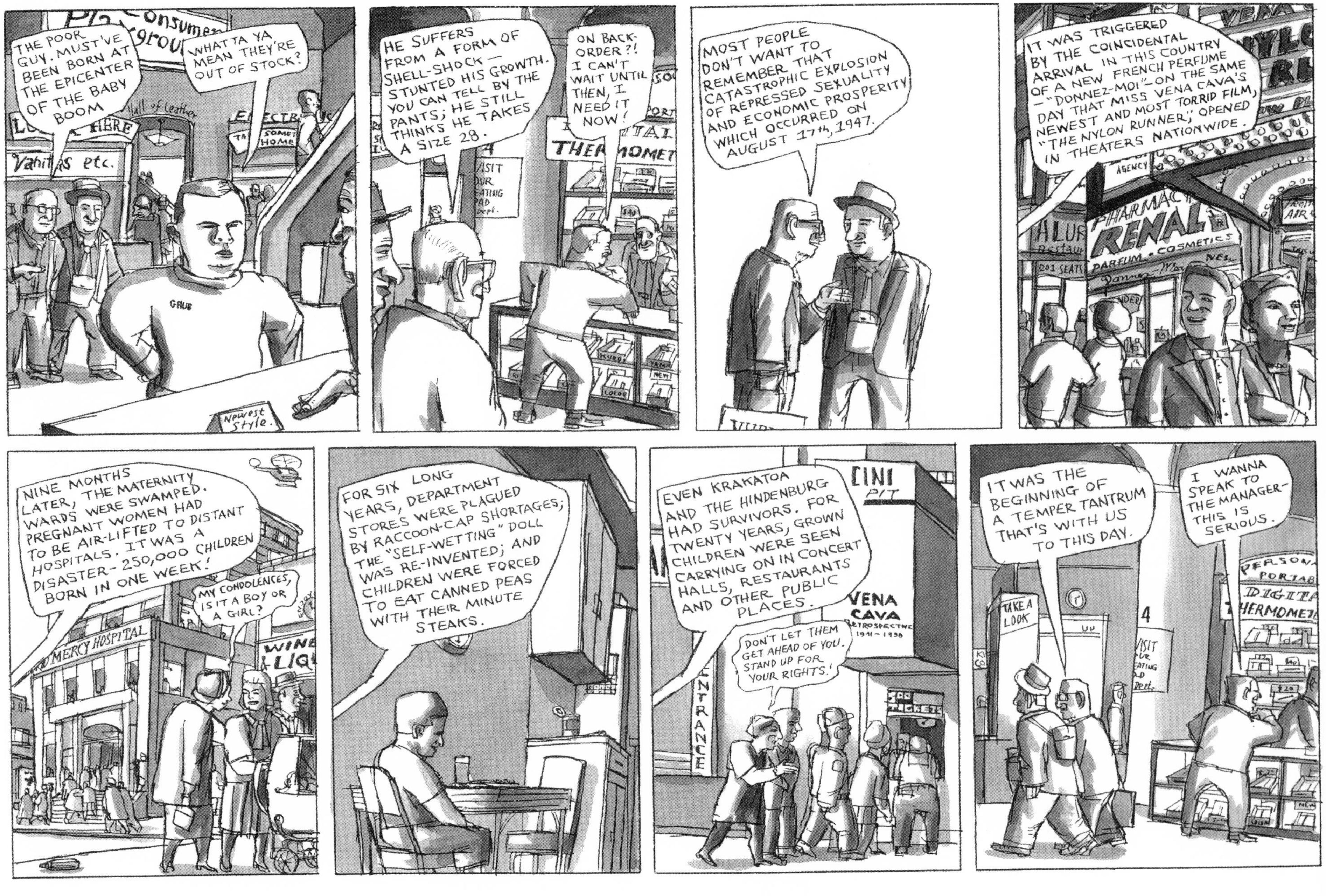
THE POOR GUY. MUST'VE BEEN BORN AT THE EPICENTER OF THE BABY BOOM
WHAT TA YA MEAN THEY'RE OUT OF STOCK?
Hall of Leather
Vanities etc.
Newest Style.
HE SUFFERS FROM A FORM OF SHELL-SHOCK — STUNTED HIS GROWTH. YOU CAN TELL BY THE PANTS; HE STILL THINKS HE TAKES A SIZE 28.
ON BACK-ORDER?! I CAN'T WAIT UNTIL THEN, I NEED IT NOW!
MOST PEOPLE DON'T WANT TO REMEMBER THAT CATASTROPHIC EXPLOSION OF REPRESSED SEXUALITY AND ECONOMIC PROSPERITY WHICH OCCURRED ON AUGUST 17th, 1947.
IT WAS TRIGGERED BY THE COINCIDENTAL ARRIVAL IN THIS COUNTRY OF A NEW FRENCH PERFUME — "DONNEZ-MOI" — ON THE SAME DAY THAT MISS VENA CAVA'S NEWEST AND MOST TORRID FILM, "THE NYLON RUNNER," OPENED IN THEATERS NATIONWIDE.
PHARMACIE RENAL
PARFUM • COSMETICS
NINE MONTHS LATER, THE MATERNITY WARDS WERE SWAMPED. PREGNANT WOMEN HAD TO BE AIR-LIFTED TO DISTANT HOSPITALS. IT WAS A DISASTER — 250,000 CHILDREN BORN IN ONE WEEK!
MY CONDOLENCES, IS IT A BOY OR A GIRL?
MERCY HOSPITAL
FOR SIX LONG YEARS, DEPARTMENT STORES WERE PLAGUED BY RACCOON-CAP SHORTAGES; THE "SELF-WETTING" DOLL WAS RE-INVENTED; AND CHILDREN WERE FORCED TO EAT CANNED PEAS WITH THEIR MINUTE STEAKS.
EVEN KRAKATOA AND THE HINDENBURG HAD SURVIVORS. FOR TWENTY YEARS, GROWN CHILDREN WERE SEEN CARRYING ON IN CONCERT HALLS, RESTAURANTS AND OTHER PUBLIC PLACES.
DON'T LET THEM GET AHEAD OF YOU. STAND UP FOR YOUR RIGHTS!
VENA CAVA RETROSPECTIVE 1941 – 1958
ENTRANCE
IT WAS THE BEGINNING OF A TEMPER TANTRUM THAT'S WITH US TO THIS DAY.
I WANNA SPEAK TO THE MANAGER — THIS IS SERIOUS.
TAKE A LOOK

I'D LIKE TO INTRODUCE YOU TO MY ACCOUNTANT'S SISTER, MYRA FINSTER.

IN THE FACE OF EACH STRANGER HE MET, ARTHUR MURMUR SAW THE GLIMMER OF A VAGUE RESEMBLANCE TO SOME WELL-KNOWN CELEBRITY.

HAS ANYONE EVER TOLD YOU THAT YOU BEAR A STRIKING RESEMBLANCE TO THE ACTRESS VENA CAVA?

NO.

WHILE EACH FORTUITOUS DISCOVERY WAS A SOURCE OF MOMENTARY ELATION,

ANOTHER VENA CAVA! I CAN'T GET OVER IT.

SHE LOOKS LIKE MYRA FINSTER TO ME.

IN PRIVATE, HE WAS QUICK TO POINT OUT THE FAILINGS OF A PERFECT MATCH.

YES, POOR GIRL, A VENA CAVA WITH A RECEDING CHIN.

LET ME GET A PAPER.

IN THE POPULATION OF A CITY THIS SIZE,

THE TENOR, GEORGE ZHAMBAY WITH A HARELIP.

HE CONCLUDED THAT MOST INDIVIDUALS WERE CURSED TO LIVE OUT THEIR LIVES AS MERE APPROXIMATIONS,

THE BALLERINA WANDA BOON WITH RICKETS.

COME ON...

OR DEFECTIVE REPLICAS, OF A GOLDEN HANDFUL OF PROMINENT ACTORS, SPORTS FIGURES AND POLITICIANS.

SENATOR HAROLD RUPIA WITH BUCKTEETH.

PLEASE.

NO ONE HAD YET NOTICED THAT ARTHUR MURMUR WAS, HIMSELF, AN ANEMIC VERSION OF THE NOTORIOUS CHILD MURDERER, CLAUDE LOUVRE.

SO TELL ME, THIS MISS FINSTER, ARE HER PARENTS STILL LIVING?

DAILY PIGEON

LOUVRE GETS 300 YEARS
NO CHANCE OF PAROLE

C. LOUVRE

NEWSPA

ON THE FIRST HOT DAY OF SUMMER, ABRAHAM CUZOR, THE DE FACTO PRESIDENT OF THE METROPOLITAN TAP-WATER RUNNERS' ASSOCIATION, INAUGURATES THE CLUB'S 105th SEASON.

YOU HAVE THE BATHROOM AND KITCHEN SINKS BOTH GOING FULL BLAST!

DON'T WORRY, I'M WATCHING.

HIS WIFE'S ANGUISHED COMPLAINTS ONLY CONFIRM THE IMPORTANCE OF HIS OFFICE.

WHY DON'T YOU GO OUT FOR A WALK? THIS IS NOT HEALTHY.

CUZOR CALCULATES THE SPEED AT WHICH THE WATER IN HIS GLASS HAD TRAVELED FROM RESERVOIR TO SINK...

150 MILES IN TWENTY MINUTES FLAT. THAT MUST BE SOME KIND OF RECORD.

AND THEN PROPOSES AN INVITATIONAL MEET BE HELD THAT AFTERNOON AT HIS FRIEND'S APARTMENT.

NOTHING'S WRONG, I JUST WANTED TO GET OUT OF THE HOUSE.

WOULD YOU LIKE SOMETHING TO DRINK?

THEY SPECULATE UPON THE WATER TEMPERATURE AT ITS SOURCE,

IT STANDS AS A SIX-STORY-HIGH COLUMN IN THESE OLD PIPES UNTIL YOU'RE THIRSTY.

UPSTATE IT STILL GETS COLD; YOU NEED A JACKET AT NIGHT.

AND MARVEL AT THE TREMENDOUS POWER OF WATER, HARNESSED AND LED BY MAN, THROUGH A FAUCET.

BE CAREFUL, OPEN HER UP EASY.

DO YOU HEAR FROM MANNY VONDLER?

BOTH MEN WAIT ANXIOUSLY,

HE NEVER FULLY RECOVERED; BUT THAT WAS ICE WATER AND HE WAS A COMPULSIVE DRINKER. LET IT RUN.

FULLY AWARE OF THE DANGER INVOLVED IN DRINKING TOO COLD A GLASS OF WATER.

LET IT RUN.

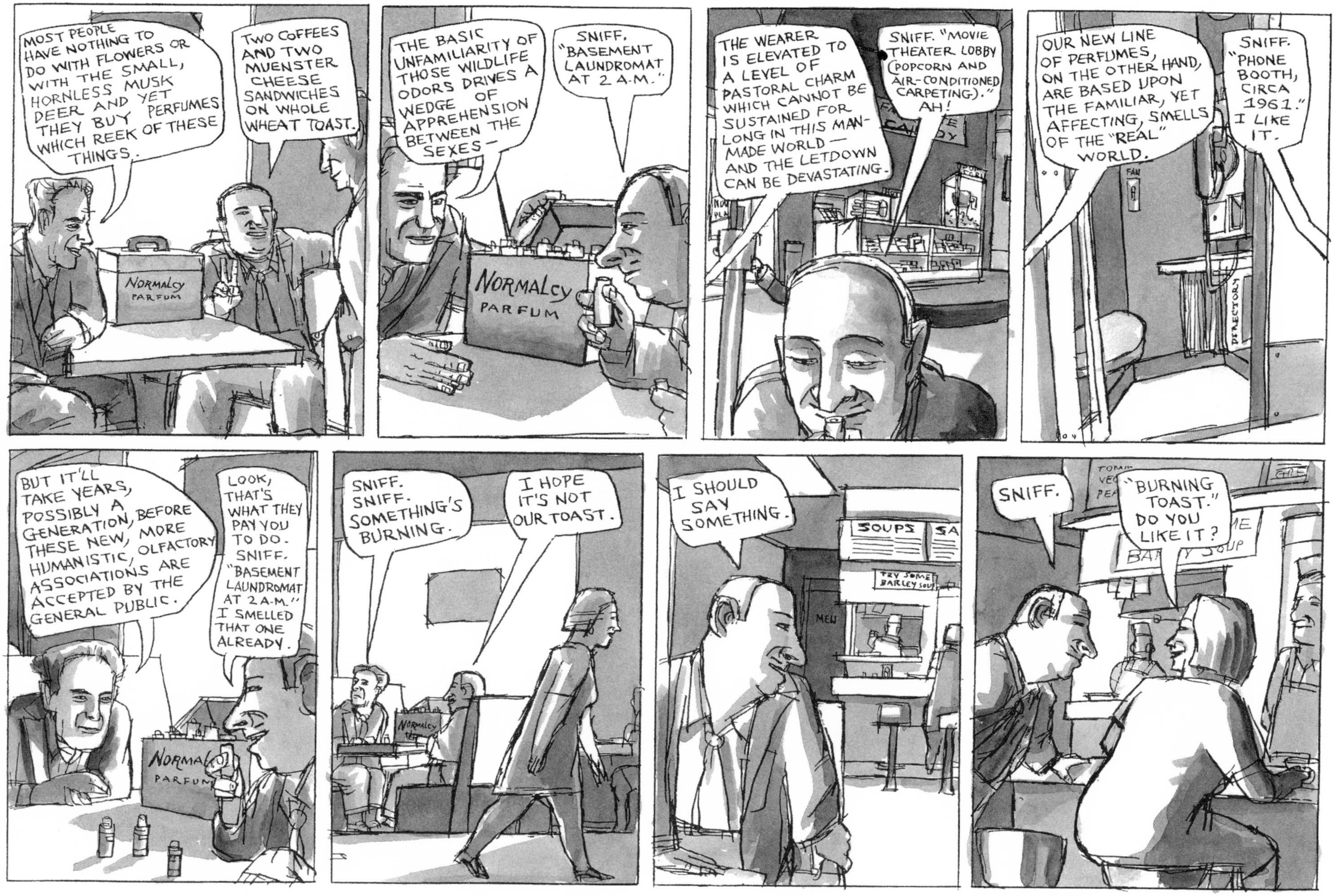
MOST PEOPLE HAVE NOTHING TO DO WITH FLOWERS OR WITH THE SMALL, HORNLESS MUSK DEER AND YET THEY BUY PERFUMES WHICH REEK OF THESE THINGS.
TWO COFFEES AND TWO MUENSTER CHEESE SANDWICHES ON WHOLE WHEAT TOAST.
NORMALCY PARFUM
THE BASIC UNFAMILIARITY OF THOSE WILDLIFE ODORS DRIVES A WEDGE OF APPREHENSION BETWEEN THE SEXES—
SNIFF. "BASEMENT LAUNDROMAT AT 2 A.M."
NORMALCY PARFUM
THE WEARER IS ELEVATED TO A LEVEL OF PASTORAL CHARM WHICH CANNOT BE SUSTAINED FOR LONG IN THIS MAN-MADE WORLD— AND THE LETDOWN CAN BE DEVASTATING.
SNIFF. "MOVIE THEATER LOBBY (POPCORN AND AIR-CONDITIONED CARPETING)." AH!
OUR NEW LINE OF PERFUMES, ON THE OTHER HAND, ARE BASED UPON THE FAMILIAR, YET AFFECTING, SMELLS OF THE "REAL" WORLD.
SNIFF. "PHONE BOOTH, CIRCA 1961." I LIKE IT.
FAN
DIRECTORY
BUT IT'LL TAKE YEARS, POSSIBLY A GENERATION, BEFORE THESE NEW, MORE HUMANISTIC, OLFACTORY ASSOCIATIONS ARE ACCEPTED BY THE GENERAL PUBLIC.
LOOK, THAT'S WHAT THEY PAY YOU TO DO. SNIFF. "BASEMENT LAUNDROMAT AT 2 A.M." I SMELLED THAT ONE ALREADY.
PARFUM
SNIFF. SNIFF. SOMETHING'S BURNING.
I HOPE IT'S NOT OUR TOAST.
I SHOULD SAY SOMETHING.
SOUPS
TRY SOME BARLEY SOUP
MEN
SNIFF.
"BURNING TOAST." DO YOU LIKE IT?

THE NORMALCY PARFUM COMPANY CONDUCTS ITS SALES TRAINING SEMINAR IN A SMALL ROOM RENTED FOR THE EVENING.
MOST OF YOUR CUSTOMERS ARE ALREADY CHOKING ON A SURFEIT OF MERCHANDISE — THEY DON'T NEED ANYTHING ELSE.
SUN BURN PARLOR
SUN BURN WHILE-U-WAIT
HOORAY GOURMET DELI
NEBULA CHAMP SNEAKERS
TAKE OUT
ITS DECOR, BORN OF THE NEGLECT OF PEOPLE WITH MORE IMPORTANT THINGS ON THEIR MIND,
HOW CAN WE CLEAR A PATH OF DESIRE THROUGH THIS BRAMBLE OF DISILLUSIONMENT?
CONSISTS OF A TV MONITOR AND VCR, A FOLDING TABLE WITH TEN CHAIRS, AND A FEW PERSPIRATION-STAINED MAPS OF THE CITY TAPED TO THE WALL.
SIMPLE, BY PUTTING A PRICE TAG ON THE RESIDUE OF EVERYDAY LIFE: THE SMELL OF A LIBRARY BOOK, THE TANG OF A BROWN PAPER BAG, THE AROMA OF DOOR-HINGE OIL — OUR NEW SPRING LINE. PASS THEM AROUND.
TWO BLOCKS AWAY STAND THE RUINS OF A ONCE-GREAT DEPARTMENT STORE — AN OBJECT LESSON TO ALL NEW SALESMEN.
VESTAL BROTHERS DEPARTMENT STORE — THEY DEVOTED THE ENTIRE GROUND FLOOR TO PERFUMES AND FRAGRANCES — NOW LOOK AT THEM!
NEW SPRING STYLES
DEPARTMENT STORE
VESTAL BROTHERS
LAST DAYS
DANGER STAY OUT
FINAL SALE
THE LECTURE PROCEEDS LATE INTO THE NIGHT.
WE OFFER THE ESSENCE OF THINGS WITHOUT THE ACCOMPANYING CLUTTER. THE DIS-EMBODIED SCENT OF A PHONE BOOTH PACKAGED IN A RECYCLABLE GLASS VIAL WITH A SIMPLE TYPEWRITTEN LABEL — LIKE A SCIENTIFIC SPECIMEN, NOT A CHOCOLATE BOX.
Pay Phone circa 1962 Normalcy Parfum
A TANKER CARRYING FIVE THOUSAND GALLONS OF "CZARINA #4" IS ANCHORED, AT THIS MOMENT, IN THE HARBOR WAITING TO DISCHARGE ITS NOXIOUS CARGO — AND WE SIT HERE MAKING SMALL TALK.
DID HE SAY ANYTHING ABOUT OUR COMMISSION?
A ROOMFUL OF MEN WHO ANSWERED A CLASSIFIED AD IN YESTERDAY'S PAPER
THEY SAY THAT WE ARE ALL CANNON-FODDER IN A HOPELESS WAR AGAINST THE HABITS OF EUROPEAN CIVILIZATION — THE DISSONANCE OF FLOWERS MASKING ANIMAL ODORS.
IT CAN'T BE STRAIGHT COMMISSION.
ARE ASKED TO SACRIFICE THEIR LIVES FOR A SMALL SALARY PLUS FIFTEEN PERCENT COMMISSION.
BUT WHAT GOOD IS YOUR SALARY AND COMMISSION IN A WORLD THAT REEKS OF LILY OF THE VALLEY?
PSST. YOU KNOW WHAT TIME IT IS?
SUN BURN PARLOR
HOORAY
SUN BURN WHILE-U-WAIT

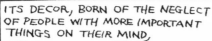

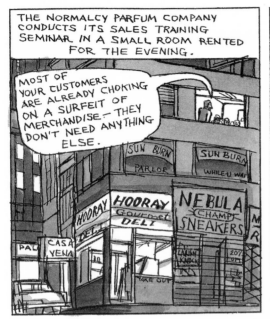

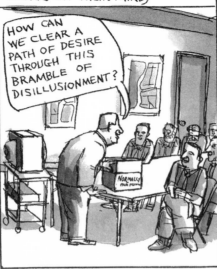

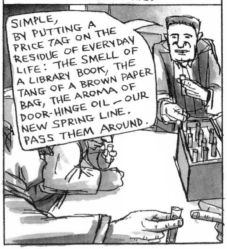

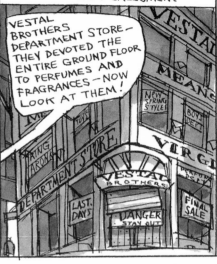

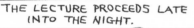

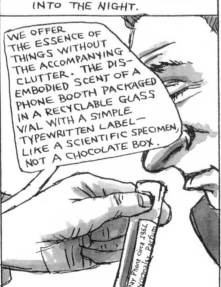

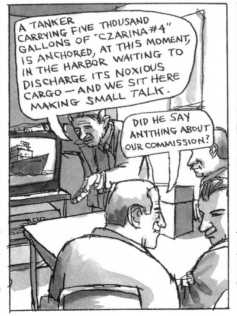

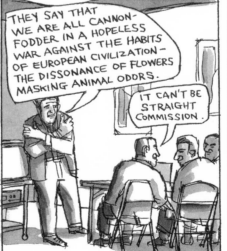

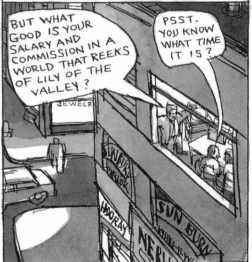

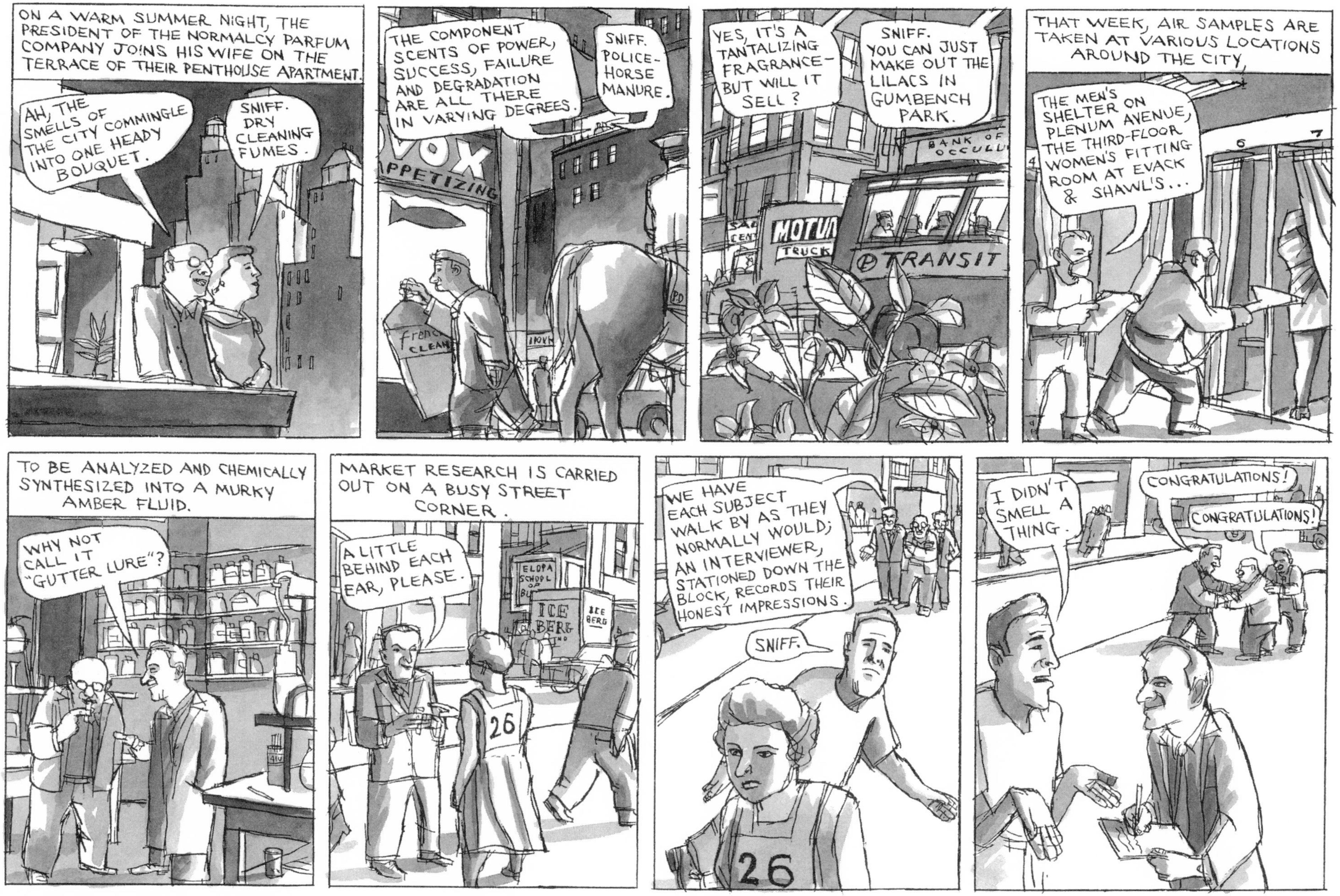
ON A WARM SUMMER NIGHT, THE PRESIDENT OF THE NORMALCY PARFUM COMPANY JOINS HIS WIFE ON THE TERRACE OF THEIR PENTHOUSE APARTMENT.
AH, THE SMELLS OF THE CITY COMMINGLE INTO ONE HEADY BOUQUET.
SNIFF. DRY CLEANING FUMES.
THE COMPONENT SCENTS OF POWER, SUCCESS, FAILURE AND DEGRADATION ARE ALL THERE IN VARYING DEGREES.
SNIFF. POLICE-HORSE MANURE.
YES, IT'S A TANTALIZING FRAGRANCE- BUT WILL IT SELL?
SNIFF. YOU CAN JUST MAKE OUT THE LILACS IN GUMBENCH PARK.
TRANSIT
THAT WEEK, AIR SAMPLES ARE TAKEN AT VARIOUS LOCATIONS AROUND THE CITY,
THE MEN'S SHELTER ON PLENUM AVENUE, THE THIRD-FLOOR WOMEN'S FITTING ROOM AT EVACK & SHAWL'S...
TO BE ANALYZED AND CHEMICALLY SYNTHESIZED INTO A MURKY AMBER FLUID.
WHY NOT CALL IT "GUTTER LURE"?
MARKET RESEARCH IS CARRIED OUT ON A BUSY STREET CORNER.
A LITTLE BEHIND EACH EAR, PLEASE.
ICE BERG
26
WE HAVE EACH SUBJECT WALK BY AS THEY NORMALLY WOULD; AN INTERVIEWER, STATIONED DOWN THE BLOCK, RECORDS THEIR HONEST IMPRESSIONS.
SNIFF.
26
I DIDN'T SMELL A THING.
CONGRATULATIONS!
CONGRATULATIONS!

EVERYWHERE YOU LOOK — FROM MALLS TO MUSEUMS; FROM NEWSPAPERS TO NETSUKE; FROM RACE TRACKS TO RAS MALI — THESE ARE THE PLAYTHINGS OF OUR ADULT LIFE.

A NEW HOPE SVENGER FILM.

EVERY CHILD OUTGROWS HIS TOYS AND GAMES TO MOVE ON TO MORE SERIOUS OCCUPATIONS AND IT'S HIGH TIME WE DID THE SAME:

"NOHTIL BOILS DACHSHUND TETHER."

A CHILD BECOMES BORED AND NATURALLY CRAVES MORE INTRICATE PASTIMES, BUT WE SEEM TO BE CONTENT TO WALLOW IN THE SAME DIRTY SANDBOX YEAR AFTER YEAR, DECADE UPON DECADE,

I KNOW OF ONLY ONE MAN WHO HAS SUCCEEDED IN TAKING THE STEP BEYOND ADULTHOOD TO WHAT HE CALLS "HOODORNAMENT."

WITH THE HELP OF HIS WIFE AND TWO BURLY MEN HIRED FOR THE JOB, HE WAS PHYSICALLY WRENCHED FROM THE PLAYTHINGS OF MIDDLE AGE. EVERYTHING WAS PUT IN A STORAGE ROOM ON RIPURIAN AVENUE FOR HIS GRANDCHILDREN.

THE VCR!

HE SITS HERE ALL DAY IN THIS COFFEE SHOP SCRIBBLING ON PAPER NAPKINS, DRINKING STRONG TEA AND CONTEMPLATING THE LUNCH MENU.

THERE IS NO DIFFERENCE BETWEEN THE VEGETARIAN CHOPPED LIVER APPETIZER AND THE SMALL VEGETARIAN CHOPPED LIVER SALAD PLATE.

IN ONE WEEK, HE'S ADDED SIX HUNDRED NEW WORDS TO THE ENGLISH LANGUAGE, AND JUST THIS MORNING DEVISED A WAY TO STREAMLINE THE MALE URINARY TRACT BY MEANS OF A PAINLESS OPERATION.

"KASTRINO" — AN UNEATEN MORSEL OF CHEESE CAKE. "FREMDING" — THE SOUND OF A STRANGE DOOR-BELL.

AH, SIT DOWN, JOIN ME. WHAT NEWS DO YOU HAVE FROM THE ADULT WORLD? ARE WOMEN STILL WEARING COLLAPSABLE HEELS? HAVE THEY DISCOVERED THE LOCATION OF THE COIN-RETURN CHUTE ON THE SODA MACHINE IN THE LOBBY OF KROWBAR UNIVERSITY? TELL ME!

PEOPLE HAVE BEEN PERSPIRING SINCE THE END OF THE LAST ICE AGE — AND YET IT WASN'T UNTIL 1952 THAT THE DEODORANT BUSINESS REALLY TOOK OFF.

THERE IS A POTENTIAL SOURCE OF INCOME HIDDEN WITHIN EACH MANIFESTATION OF NATURE, BUT SOMEONE HAS TO TURN OVER THE ROCK, PEER UNDER THE LEAF, IN ORDER TO DISCOVER IT — LOOK AT SUNGLASSES, DISPOSABLE DIAPERS, MAPLE SYRUP, DUNE-BUGGIES...

THE PHENOMENON OF RAIN HAS SPAWNED A VAST INDUSTRY OF UMBRELLAS, WATER-PROOF COATS AND RUBBER SHOES...

BUT I AM CONVINCED THAT NO ONE HAS YET EXPLOITED THAT MOMENT OF CLEARING AFTER A RAIN SHOWER WHEN THE CLOUDS DEPART AND THE SUN RETURNS.

YOU HAVE, IN THIS CITY ALONE, EIGHT MILLION PEOPLE WALKING AROUND WITH WET UMBRELLAS AND AN EQUAL NUMBER LOOKING FOR SOMETHING TO DRY THEMSELVES ON.

SURELY THERE'S AN UNTAPPED MARKET HERE FOR SOME KIND OF DISPOSABLE TOWELING PRODUCT — AND THE INVENTION OF THE UMBRELLA STAND HASN'T BEEN IMPROVED UPON SINCE THE EARLY 19th CENTURY.

I'D INVEST A FEW THOUSAND DOLLARS.

NO, NO, NO, THESE IMMENSE PROFITS ARE NOT FOR US TO REAP — THEY WAIT FOR YOUNG MEN WITH ENERGY AND AMBITION.

THE PUDDLES ON THE MAIN THOROUGH-FARES OF THIS CITY HAVE YET TO BE MAPPED AND CHARTED — IT'S A HERCULEAN TASK, NOT FOR TWO MIDDLE-AGED MEN IN WET SHOES.

A NUMBER OF STOREFRONTS, SUBDIVIDED OVER THE YEARS INTO SPACES NO WIDER THAN THE CHEST OF AN ADULT MALE, CAN NOW ONLY ACCOMMODATE A SPECIES OF "DROP-OFF" BUSINESS.

PHOTO PROCESSORS, DRY CLEANERS, NEXT-DAY URINALYSIS LABS...

A MUSCLE-BOUND YOUNG MAN SITS BEHIND THE COUNTER OF A CHEWING-GUM REMOVAL SERVICE.

A CLOTHES RACK, A CASH REGISTER, A FEW PLYWOOD SHELVES AND A WOBBLY STOOL.

IT IS ONE OF SIX DROP-OFF POINTS FOR A LARGE COMMERCIAL CHEWING-GUM REMOVAL PLANT.

REGULAR DRY CLEANERS WON'T TOUCH THIS STUFF.

THE DRIVER, WHO MAKES HIS DAILY PICK-UPS AROUND THE CITY, THRIVES ON FRESH AIR AND CHANGING SCENERY.

HE KEEPS THE DOOR CLOSED.

THE CLERK'S DAY IS A SUCCESSION OF ENCOUNTERS WITH CUSTOMERS WHO SHOW HIM GUM-DAMAGED ARTICLES AND ASK HIS OPINION OF THE CHANCES FOR THEIR SUCCESSFUL CLEANING.

HERE, ON THE SEAT OF MY PANTS— YOU CAN STILL SMELL THE SPEARMINT.

HE PRETENDS TO UNDERSTAND THE POWER OF INDUSTRIAL SOLVENTS AND, IN MANY CASES, DISPENSES FALSE HOPE.

FROM THE BOTTOM OF MY SHOE TO THE ELBOW OF MY JACKET.

IT'S NOTHING, I'VE SEEN WORSE. IT'LL BE LIKE NEW AGAIN.

IN FACT, HE HAS ONLY A VAGUE IDEA OF WHERE THE ITEMS ARE TAKEN TO BE CLEANED,

UNDALETCH... HUNTALEDGE VALLEY? SOMEWHERE ON THE OUTSKIRTS OF THE CITY.

AND CAN ONLY HOPE HIMSELF THAT THEY'LL BE RETURNED ON TIME.

KOLBAR... KOLBAR, MAURICE. MAYBE THEY PUT IT UNDER "M."

A DEALER IN ANTIQUE OFFICE SUPPLIES EXPLORES A DISUSED CORRIDOR OF THE GOULASH BUILDING ON NICKNAM AVENUE.

THESE DAYS I'M LUCKY TO FIND A PACKAGE OF DRIED-UP CARBON PAPER OR AN UNOPENED BOX OF NON-SKID PAPER CLIPS.

BUT HERE, WHAT'S THIS? AN UNUSED WATER-COOLER BOTTLE FROM 1962! THEY MUST'VE FORGOTTEN TO PICK IT UP.

IT'S GLASS AND IN FAIRLY GOOD CONDITION. THIS MAY BE WORTH SOMETHING. I'LL HAVE TO MAKE A FEW PHONE CALLS.

LATER THAT NIGHT IN HIS SHOP...

I SURMISE THAT IT CAME FROM A SUCCESSFUL LAW OFFICE OR ADVERTISING AGENCY — IN THOSE DAYS BOTTLED WATER WAS A LUXURY — MOST PEOPLE JUST REFILLED THE SAME BOTTLE WITH TAP WATER.

THE LABEL READS: "SVONNY RIVER PURE DRINKING WATER CO., 287 LATREEN AVE." YES, YES, THAT'S THE REMARKABLE THING — IT WAS NEVER OPENED! WOULDN'T YOU BE CURIOUS TO HAVE A TASTE OF 1962 VINTAGE WATER?

THIS BOTTLE GOES WAY BACK BEFORE FLUORIDATION — WHEN THE UPSTATE RESERVOIR WAS REALLY UPSTATE. THIS IS THE SAME WATER NORMAN MELBAR MIXED WITH SCOTCH WHILE WRITING "THE DISPOSABLE MUSE" IN 1962. THIS IS WHAT WAS IN THE GLASS ON PRESIDENT DIAMINT'S LECTERN DURING THE FAMOUS TELEVISED DEBATE WITH SENATOR MILES HURON... NOT INTERESTED? NOT YOUR KIND OF THING? OKAY, I UNDERSTAND.

UNLIKE WINE, THIS STUFF WAS NOT BOTTLED TO LAST — IT DOESN'T AGE WELL — PROBABLY SUBJECT TO ALL KINDS OF BACTERIAL CON-TAMINATION. THERE SEEMS TO BE A SCUM ON THE TOP... BUT STILL, I'M TEMPTED TO HAVE A GLASS.

"KUROS VANDER, NOTED ANTIQUE DEALER, AGE 69, DIED LAST NIGHT OF COMPLICATIONS FOLLOWING A SEVERE BOUT OF DISILLUSIONMENT."

TWENTY-FIVE YEARS AGO, A TRUCK, CARRYING FROZEN FISH-STICKS, ACCIDENTLY BACKED UP ONTO THE SIDEWALK AND INTO THE MAIN ENTRANCE OF FELZ' DEPARTMENT STORE.

HE DROVE ALL THE WAY FROM MAINE.

TWENTY YEARS LATER, AN ENTHUSIASTIC WINDOW-SHOPPER PUT HIS HEAD THROUGH THE PLATE OF GLASS BEFORE A SPRING SPORTSWEAR DISPLAY.

LIKE MOTHS TO A FLAME.

THE LURE OF DISCOUNT MERCHANDISE.

INSPIRED BY THE IDEA OF A COASTAL LIGHTHOUSE, MR. FELZ DECIDED TO ERECT A WARNING BEACON ON THAT ONE TREACHEROUS CORNER OF HIS BUILDING.

WHO NEEDS THE SEAGULLS? IF IT WORKS, IT WORKS.

A WEATHERPROOF 800-WATT LAMP SET ON A REVOLVING BRASS FIXTURE

ONCE EVERY ELEVEN SECONDS, OR, THE TIME IT TAKES TO EAT A POTATO CHIP.

CASTS A REASSURING BEAM OF LIGHT INTO THE EYES AND MINDS OF PEDESTRIANS AND MOTORISTS—

A PENETRATING BEACON VISIBLE FROM A REAR BOOTH IN ALI WALLAH'S KASH-BAR RESTAURANT—SIX BLOCKS AWAY!

MUST BE A CLEAR NIGHT.

PEOPLE ARE NOT PURPOSELY GOING OUT OF THEIR WAY TO BUMP INTO OUR BUILDING, BUT IT'S HAPPENED—THE SCARS ARE STILL VISIBLE.

BUT IN THE PAST FIVE YEARS, NOT A SCRATCH.

YOU HAVE HERE THE CONFLUENCE OF TWO MIGHTY AVENUES: HYMOT AND DEPEWER. THE LOCAL PEOPLE ARE ACCUSTOMED TO THE SOUND OF SHATTERING GLASS AND TWISTED METAL. EVEN WITH ALL POSSIBLE PRECAUTIONS IN PLACE, THEY KNOW THAT IT'S JUST A MATTER OF TIME BEFORE THEY'RE AGAIN CALLED TO THEIR WINDOWS TO VIEW THE WRECKAGE OF ANOTHER SOUL UPON THIS CURSED EDIFICE.

LOST IN THE CHEST-HAIR OF TEN THOUSAND BUSY MEN,

HERE, READ IT FOR YOURSELF.

DANGLING AT THE END OF A PHONY 18-CARAT GOLD CHAIN, IS A TINY AMULET OF DUBIOUS VALUE.

"THE SHORTEST DISTANCE BETWEEN TWO POINTS IS A STRAIGHT LINE."

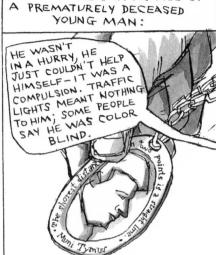

A THIN COPPER MEDAL STAMPED WITH THE HEAD-IN-PROFILE OF A PREMATURELY DECEASED YOUNG MAN:

HE WASN'T IN A HURRY, HE JUST COULDN'T HELP HIMSELF—IT WAS A COMPULSION. TRAFFIC LIGHTS MEANT NOTHING TO HIM; SOME PEOPLE SAY HE WAS COLOR BLIND.

MUNI TYMUS, THE UNOFFICIAL "PATRON SAINT" OF JAYWALKERS AND MID-BLOCK CROSSERS.

POOR GUY, HE WAS ON HIS OWN AND PAID THE ULTIMATE PRICE SO THAT ALL OF US CAN NOW CROSS WITH-OUT LOOKING.

HE'S WITH ME ALL THE TIME—EVEN IN THE SHOWER. HE LOOKS BOTH WAYS FOR ME.

WITH HIS HELP, WE CAN MAKE IT TO THE OTHER SIDE OF THE STREET—BUT MUNI'S NOT A LUCKY CHARM. MOST OF US END UP SICK, PENNILESS AND ESTRANGED FROM OUR FAMILIES. THE RECKLESSNESS OF OUR STREET-CROSSING HABITS EXTENDS INTO ALL AREAS OF OUR PRIVATE LIFE.

HE'S A SILENT COMPANION TO THE LONELY MAN WHO HAS ANTS IN HIS PANTS. HERE! NOW! LET'S GO!

'BEEP' 'BEEP'

'BEEP'

MY FATHER WORE "HIM" AND SO I WEAR "HIM", AND WHEN MY CHILD IS OLD ENOUGH TO CROSS BY HIMSELF, HE'LL WEAR "HIM" TOO.

'PANT' 'PANT'

A SPARK OF RECOGNITION ON A BUSY MIDTOWN STREET

YES, YES I KNOW YOU.

IGNITES A VAT OF GREASY MEMORIES.

KNIPL, THE PHOTOGRAPHER, IN THAT BUILDING ON ROSSEL AVENUE WITH THE TERRIBLE RESTAURANT IN THE BASEMENT. THAT SANDWICH I ATE SIX WEEKS AGO IS STILL REPEATING ON ME.

YOU MEAN THE PARNASSIAN COFFEE SHOP.

YES, IT'S A DISGUSTING PLACE, AND DIRTY TOO, I ALMOST BROKE MY NECK ON THEIR STAIRCASE—BEEF FAT MIXED WITH CABBAGE WATER. BUT TELL ME, HOW ARE YOU DOING?

I'M OKAY.

AN UNFORTUNATE ASSOCIATION FORMED BY THE CHANCE PROXIMITY OF ONE BUSINESS TO ANOTHER.

I'M ON THE THIRD FLOOR, THEY'RE IN THE BASEMENT.

I KNOW. I KNOW.

OVER THE COURSE OF TWENTY YEARS, I MAY HAVE EATEN THERE ONCE OR TWICE.

I REMEMBER A BIG SNOWSTORM IN 1983. WE WERE ALL TRAPPED IN THE BUILDING WITH NOTHING TO EAT. THEY HAD A PEA SOUP WHICH WASN'T BAD.

HELLO, THIS IS JULIUS KNIPL, THE REAL ESTATE PHOTOGRAPHER...

YOU KNOW, UPSTAIRS FROM THE PARNASSIAN COFFEE SHOP.

THE IRON GATE ON THE KITCHEN WINDOW OF APARTMENT 3-G WAS DESIGNED TO ALLOW FOR THE PLACEMENT OF AN 8-INCH DUAL FAN,

A THERMOMETER TO MEASURE THE OUTSIDE AIR TEMPERATURE, A SILL-SIDE SOLAR DEFROSTING PAN AND A "QUIK-LOOK" PIGEON FEEDER.

INSIDE, FELOR BOOTH SCRAPES THE LAST FEW TEASPOONFULS OF HONEY FROM THE BOTTOM OF A STICKY JAR.

HMM? "PLASTIC BEEHIVE KIT — ATTACHES EASILY TO ANY WINDOW FRAME. PROVIDES HOURS OF EDUCATIONAL FUN. $12.95 POST-PAID"

A YOUNG MAN, LURKING ON A BACK ROOFTOP, IS DISSUADED FROM BURGLARIZING THIS PARTICULAR APARTMENT.

WHY GO THROUGH ALL THAT TROUBLE FOR THE SAME LOUSY TELEVISION SET AND PEARL NECKLACE?

BUT THEN, TWENTY MINUTES LATER, WHILE HAVING LUNCH AT A PIZZA PLACE AROUND THE CORNER, HIS EYE IS CAUGHT BY THE SIGHT OF AN OPEN WINDOW AT THE FRONT OF THAT SAME APARTMENT.

WATCH MY SLICE. I'LL BE RIGHT BACK.

HE SCALES THE FACADE OF A LIQUOR STORE AND ENTERS A COOL, DARK BEDROOM.

REGINA, IS THAT YOU?

WITH ONE EFFORTLESS BLOW, HE KNOCKS THE OCCUPANT UNCONSCIOUS

ARTIFICIAL.

AND THEN LEAVES BY THE FRONT DOOR WITH ALL HE CAN CARRY.

TWENTY-SEVEN-INCH COLOR.

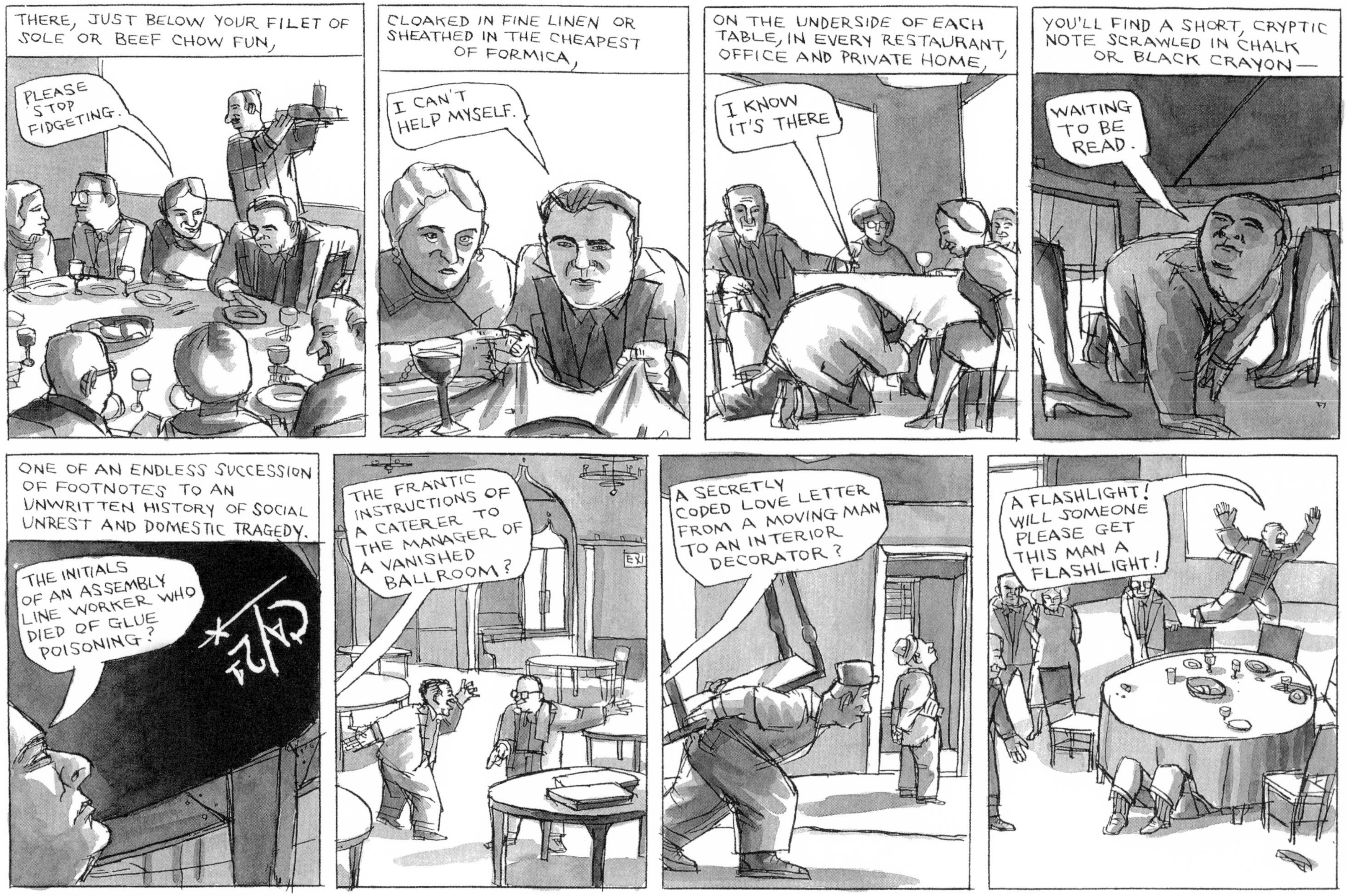
THERE, JUST BELOW YOUR FILET OF SOLE OR BEEF CHOW FUN,
PLEASE STOP FIDGETING.
CLOAKED IN FINE LINEN OR SHEATHED IN THE CHEAPEST OF FORMICA,
I CAN'T HELP MYSELF.
ON THE UNDERSIDE OF EACH TABLE, IN EVERY RESTAURANT, OFFICE AND PRIVATE HOME,
I KNOW IT'S THERE
YOU'LL FIND A SHORT, CRYPTIC NOTE SCRAWLED IN CHALK OR BLACK CRAYON—
WAITING TO BE READ.
ONE OF AN ENDLESS SUCCESSION OF FOOTNOTES TO AN UNWRITTEN HISTORY OF SOCIAL UNREST AND DOMESTIC TRAGEDY.
THE INITIALS OF AN ASSEMBLY LINE WORKER WHO DIED OF GLUE POISONING?
THE FRANTIC INSTRUCTIONS OF A CATERER TO THE MANAGER OF A VANISHED BALLROOM?
A SECRETLY CODED LOVE LETTER FROM A MOVING MAN TO AN INTERIOR DECORATOR?
A FLASHLIGHT! WILL SOMEONE PLEASE GET THIS MAN A FLASHLIGHT!

ON THE FOURTH FLOOR OF AUROCH'S DEPARTMENT STORE, DEEP WITHIN THE RACKS OF BETTER MENSWEAR...

THANK YOU FOR COMING WITH ME. WHEN WE'RE FINISHED, I'LL TAKE YOU FOR A NICE LUNCH AT "THE CARPATHIAN PEEPHOLE," ON ME.

TAKE YOUR TIME, I HAD A LATE BREAKFAST.

WILL A SALESMAN EVER FIND US HERE?

NO, WE'RE ON OUR OWN.

AH, THIS IS EXACTLY WHAT I'M LOOKING FOR — A DARK WOOLEN SUIT WITH TWO PAIRS OF PANTS.

HOW MUCH IS IT?

AS THOUGH STEADYING HIMSELF TO VIEW A DISTANT VISTA FROM THE HEIGHT OF A TREACHEROUS PLATEAU, THE HEAVY-SET MAN STOOPS TO READ THE PRICE TAG.

LET'S SEE WHAT I CAN MAKE OUT. GIVE ME ROOM.

HE PULLS THE TAG FROM THE JACKET SLEEVE, SHIELDS HIS EYES AND SQUINTS, WHILE FIGHTING A SUDDEN WAVE OF DIZZINESS.

LOOKS LIKE TWO HUNDRED AND SIXTY-FOUR DOLLARS AND NINETY-FIVE CENTS.

HE STAGGERS BACKWARDS, JUST MANAGING TO CATCH HIMSELF ON A RACK OF FLANNEL BATHROBES.

THANK GOD YOU'RE HERE. NOW YOU SEE WHY I COULDN'T COME ALONE— I WOULD BE LOST.

PLEASE TAKE A LOOK, TELL ME WHAT YOU SEE. ARE THEY REALLY ASKING $264.95? I SOME-TIMES DOUBT MY OWN EYES.

MAYBE WE SHOULD CALL FOR A SALESMAN.

MR. KNIPL GRABS THE PERFORATED TAG AND STARES INTO THE GLARING FACTS OF RETAIL PRICING.

AH WOOOO!

THE HEADWAITER AT THE GYPSY MOTH HOUSE EXPLAINS...

EVERY OTHER DAY WE CATCH SOMEONE IN THE ACT — THEY'RE FAIRLY BLATANT ABOUT IT.

TAKE IT TO GO SOMEWHERE ELSE!

THEY BRING THE FOOD FROM HOME OR FROM SOME CHEAP TAKE-OUT PLACE...

LIVER AND ONIONS, TO GO.

AND COME HERE JUST FOR THE ATMOSPHERE.

TABL FOR ONE, PLEASE.

THEY'LL ORDER A CUP OF TEA OR A SMALL SALAD, BUT DOWN BELOW, ON THEIR LAP, THEY'RE HARD AT WORK IN AN ALUMINUM CONTAINER OF BEEF STEW OR CHICKEN BIRYANI.

AND TOMORROW NIGHT, VEAL PARMAGIANA AT THE SIAMESE DAIRY RESTAURANT.

THERE ARE THE "SOCIAL EATERS" — PEOPLE WHO ARE PHYSICALLY INCAPABLE OF EATING AT HOME, BUT CAN'T AFFORD THE NIGHTLY EXPENSE OF RESTAURANT DINING.

SNIF SNIF LIVER AND ONIONS?

ONLY IN THE COMPANY OF OTHER HAPPY DINERS ARE THEY ABLE TO FORGET THEIR SPASTIC ESOPHAGUS AND THICKENED TONGUE AND HOLD DOWN A BALANCED MEAL.

BUT THE MAJORITY OF THEM ARE SHAMELESS VOLUPTUARIES!

ON WEDNESDAY, ROPA VIEJA AT THE YISROEL DYNASTY EAST...

IN A CITY OF TEN THOUSAND RESTAURANTS, THEY INSIST UPON EATING THE FOOD OF ONE IN THE ATMOSPHERE OF ANOTHER.

AND ON THURSDAY, CORNED BEEF AND CABBAGE AT THE HATSHEPSUT SNACK-BAR.

BY CHANCE, MR. KNIPL SITS NEXT TO A YOUNG MAN STRUGGLING TO READ A BATTERED PAPERBACK NOVEL.

"JUBILATION ALLEY" BY CONSTANTINE HOOPLE?

HERE, THE TOP OF PAGE 218.

THANK YOU, THANK YOU. MOST PEOPLE DON'T UNDERSTAND.

THEY SAY "WHY NOT GO OUT AND BUY A FRESH COPY? YOU CAN FIND ONE IN ANY BOOKSTORE—IT MUST STILL BE IN PRINT."

WHY BOTHER RECOVERING THAT CRUMBLING COPY WITH CHRISTMAS WRAPPING PAPER? WHY WASTE TIME SHUFFLING THE LOOSE PAGES BACK INTO ORDER EACH TIME YOU PICK IT UP TO READ? WHY DEPEND UPON A RUBBER BAND TO HOLD THE ENTIRE FOUR-HUNDRED-PAGE MASTER-PIECE TOGETHER?"

BUT, YOU SEE, THIS COPY IS AN HEIRLOOM. PURCHASED ON AN IMPULSE BY MY GRANDMOTHER AT THE PORT AUTHORITY BUS TERMINAL IN 1958 ON HER WAY TO LAKE OLSWALO, IT WAS HER SUMMER READING MATERIAL. SHE GOT ONLY HALF WAY THROUGH, BUT FOREVER CONSIDERED IT HER FAVORITE BOOK.

IT SAT FOR MANY YEARS ON THE BOTTOM SHELF OF HER TELEPHONE TABLE AND THEN, WHEN SHE DIED IN 1964, PASSED INTO THE POSSESSION OF MY MOTHER, WHO READ IT FOUR TIMES WHILE ON JURY DUTY IN THE EARLY 70S.

MY OLDER SISTER PREFERRED IT TO HER HIGH SCHOOL READING ASSIGNMENTS; THE BEGINNING OF CHAPTER THIRTY-TWO WAS ALREADY MISSING. IT WAS OF NO INTEREST TO ME; I WAS BUSY WITH THE TELEVISION BY THEN.

BUT NOW THAT I'M FINISHED WITH SCHOOL, I FEEL THAT IT'S TIME FOR ME TO TAKE THE PLUNGE AND SEE FOR MYSELF WHAT MADE THIS ONE BOOK ENDURE OVER THE YEARS WHILE OTHERS WERE LOST AND FORGOTTEN.

HERE, PAGE 378.

ON THE FLOOR OF A BUSY PHARMACY, FREDERICK MATINÉE WITNESSES A RARE MOMENT OF INSPIRATION IN A FELLOW POET.

SHE SWALLOWS CALMLY LIKE A QUEEN/ HER CHOSEN BRAND OF ASPIREEN...

FOLLOWED BY AN AGONIZING DISCOVERY.

OUT OF INK! WITHOUT A SIGN, WITHOUT A SKIP!

HE RUSHES FORWARD WITH AN OFFER OF CONSOLATION.

THE PRODUCTION OF THESE CHEAP WRITING INSTRUMENTS HAS FAR OUT-STRIPPED THE DEMANDS OF POETIC INSPIRATION, AND SO, AS A RESULT, YOU HAVE HUNDREDS OF THOUSANDS OF PENS GOING DRY THROUGH DISUSE. REFILLS ARE SOLD IN PACKAGES OF A DOZEN, FURTHER WIDENING THE GAP.

WHAT DID I WRITE? A SHORT SHOPPING LIST, A FEW PHONE NUMBERS, A "BACK IN TEN MINUTES" NOTE FOR MY FRONT DOOR? AND THEN SUDDENLY, NOTHING.

NO, MY FRIEND, YOU DON'T UNDERSTAND. THE CHANNEL BETWEEN THE RESERVOIR AND THE BALL-POINT IS BLOCKED BY A MICROSCOPIC DAM OF STAGNANT INK. IF YOU HOLD IT UP TO THE LIGHT, YOU CAN SEE IT'S PERFECTLY FULL.

YOU CAN TRY APPLYING THE HEAT OF A MATCH OR RUNNING IT UNDER HOT WATER. SOME PEOPLE TAKE UP ABSENT-MINDED DOODLING JUST TO KEEP THE INK STREAM IN MOTION.

"YOUR SWALLOW FOLLOWS LIKE A QUEEN..." HOW DID IT GO?

WHOEVER SOLD THESE PENS SHOULD HAVE ISSUED A WARNING. DID YOU DO ANYTHING THAT MIGHT HAVE LED THE SALESMAN TO BELIEVE THAT YOU WERE A PROLIFIC AUTHOR?

NO, I WAS JUST TRYING TO SAVE MONEY.

IN DESK DRAWERS, ATTACHÉ CASES AND SHIRT POCKETS ALL OVER THE CITY, THESE EXPIRATION DATES COME AND GO WHILE PEOPLE WAIT FOR THE IMPULSE OR OCCASION TO WRITE.

ONE BOTTLE OF FEX-LAX AND SIX FINE-POINT PENS.

A NONDESCRIPT WAREHOUSE, VISIBLE FOR A MOMENT FROM THE NORTHBOUND LANES OF THE PRECUSKO EXPRESSWAY,

THE PROFOUND CONVOLUTIONS ON THE SURFACE OF A DRIED CHERRY.

SERVES AS THE TEMPORARY RESTING PLACE FOR THE HAVERPEASE COLLECTION OF EUROPEAN DRIED FRUIT.

THE FOREBODING SHEEN OF AN EXTRA-LARGE DATE.

DO YOU REMEMBER WANDERING, AS A CHILD, THROUGH THOSE DARK WOODEN STOREFRONT GALLERIES

PEARS DRIED IN THE FORM OF GENITAL ORGANS.

WHERE EVERYTHING WAS DISPLAYED IN POORLY LABELED, ROACH-PROOF BINS?

APRICOT HALVES LIKE THE EARS OF CHERUBIM.

IN 1962, THE UNSOLD STOCK WAS PURCHASED BY MAURICE HAVERPEASE, A WEALTHY PRUNE-JUICE BOTTLER, AND CONSOLIDATED TO FORM THE CORE COLLECTION.

AS AN ART FORM IT LIES SOMEWHERE BETWEEN STILL-LIFE PAINTING AND PLUMBING.

UPON HIS DEATH, IN 1967, A QUARTER OF THE ITEMS WERE SOLD OFF FOR COMPOTE TO A HIGH-CLASS HOTEL RESTAURANT.

UNSUSPECTING GUESTS WERE SERVED STEWED, TURN-OF-THE-CENTURY TURKISH FIGS FOR BREAKFAST.

THE REST OF THE COLLECTION REMAINS HERE, STORED IN PLAIN BROWN PAPER BAGS, UNTIL FUNDS CAN BE RAISED TO BUILD A PERMANENT MUSEUM AND STUDY CENTER.

A SHOE MADE OF APRICOT LEATHER FOR THE DAUGHTER OF A CZAR.

THE VISIONARY ARCHITECT, SELLADORE, WAITS UNTIL DESSERT IS SERVED TO ANNOUNCE HIS LATEST PET SCHEME.

YOU'VE ALL TRAVELED THROUGH THESE PLACES ON YOUR WAY SOMEWHERE ELSE — THE SMALL TOWNS AND SUBURBAN TRACTS OF THIS SAD COUNTRY.

AT ONE TIME, THERE WERE REASONS FOR PEOPLE TO WALK THESE OBSCURE SIDEWALKS. THERE WERE NEIGHBORHOOD GROCERIES, MOVIE THEATERS, SHOE REPAIR SHOPS...

FARNESE LUNCH

FARNESE SANDWICH

TODAY'S TOWN PLANNING COMMISSIONS STILL FEEL OBLIGATED TO INCLUDE SUCH WALKWAYS ALONGSIDE THEIR MAJOR AND MINOR ROADS.

SALAAM ELECTRIC

BUT THE FACT IS THAT THERE ARE PARTICULAR STRETCHES OF SIDEWALK THAT ARE NEVER USED. THE ONLY WEAR THEY GET IS FROM THE RAIN AND THE EYES OF PASSING MOTORISTS.

HERE, HAVE ANOTHER DRINK.

YES, YES, OCCASIONALLY YOU'LL SEE A POOR MAN OR WOMAN WHO'S BEEN FORCED BY DIRE CIRCUMSTANCES TO WALK — THEY COULDN'T WAIT ANY LONGER FOR THE BUS AND DON'T OWN A CAR.

DRIVE-IN

BUS STOP

EASY DRIVE-IN

FOR A FRACTION OF WHAT THE LOCAL GOVERNMENT SPENDS ON THE UPKEEP OF SIDEWALKS AND THE PRETENSE OF A WALKABLE ENVIRONMENT, THESE POOR SOULS COULD BE PROVIDED WITH CHAUFFEURED LIMOUSINES.

MARIPOSA TIRE Co.

SALE

I PROPOSE THE IMMEDIATE EXTIRPATION OF ALL THESE UNUSED SIDEWALKS! WITH THE AMASSED RUBBLE, WE CAN CONSTRUCT A GREAT PEDESTRIAN BRIDGE TO HAWAII!

LOWBALL CLUB

PARK

TOY

IN THE TRENCHES LEFT ON EITHER SIDE OF THESE ROADS, LET THEM PLANT LILIES OR SOME OTHER FUNEREAL FLOWER.

HERE.

A LONG-VACANT OFFICE ON MR. KNIPL'S FLOOR IS SUDDENLY OCCUPIED BY A GROUP OF EARNEST YOUNG MEN.

I HOPE THEY'RE NOT TOO NOISY.

407

MISSPENT YOUTH CENTER

INSTEAD OF THE CASUAL FURNITURE ASSOCIATED WITH SOCIAL WORK, A WALL OF TELLER'S WINDOWS IS INSTALLED.

AND THEN, ONE MORNING, A LINE OF REMORSEFUL INDIVIDUALS BEGINS TO FORM IN THE HALLWAY.

BOOKS BOUGHT BUT NEVER READ.

TICKETS TO TRASHY MOVIES.

NEXT

STRETCHING FROM THE OFFICE DOOR DOWN THE STAIRS INTO THE STREET, THEY WAIT IN HOPE OF RECLAIMING SOME PART OF THEIR MISSPENT YOUTH.

EXTRAVAGANT HAIRCUTS.

RACKS OF TRENDY CLOTHING.

JUNK FOOD.

INSIDE, CRISP NEW TEN- AND TWENTY-DOLLAR BILLS ARE, FOR A SMALL FEE, EXCHANGED FOR THE WORN AND TATTERED CURRENCY OF THE PAST.

A 1968 FEDERAL RESERVE BANKNOTE FROM WASHINGTON, D.C. FOR TWENTY DOLLARS.— THAT'S CLOSE ENOUGH! I NEVER THOUGHT I'D SEE ONE AGAIN.

CREDIT CARDS ACCEPTED

ALL THE THINGS WE PURCHASED ARE LONG GONE—BROKEN OR IRRETRIEVABLY LOST— BUT THE MONEY ITSELF, WHICH PASSED THROUGH OUR HANDS, CAN BE RELOCATED BY DATE AND SERIAL NUMBER.

EACH EVENING, A SMALL, AGITATED CROWD CONGREGATES OUTSIDE THE BUILDING.

MOST PRE-1950s BILLS HAVE BEEN TAKEN OUT OF CIRCULATION— FOR THOSE PEOPLE IT'S TOO LATE.

THERE'S NOTHING WE CAN DO.

SIX MONTHS LATER, PLANS ARE ANNOUNCED TO MOVE TO A MORE COMMODIOUS OFFICE SOMEWHERE UPTOWN.

407

NOTICE

MISSPENT YOUTH CENTER

NOTICE

MISSPENT YOUTH CENTER - I   55

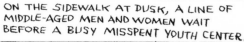

ON THE SIDEWALK AT DUSK, A LINE OF MIDDLE-AGED MEN AND WOMEN WAIT BEFORE A BUSY MISSPENT YOUTH CENTER.

WILL I EVER SEE AGAIN THE FORTY DOLLARS I SPENT ON A USED NINETEEN-INCH TELEVISION SET IN 1968?

SIMON MAGUS MISSPENT YOUTH CENTER NO. 12

NO LOITERING

247

WITH A CREDIT CARD OR PESONAL CHECK THEY HOPE TO RECLAIM THE PRECIOUS CASH OF THEIR SQUANDERED YOUTH.

WHAT BECAME OF THE $3.95 I PAID FOR A PAPERBACK EDITION OF MOLT'S "SEXUAL HISTORY OF THE SHOWER CAP IN ANCIENT ROME," BUT NEVER READ?

AS LESS AND LESS OF THE PAPER CURRENCY FROM THE 1950s AND 60s REMAINS IN CIRCULATION, THE MECHANISM FOR COLLECTING IT BECOMES INCREASINGLY COMPLEX.

WE'RE ALL OUT OF TWENTY-DOLLAR BILLS FROM 1968.

CLOSED

OUR ENTIRE PROGRAM DEPENDS UPON A LOOSELY ORGANIZED WEB OF VOLUNTEERS — YOU'LL FIND AT LEAST ONE IN EACH CITY AND SMALL TOWN. THEY'RE SELF-APPOINTED GATHERERS, WHO, IN THEIR SPARE TIME, MAKE IT THEIR BUSINESS TO KNOW WHERE TO LOOK FOR SUCH MONEY.

HERE, ON PETREL AVENUE, THE HANSEATIC BARBER SHOP.

BANK NOTES OF THIS VINTAGE CAN BE FOUND IN THE PURSES OF ELDERLY MEN AND TAPED TO THE WALLS OF BARBER SHOPS...

EXCUSE ME...

UNDER THE CASH REGISTER DRAWERS OF OUT-OF-THE-WAY VACUUM CLEANER/SEWING MACHINE STORES AND IN THE BARGAIN BINS OF SMALL-TOWN NUMISMATIC SHOPS...

BUT WOULD YOU HAPPEN TO HAVE...

COIN CORNER

WONDER VUUMING HOME CENTER

GOLD   PAPER

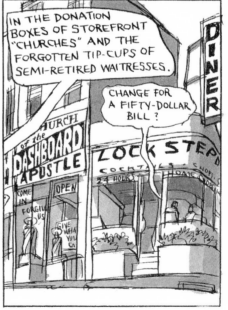

IN THE DONATION BOXES OF STOREFRONT "CHURCHES" AND THE FORGOTTEN TIP-CUPS OF SEMI-RETIRED WAITRESSES.

CHANGE FOR A FIFTY-DOLLAR BILL?

DINER

CHURCH OF THE DASHBOARD APOSTLE

LOCK STEP

OPEN

AND FOR THEIR CEASELESS EFFORTS IN THIS STRUGGLE AGAINST THE PASSAGE OF TIME, WHAT THANKS DO THEY RECEIVE?

SORRY, NO CHANGE WITHOUT A PURCHASE.

A MAN IN THE SUBWAY READS FROM THE PAGES HELD IN A FOUR-INCH-THICK LOOSE-LEAF BINDER.

"THE GROSS RECEIPTS OF PLEASURE." ...A HOME-STUDY COURSE? A CORPORATE MANUAL?

AT THE NEXT STOP, HE STUFFS THE BINDER INTO A VINYL POUCH EMBLAZONED WITH THE WORDS: "DELUGE ORANGEADE" AND GETS OUT.

WITH A YELLOW MARKING-PEN IN HAND, HE EATS A THREE-COURSE MEAL.

"BE OF GOOD CHEER AS YOU ACCENTUATE THE WORTHLESSNESS OF OTHERS."

HALFWAY DOWN THE BLOCK FROM THE RESTAURANT, HE FEELS THAT HE'S BEEN POISONED

"BE THE ONE TO PUT THE FINISHING TOUCHES ON THE RUBBISH HEAP."

AND STOPS AT A CORNER BAR TO ORDER THE ANTIDOTE.

A CHARTREUSE DRIZZLE.

HOURS LATER, HE WALKS HOME QUOTING MEMORABLE PASSAGES AT THE TOP OF HIS VOICE.

"HE WAS AS CHARMING AS THE LOOKOUT MAN IN A PUBLIC RESTROOM."

IN A GARBAGE CAN, BEFORE HIS APARTMENT HOUSE, HE FINDS AN UNOPENED LETTER ADDRESSED TO HIMSELF FROM THE BROKEN NECTAR BEVERAGE COMPANY.

"TO SPARE FUTURE READERS FROM THESE NOXIOUS IDEAS, WE ASK YOU TO REMOVE PAGES 217 THRU 219, SECTION 'H', FROM OUR CURRENT HANDBOOK."

EARLY THAT MORNING, IN A STATE OF HALF-SLEEP, HE CATCHES HIMSELF IN THE POWERFUL SPRING MECHANISM OF THE RING BINDER.

EACH NIGHT, IN BEDS THROUGHOUT THE CITY, A DEEP-SEATED SUBCONSCIOUS RESENTMENT FINDS EXPRESSION

"ENIMOL'S DRUG AND BEAUTY CENTER."

IN THE FORM OF A COMMON DREAM DEPICTING THE SWIFT FAILURE OF THE CITY'S MOST POPULAR CHAIN STORES.

WHAT HAPPENED?

ENIMOL'S DRUG & BEAUTY CENTER DISCOUNT

CLOSING THIS LOCATION

FAREWELL TO ALL

THESE INSTITUTIONS OF FAST FOOD, CUT-RATE DRUGS AND POORLY MADE SHOES ARE SUDDENLY PLUNGED INTO ECONOMIC RUIN BY A MYSTERIOUS TURN OF EVENTS.

THEY FELL ASLEEP WITH THEIR MOUTHS OPEN AND EVERYTHING WENT DRY.

VEAL LURE RESTAURANT EAT 'N RUN STYLE

PARKING

LAST 4 DAYS

IN A BURST OF ACCELERATED MOTION, THEY ARE STRIPPED OF THEIR FIXTURES AND MERCHANDISE.

HURRY! OUR DAY ENDS AT SUNRISE.

CLUB FOOT SHOES WOMEN - MEN

EVERYTHING MUST GO

FINAL SALE

A FEW OLD SHOPPING BAGS REMAIN IN CIRCULATION TO BE NOTICED BY CHILDREN AND MELANCHOLIC BACHELORS—

ENIMOL'S DRUG & BEAUTY CENTER 372 FRICTION AV.

FOR IN THE COMMERCIAL LIFE OF A CITY, THE DEMISE OF EVEN THE MOST DESPISED BUSINESS IS FOLLOWED BY A LONG PERIOD OF MOURNING AND WEARY SPECULATION.

RELIGIOUS SUPPLY STORES, RENTAL LIBRARIES, CLOUDY LEMONADE STANDS OR SOMETHING WORSE.

FOR RENT CALL: ABULAR 237-012

IN THE MORNING, THE DREAM IS COMPLETELY FORGOTTEN AND LIFE GOES ON.

WEEKS LATER, UPON ENCOUNTERING ONE OF THESE THRIVING CHAIN STORES, THE WAKING SUBJECT IS FILLED WITH AN INEXPLICABLE SENSE OF RELIEF.

HOW NICE TO SEE THEY'RE DOING WELL.

ENIMOL'S DRUG & BEAUTY CENTER DISCOUNT

SPECIAL

PERFUME

IN THE MIDDLE OF AN OTHERWISE PLEASANT CONVERSATION

TO KEEP A LIVING THING ON A WINDOW SILL IS, TO ME, INHUMAN.

AND TODAY, THEY MAKE SUCH BEAUTIFUL ARTIFICIAL PLANTS!

MR. KNIPL'S FRIEND NOTICES A BOX OF POWDERED MILK ON THE REAR OF A KITCHEN SHELF.

OH, I SEE... EMERGENCY SUPPLIES.

FERTILE CRESCENT BRAND POWDERED DRY MILK 24 ENVELOPES

PEAS

YES, WE'VE BEEN SPARED TILL NOW, BUT IT'S INEVITABLE. THESE CATASTROPHES WE READ ABOUT IN THE NEWSPAPER EVERY DAY IN SOME FAR-AWAY LAND WILL EVENTU-ALLY VISIT THEMSELVES UPON OUR FAIR CITY.

WHEN I FIRST MOVED IN HERE, IT WAS A NECESSITY.

I UNDERSTAND. OF COURSE NO ONE LIKES TO ADMIT IT, BUT WE'RE LONG OVERDUE.

LATE AT NIGHT, IF YOU'D RUN OUT OF MILK THERE WAS NO PLACE TO GO — IT WAS TERRIBLE...

FREEZE

SOME PEOPLE CAN'T WAIT FOR IT TO HAPPEN — THEY'RE DYING FOR A CHANCE TO WIPE THE SLATE CLEAN.

THE ONLY SUPERMARKET CLOSED AT 6:30.

IN THE AFTERMATH OF A LARGE-SCALE VOLCANIC ERUPTION OR EARTHQUAKE, HOW LONG DO YOU THINK YOUR SUPPLIES WOULD LAST? YOU'D HAVE TO SHARE THEM WITH THE OTHER TENANTS ON THIS FLOOR — POSSIBLY THE WHOLE BLOCK!

I ALSO KEEP CRACKERS AND A JAR OF PEANUT BUTTER, BUT THAT DOESN'T MEAN I EXPECT THE WORLD TO END TOMORROW.

LOOK, THEY TELL YOU: EACH ENVELOPE MAKES ONE MEASLY QUART OF MILK.

I'VE HAD THE SAME BOX FOR TWO YEARS.

DELI DEL

MILK 79¢

235

AND ASSUMING YOU KILL OFF YOUR NEIGHBORS AND THEIR CHILDREN — IN SELF-DEFENSE, OF COURSE — WHERE WILL YOU GET UNCONTAMINATED WATER WITH WHICH TO MIX YOUR DELICIOUS MILK?

THEY OPENED UP SIX MONTHS AGO. FRESH MILK, BAGELS — ANYTHING YOU WANT — 24 HOURS A DAY.

COLD CUTS

IN THAT SANCTIONED MOMENT OF PHYSICAL AND EMOTIONAL RELEASE

BETWEEN THE ANDANTE AND FINAL PRESTO MOVEMENTS OF CANOPENA'S "QUARTET FOR PAWNED INSTRUMENTS,"

A YOUNG MAN PUSHES HIS WAY THROUGH A FLURRY OF COUGHS AND THROAT CLEARINGS.

THE WOMAN AT THE COAT-CHECK CONCESSION ALLOWS HIM TO CHOOSE FROM AMONG THE SIX HUNDRED GARMENTS IN HER CARE.

HE LEAVES THE CONCERT HALL WEARING A STRANGE WOMAN'S FUR COAT

AND FINDS HIMSELF ON A BUS, TRAVELING IN THE OPPOSITE DIRECTION FROM HIS HOME.

IN A MOTEL ROOM ON THE EDGE OF THE CITY, HE IS SEVERELY BEATEN.

THE POLICE ARE ONLY ABLE TO IDENTIFY HIM BY MEANS OF A TICKET STUB FOUND IN HIS SHIRT POCKET.

EACH MORNING, REGARDLESS OF MONTH OR DAY, THESE MIDDLE-AGED MEN RESOLVE TO CLAIM THEIR BIRTHRIGHT.

NOVEMBER 25th AT LAST!

A CASE OF ARRESTED DEVELOPMENT PLAYED OUT IN A BRUTAL ADULT WORLD.

ON THIS VERY DAY, FORTY-SEVEN LONG YEARS AGO, I WAS BROUGHT INTO THIS GLORIOUS WORLD.

A PATHETIC ATTEMPT TO REGAIN A BIT OF LEVERAGE NEVER FULLY USED DURING ONE'S CHILDHOOD.

HOW OLD DO YOU THINK I LOOK?

HERE, HAVE A DESSERT — ON THE HOUSE. HAPPY BIRTHDAY!

A CLAIM — OF SUCH TOTAL INNOCENCE THAT NO ONE WOULD EVER DOUBT IT—

I THROW IN THE NECKTIE AS A PRESENT — WHY NOT?!

REAPING BENEFITS OF SUCH MINUSCULE WORTH AS TO BE NEGLIGIBLE.

IMAGINE EATING HERE ALL ALONE ON YOUR BIRTHDAY.

YOUR BIRTHDAY?

THIS SO-CALLED "BIRTHDAY BOY SCAM" FALLS BELOW THE THRESHOLD OF SOCIETAL CENSURE; A CRIME HARDLY WORTH RECOGNIZING.

WE STOP THE METER NOW 'CAUSE IT'S YOUR BIRTHDAY.

AND YET, THESE SMALL GAINS, COMPOUNDED OVER THE 365 DAYS OF A YEAR

I HAD A WONDERFUL BIRTHDAY — I DID.

AMOUNT, IN THE END, TO A GREAT WINDFALL — A VAST INHERITANCE JUST WAITING TO BE CLAIMED.

TOMORROW, NOVEMBER 26th —AT LAST!

IN A SUNNY DEPARTMENT STORE AISLE, TWO WOMEN ENCOUNTER A FAMILIAR NAME.

HERE, BETWEEN THE AFTER-SHAVE LOTIONS AND DESIGNER SHOE POLISH...

"DOURMAT'S MUD APPLIQUÉ"

THAT'S HAROLD DOURMAT—THE SCION OF A WEALTHY CEMENT MANUFACTURING FAMILY. HE'S SINGLE.

A TWO-OUNCE BOTTLE SELLS FOR FIFTY DOLLARS.

A DOZEN PHONE CALLS ARE MADE.

ANY NIGHT, ANY WEEK—AN INFORMAL GET-TOGETHER.... YOU SAY HE WAS CONCEIVED FORTY-THREE YEARS AGO THIS COMING THURSDAY?

AND ON THAT THURSDAY EVENING, A PARTY IS HELD AT SYLVIA DOURMAT'S APARTMENT ON ROMAN BOULEVARD.

MY SON HAROLD SHOULD BE HERE ANY MINUTE; HE'S FLYING IN FROM THE CALAPEENA SWAMPS.

THE SHOE-SHINE MEN LOVE HIM—HE'S RESPONSIBLE FOR THE POPULARITY OF THE MUDDIED-SHOE, COUNTRY SQUIRE LOOK.

SLOWLY, OVER THE PAST HUNDRED YEARS, THE CONCRETE AND CEMENT BUSINESS HAS PAVED ITSELF INTO A CORNER. WHAT FUTURE IS THERE FOR AN AMBITIOUS YOUNG MAN TO RIP UP AND REPOUR THE SAME SIDEWALK FOR THE DOZENTH TIME?

IN A PRIVATE BATHROOM, HAROLD'S YOUNGER BROTHER, LAERTES, TOUCHES UP HIS SHOE RIMS AND PANT'S CUFFS WITH A SMALL BUILT-IN APPLICATOR BRUSH...

"FECAL OCHRE" —MY FAVORITE SHADE OF MUD.

AND THEN MAKES HIS ENTRANCE.

I'M JUST IN FOR THE EVENING FROM UPSTATE—BEASTLY WEATHER WE'RE HAVING.

HE'S A HALF-BROTHER VIA IN VITRO.

AT ELEVEN-THIRTY, THE PARTY COMES TO AN UNSATISFYING CONCLUSION.

HAROLD'S PLANE WAS STUCK. HE'S VERY SORRY AND LOOKS FORWARD TO MEETING YOU ALL SOMEDAY.

"FECAL OCHRE" —EITHER YOU LIKE IT OR YOU DON'T.

HAROLD DOURMAT, A PURVEYOR OF FINE MUD, TELEPHONES HIS MOTHER FROM A HOTEL IN THE CALAPEENA SWAMP.

IT'S TERRIBLE, TERRIBLE, MA. I LOST A SHOE. THE MUD'S KNEE-DEEP.

LET'S SEE WHO'S KNEE IS DEEPER.

SHHH... THEY THINK I'M AT THE AIRPORT.

ALL THE PLANES ARE STUCK... AT LEAST UNTIL NEXT WEEK. IT'S IMPOSSIBLE TONIGHT. TWO JUMBO JETS WERE LOST IN THE RUNWAY SLUDGE. TELL EVERYONE I'M SORRY AND THAT I LOOK FORWARD TO MEETING THEM ALL SOMEDAY... BUT TONIGHT IS IMPOSSIBLE!

FOR THE THIRD TIME THAT EVENING, HE EXPLAINS HIS BUSINESS TO MALUTA, A NATIVE GIRL.

OURS IS AN ARTIFICIALLY PRODUCED MUD. THE LEFTOVER BREAKFAST BEVERAGES FROM THIS HOTEL, AND OTHERS IN THE AREA, ARE DUMPED EACH MORNING INTO AN EARTHEN PIT NOT FAR FROM HERE.

COFFEE, TEA AND ORANGE JUICE?

IT CONTAINS LESS BACTERIA THAN IS NATURALLY FOUND IN MUD AND WE'RE ABLE TO PRECISELY CONTROL ITS CONSISTENCY. OF COURSE THESE FACTS ARE NOT PUBLICIZED. PEOPLE LIKE TO THINK THEY'RE GETTING "THE REAL THING"—WHATEVER THAT IS.

TOMORROW MORNING, I'LL TAKE YOU ON A TOUR OF THE DOURMAT MUD PUDDLE. AS YOU KNOW, THIS AREA WAS COMPLETELY PAVED OVER BACK IN THE 1950s— A RECLAIMED SWAMP. WE CHOSE IT FOR ITS NAME AND BEAUTIFUL WEATHER.

CA-LA-PEE-NA.

IN BUSINESS, IT'S SOMETIMES NECESSARY TO TELL A FEW WHITE LIES.

BUT YOU REALLY ARE A MILLIONAIRE ... OR MULTI-MILLIONAIRE?

IN HIS MOTHER'S APARTMENT, THREE-THOUSAND MILES AWAY, APOLOGIES ARE MADE.

HAROLD SAYS HE'S VERY SORRY AND LOOKS FORWARD TO MEETING YOU ALL SOMEDAY.

HE LIVES IN CONSTANT DANGER OF MUD SLIDES AND ANGRY NATIVES, BUT SEEMS TO ENJOY IT.

IN THE MIDDLE OF THE NIGHT, HAROLD DOURMAT, THE MUD IMPORTER, AND HIS NATIVE FRIEND, MALUTA, LEAVE THEIR HOTEL ON A LIBIDINOUS ERRAND.

IF YOU INSIST UPON DOCUMENTATION, I CAN PRODUCE IT.

A TAX RETURN OR NOTARIZED STATEMENT OF PROFITS AND LOSS — ANYTHING WILL DO.

THEY SPEED THROUGH THE CROWDED STREETS OF DOWNTOWN CALAPEENA,

I UNDERSTAND... EVERYONE'S A MULTI-MILLIONAIRE, BUT YOU WANT TO SEE THE ACTUAL FIGURES.

LIKE A BIRTHMARK OR BEAUTY-SPOT — I FIND THESE THINGS TREMENDOUSLY ALLURING.

PAST THE STORES AND RESTAURANTS WHICH HE PATRONIZES ON A DAILY BASIS.

THERE, LOOK, MOE LURAY'S GRISTLE HOUSE. IN THAT RESTAURANT ALONE, I SPEND TEN THOUSAND DOLLARS A MONTH.

ALL OF MY SUITS, AND EVEN THESE PAJAMAS, COME FROM PHYFE & DYAM'S.

$375.00

AND THAT'S MY DRY CLEANER. I PUT HIS THREE CHILDREN THROUGH COLLEGE —

ALL FROM MUD!

THEY ARRIVE AT THE STUCCO VILLA OF HIS ACCOUNTANT

HE MAY ALREADY BE SLEEPING.

THIS IS AN EMERGENCY.

AND ARE USHERED INTO A BASEMENT OFFICE.

SO, HOW LONG HAVE YOU KNOWN EACH OTHER?

FORTY-FIVE MINUTES... MAYBE AN HOUR.

THIS YEAR, THINGS DON'T LOOK SO ROSY — A SEVEN-HUNDRED-THOUSAND-DOLLAR DEFICIT. YOU MAY HAVE TO LAY OFF YOUR OWN BROTHER,

WAIT, WAIT, WAIT... MALUTA, COME BACK!

UPON LEARNING OF HAROLD DOURMAT'S LOSSES IN THE MUD BUSINESS, MALUTA, HIS NATIVE GIRLFRIEND, FLEES FROM THE ACCOUNTANT'S OFFICE.

SALES ARE OFF BY FORTY PERCENT, YOUR OVERHEAD HAS DOUBLED AND THE FOOD AND DRUG ADMINISTRATION IS INVESTIGATING YOUR "ORIGINAL" FORMULA.

WAIT, AT LEAST LET HIM FINISH!

WHERE DID SHE GO? WAS IT SOMETHING I SAID?

NO, NO, NO, THE FIGURES SPEAK FOR THEMSELVES.

THE PUBLIC'S INTEREST IN MUD HAS MOMENTARILY FLAGGED. THESE THINGS RUN IN CYCLES—SHE'LL BE BACK.

YOU'RE PAYING THE NATIVE BOYS FAR TOO MUCH—THAT'S YOUR PROBLEM!

HE DRIVES TOWARD THE VAST DOURMAT FAMILY MUD PUDDLES ON THE OUTSKIRTS OF CALAPEENA.

CAN YOU BLAME HER? WHAT DOES SHE KNOW OF MUD? SHE'S LIVED HER ENTIRE LIFE, HERE, ON SIDEWALKS AND ASPHALT DRIVEWAYS. SHE'S A CREATURE OF THE PAVEMENT.

HE TRAMPS THROUGH THE FRESH MIRE OF PUDDLE NO. 6.

WHEN I MET HER, EARLIER THIS EVENING, SHE WAS A SHOE-SHINE GIRL IN THE HOTEL LOBBY. HER MOTHER WAS A SHOE-SHINE GIRL BEFORE HER, AND HER MOTHER'S MOTHER WAS A SHOE-SHINE GIRL BEFORE THAT.

AND NOW SUDDENLY, SHE'S A FINANCIAL ANALYST.

HE DRIVES BACK TO HIS HOTEL

WHAT MADE ME THINK I COULD CHANGE HER?

WHERE MALUTA WORKS THE EARLY MORNING CROWD.

SHINE, MISTER?

FROM THE CRAMPED BASEMENT ROOM OF A NEGLECTED APARTMENT HOUSE

I HAVE SOMETHING FOR YOU... A REMARKABLE TWO-BEDROOM.

—A ROOM ILLEGALLY CONVERTED THIRTY YEARS EARLIER FROM A SUB-GRADE COAL BIN—

I CAN TRY TO DESCRIBE IT, BUT REALLY, YOU MUST SEE IT. IT'S SOMETHING OUT OF THE ORDINARY.

FRANKLIN HOORAY CONDUCTS A SUCCESSFUL REAL-ESTATE BUSINESS.

YOU WALK IN AND THERE BEFORE YOU IS AN EXPANSE OF DEEP-PILE CARPETING—WHICH RUNS EAST AND WEST FOR AS FAR AS THE EYE CAN SEE—A BREATHTAKING FOYER!

A PLYWOOD BOARD COVERS THE RIVULET OF AN OPEN SEWER WHICH RUNS BY THE FOOT OF HIS SWIVEL CHAIR.

YOU PROCEED TO YOUR LEFT, PAST THREE WALK-IN CLOSETS, TO A POST-MODERN HOLLY-WOOD KITCHEN OUTFITTED WITH BUILT-IN FILE CABINETS FOR ALL YOUR TAKE-OUT MENUS. IN THE WALL, NEXT TO THE ELECTRIC LUKEWARMER, IS A HIGH-PRESSURE DUCK-SAUCE DISPENSER.

AN UNHEALTHY MILDEW, VISIBLE ON THE SAGGING SHEETROCK CEILING, HAS SPREAD OVER THE YEARS INTO THE DESK DRAWER HOLDING HIS THREE-DAY SUPPLY OF UNDERWEAR,

TO YOUR RIGHT IS AN EAT-IN DINING ROOM WITH STAINLESS STEEL WAINSCOTING AND MOTHER-OF-PEARL MOPBOARDS... HOLD ON, I HAVE A CALL ON THE OTHER LINE.

BY PREARRANGEMENT, HE HAS FULL USE OF A COFFEE SHOP'S TOILET ACROSS THE STREET,

MARASCHINO
BURGERS · SANDWICH · DON

HIS SLEEPING PALLET AND STERNO STOVE ARE KEPT IN A DANK CLOSET ORIGINALLY BUILT TO HOLD TOXIC EXTERMINATING SUPPLIES.

THEN WE COME TO THE LIVING ROOM. TELL ME, HAVE YOU EVER BEEN OUT WEST TO THE GRAND CANYON? THE BEDROOMS ARE SEPARATED BY A GROVE OF PINE TREES IN BAS-RELIEF—THE PREVIOUS OWNER WAS A NATURE LOVER WHO WALKED IN HIS SLEEP.

NO, NOT FOR YOU? YOUR WIFE HATES MOTHER-OF-PEARL... PREFERS THE FAUX TOMATO-PASTE MOLDINGS WE SAW ON RECESS AVENUE? OF COURSE, I UNDERSTAND... NOTHING'S PERFECT.

HOORAY REALTY CO.

MR. KNIPL GAZES INTO THE WINDOW OF A NEWLY OPENED STORE.

ELECTRIC TRAINS, PANTYHOSE, MALTED MIXERS, A CAFE AND WHO KNOWS WHAT ELSE!

THOSE SIMPLISTIC CATEGORIES OF BUSINESS THAT YOU FIND IN THE TELEPHONE BOOK ARE A THING OF THE PAST.

THESE NEW-STYLE ENTREPRENEURS ARE CHARTING THEIR OWN FREE-ASSOCIATIVE URGES AND THOSE OF THEIR CUSTOMERS-- ANYTHING GOES-- AS LONG AS IT SELLS!

AND LOOK HERE!

CHOCOLATE COVERED PRUNES FROM RUSSIA, HAMMERS, SICKLES AND OTHER IDEOLOGICAL HARDWARE, A TASTEFUL SELECTION OF SURGICAL SUPPLIES AND A CAFE.

SOMETIMES THE CONNEC- TIONS ARE NOT SO APPARENT, BUT WHEN IT WORKS, IT SETS UP AN IRRESISTIBLE CHAIN REACTION OF PURCHASES AND AT THE END, EVERYONE LIKES TO SIT DOWN AND HAVE A CUP OF COFFEE.

AS THESE SUBCONSCIOUS DEMANDS ARE ALLOWED TO SURFACE, THE SUPPLIERS WILL BE THERE TO SATISFY THEM. WHAT SEEMS LIKE MADNESS TODAY WILL, IN THE FUTURE, BE PERFECTLY NORMAL.

HANDMADE TOILET PAPER, PASTA AND EXPLOSIVES?

HOW ARE THESE STORES ANY DIFFERENT FROM THE OLD NEIGHBORHOOD VARIETY STORES THAT CARRIED A VAST ASSORTMENT OF MERCHANDISE?

IT'S THE DIFFERENCE BETWEEN A DICTIONARY AND A SHORT POEM. THESE NEW BUSINESSES CAN ONLY BE DESCRIBED BY MOOD AND ATMOSPHERE-- THUS, THEIR ANNOYINGLY OBLIQUE NAMES.

TODAY, WE KNOW THAT A WOMAN LOOKING FOR SHOES IS REALLY IN THE MARKET FOR A STURDY WOODEN LADDER, AND THAT A FEW MINUTES AFTER A PASTRY SHOP ONE'S MIND TURNS TO PLUMBING SUPPLIES. THESE ARE PROVEN PSYCHOLOGICAL FACTS!

ONLY THE POOREST PEOPLE WILL GO SHOPPING FOR SPECIFICS; THE REST OF US WILL GO FOR THE EXPERIENCE, THE CHANCE ENCOUNTER, THE FORTUITOUS DISCOVERY!

OF COURSE, THESE NEW MARKETING STRATEGIES ARE STILL IN THEIR INFANCY. NEITHER OF US WILL LIVE TO SEE THE ESTABLISHMENT OF CORSET SALONS THAT OFFER TROPICAL FRUIT JUICE DRINKS AND CANTORIAL RECORDINGS!

IMPORTED ASPIRINS, BOXING GLOVES AND WEDDING CAKE DECORATIONS?

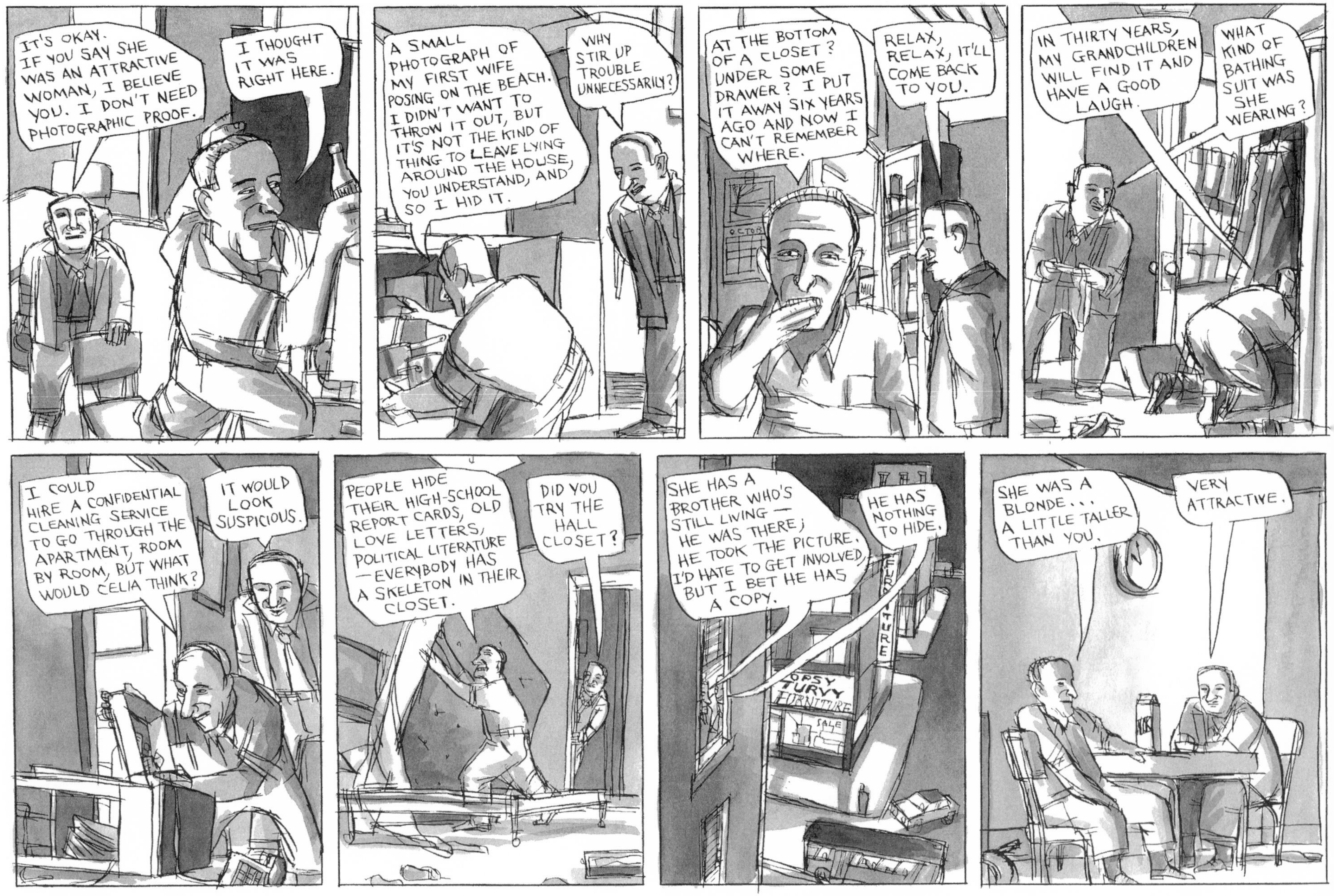
IT'S OKAY. IF YOU SAY SHE WAS AN ATTRACTIVE WOMAN, I BELIEVE YOU. I DON'T NEED PHOTOGRAPHIC PROOF.
I THOUGHT IT WAS RIGHT HERE.
A SMALL PHOTOGRAPH OF MY FIRST WIFE POSING ON THE BEACH. I DIDN'T WANT TO THROW IT OUT, BUT IT'S NOT THE KIND OF THING TO LEAVE LYING AROUND THE HOUSE, YOU UNDERSTAND, AND SO I HID IT.
WHY STIR UP TROUBLE UNNECESSARILY?
AT THE BOTTOM OF A CLOSET? UNDER SOME DRAWER? I PUT IT AWAY SIX YEARS AGO AND NOW I CAN'T REMEMBER WHERE.
RELAX, RELAX, IT'LL COME BACK TO YOU.
IN THIRTY YEARS, MY GRANDCHILDREN WILL FIND IT AND HAVE A GOOD LAUGH.
WHAT KIND OF BATHING SUIT WAS SHE WEARING?
I COULD HIRE A CONFIDENTIAL CLEANING SERVICE TO GO THROUGH THE APARTMENT, ROOM BY ROOM, BUT WHAT WOULD CELIA THINK?
IT WOULD LOOK SUSPICIOUS.
PEOPLE HIDE THEIR HIGH-SCHOOL REPORT CARDS, OLD LOVE LETTERS, POLITICAL LITERATURE — EVERYBODY HAS A SKELETON IN THEIR CLOSET.
DID YOU TRY THE HALL CLOSET?
SHE HAS A BROTHER WHO'S STILL LIVING — HE WAS THERE; HE TOOK THE PICTURE. I'D HATE TO GET INVOLVED, BUT I BET HE HAS A COPY.
HE HAS NOTHING TO HIDE.
FURNITURE
TURVY
FURNITURE
SALE
SHE WAS A BLONDE... A LITTLE TALLER THAN YOU.
VERY ATTRACTIVE.

A DROP OF FLUID, THE CONSISTENCY OF FRESH CREAM, FALLS UPON MR. KNIPL'S RIGHT SHOULDER

HE LOOKS TO THE UPPER FLOORS OF THE SURROUNDING BUILDINGS AND INTO THE BRILLIANT SKY, BUT SEES NOTHING.

AN OVERFED PIGEON ON THE FIRST WARM DAY OF SPRING?

TWO MORE DROPS HIT THE PAVEMENT AND HE RUNS FOR COVER INTO THE NEAREST STORE.

NO, SNIFF, SNIFF, IT'S STRAWBERRY ICE CREAM!

I THOUGHT IT WAS...

IT'S A FAMILY WITH A TERRACE ON THE THIRTY-FOURTH FLOOR.

THIS LOOKS LIKE A SWEET CHUTNEY.

RIGHT NOW, THEY'RE HAVING DESSERT A LITTLE TOO CLOSE TO THE BALUSTRADE.

SO I CAME ALONG AT JUST THE RIGHT TIME.

THE STRANGER POINTS TO A RIND OF CAMEMBERT NEAR THE CURB.

YES, YOU NEVER KNOW WHAT THEY'LL HAVE FOR LUNCH.

THERE'S A WINE STAIN ON YOUR TIE.

A MAN IN LIVERY SURVEYS THE SIDEWALK.

HERE, YOU SEE, THEY ALWAYS SEND SOMEONE DOWN TO APOLOGIZE.

IT'S NOTHING. A DRIPPING ICE CREAM ON A WARM DAY— NO HARM DONE.

PLEASE ALLOW US TO COVER YOUR DRY CLEANING EXPENSES!

HERE! HERE'S THE FELLOW YOU HIT.

WE NEED HIS NAME, ADDRESS AND SOCIAL SECURITY NUMBER FOR INSURANCE PURPOSES.

AND I THOUGHT IT WAS JUST A PIGEON.

SHHH. IF YOU'RE LUCKY THEY'LL INVITE YOU TO DINNER WITH THEIR UNMARRIED DAUGHTER.

MR. KNIPL IS HAPPY TO LEARN THAT HIS JACKET, SOILED BY DRIPPING ICE CREAM, WILL BE CLEANED AT THE EXPENSE OF AN ECCENTRIC UPSTAIRS FAMILY.

IT'LL BE READY AT NINE.

DR. RUSHOWER, THE WORLD FAMOUS ELECTROLYSIST, AND HIS FAMILY WOULD LOVE TO HAVE YOU JOIN THEM FOR AN EARLY DINNER.

MOMENTS LATER ON THE TERRACE OF THAT SAME BUILDING'S THIRTY-FOURTH FLOOR PENTHOUSE.

LUMIN RUSHOWER, THIS IS MY EX-WIFE, MINA, AND OUR STEP-DAUGHTER, GINGIN. WE ARE TERRIBLY SORRY FOR WHAT HAPPENED. — OUR FAULT, IN PART— THANK YOU FOR COMING.

REGARDLESS OF OUR WISHES, THIS ACCIDENT HAS INEXTRICABLY LINKED US TOGETHER IN A WONDERFUL WAY. THE ICE CREAM STAIN WILL, HOPE- FULLY, BE REMOVED, BUT THE TRUE IMPORT OF THIS ACCIDENT HAS PENETRATED FAR DEEPER INTO THE FABRIC OF OUR LIVES. TELL ME, WHAT BROUGHT YOU TO THIS PARTICULAR STREET AT THIS PARTICULAR MOMENT — JUST AS WE WERE HAVING DESSERT? DO YOU EVEN KNOW YOURSELF?

I WAS GOING TO THE CORNER FOR A NEWSPAPER.

AH, YOU SEE, THERE ARE ALREADY VAGUE POLITICAL MOTIVES BEHIND THIS INCIDENT, DON'T TELL ME WHICH PAPER YOU READ, LET ME GUESS. WHY TAKE THE TIME AND TROUBLE TO INVESTIGATE THE ULTIMATE CAUSES OF THOSE LITTLE "ACCIDENTS" OF WHICH LIFE IS COMPOSED? MOST PEOPLE ARE ETHICAL HIT-AND-RUNNERS. IF THERE ARE NO WITNESSES, THEY'RE HAPPY TO GET AWAY WITH A THOUSAND CRIMES IN THE COURSE OF AN AFTERNOON.

TELEPHONE FOR DR. RUSHOWER!

MY FATHER HAS MANY FRIENDS. NEXT MONTH, YOU'LL BE INVITED TO A BANQUET ALONG WITH TWO HUNDRED OTHER INDIVIDUALS WHO, LIKE YOURSELF, HAPPENED TO WANDER BELOW OUR TERRACE AT LUNCH TIME. HE MULLS OVER THE MINUTE DETAILS OF EACH ACCIDENT AND THEN ERECTS AN ENTIRE SOCIAL STRUCTURE BASED UPON THEM.

LUMIN HAS A REMARKABLE MEMORY.

YES, YES, OF COURSE I REMEMBER: OSCAR PONTE, THE POOR FELLOW STRUCK ON THE HEAD BY A MORSEL OF PIE CRUST LAST CHRISTMAS EVE. HOW ARE YOU DOING? AND THE CANNED SPAGHETTI BUSINESS? AND YOUR FAMILY? COMING INTO TOWN THIS WEEK...YES, WE MUST GET TOGETHER!

SNIFF. I CAN SMELL THE DRY CLEANING FUMES— THE 8:45 CYCLE MUST ALMOST BE OVER. GINGIN, BE A GOOD GIRL AND GO DOWN TO PICK UP MR. KNIPL'S JACKET.

KNIPL? NO, HE'S NOT MY TYPE.

FROLIK

ON THE SIDEWALK, FAR BELOW DR. RUSHOWER'S PENTHOUSE APARTMENT, TWO AMBITIOUS YOUNG MEN LAY THEIR CLOTHES OUT FOR THE EVENING.

RICARDO SWORE THAT LAST NIGHT, AT THIS TIME, IT WAS RAINING BOUILLABAISSE.

THEY COULD NEVER GET THE STAINS OUT.

THIS RUSHOWER FELLOW TOOK HIM IN LIKE A SON. HE'S DATING THE GUY'S STEP-DAUGHTER AND WAS PROMISED A JOB ON THE BOARD OF THE FAMILY'S FOUNDATION.

PLUS THEY PICKED UP THE CLEANING BILL.

DR. RUSHOWER'S STEP-DAUGHTER, GINGIN, EMERGES FROM THE BUILDING'S LOBBY, A PALE GREEN RECEIPT IN HER DELICATE HAND.

THE SUN SETS TWELVE MINUTES EARLIER ON THE GROUND FLOOR; IT'S ALREADY NIGHT DOWN HERE.

SHE GAZES INTO THE WINDOW OF A BUSY COFFEE SHOP.

AH, THE SMELL OF KETCHUP, HOT GREASE AND MAYONNAISE RUN-OFF! THESE PEOPLE EAT WITH UTTER ABANDON.

EVERYWHERE YOU LOOK THERE'S A STAIN, SPOT OR BIT OF INCRUSTATION.

SOMETIMES A WEEK GOES BY BEFORE THEY EVEN NOTICE, AND THEN IT BECOMES A BIG MYSTERY.

HOW DID THIS TARTAR SAUCE GET ONTO MY SHIRTSLEEVE? I HAVEN'T BEEN TO THE SEASHORE SINCE LAST SUMMER, WHO PUT THIS SPOT OF PEA SOUP ON MY FAVORITE NECKTIE? EXTRAORDINARY FEATS OF SELF-DELUSION!

MY STEP-FATHER TAKES THIS ALL VERY SERIOUSLY.

WE PUT UP MIRRORS AT EACH TABLE AND POLISHED THE NAPKIN DISPENSERS, BUT YOU CAN'T FORCE PEOPLE TO STOP AND EXAMINE THEMSELVES IN THE HEAT OF A MEAL.

HE'S ENDOWED A FOUNDATION TO STUDY THE PROBLEM.

OUTSIDE, IT BEGINS TO RAIN CHOP SUEY.

A CLEAN NAPKIN DAMPENED WITH A LITTLE COLD SELTZER WATER, THAT'S ALL YOU NEED!

ON A QUIET WEEKDAY MORNING, TWO VISITORS ADMIRE THE FRESH DUST MOTES IN A SUN-FILLED GALLERY OF THE RECENTLY OPENED MULETEAM MUSEUM OF IMMANENT ART.

THE DISPLAY COPY OF A CATALOG FOR A TOURING EXHIBITION OF RECENT AMERICAN SHOWER-CAPS SLIPS TO THE FLOOR OF THE BUSY GIFT SHOP.

IN THE BASEMENT CAFETERIA, SOMEONE UNINTENTIONALLY RECREATES THE SCUMBLING TECHNIQUE OF A 16th CENTURY VENETIAN PAINTER.

THE DIRECTOR OF THE SECOND-FLOOR WIDOW'S LOUNGE BUYS ONLY THOSE TISSUES PACKAGED IN THE DISTINCTIVE STYLE OF A FAMOUS MODERN PAINTER.

ONE ROOM IS DEVOTED TO THE WORK OF AN INFLUENTIAL 19th CENTURY PICTURE HANGER.

AT NOON, ONE OVERWEIGHT GUARD RELIEVES ANOTHER ON THE MOTORIZED WALKWAY CONNECTING THE ERASURE WING TO THE NOT-YET-FOUND SCULPTURE COURT.

A BOARD MEMBER DEFENDS HIS PROPOSAL TO RENT OUT CERTAIN GALLERIES FOR USE AS MOTEL ROOMS EACH NIGHT AFTER MUSEUM HOURS.

A SMALL TURPENTINE FOUNTAIN FILLS THE MUSEUM'S ENTRANCE HALL WITH THE SMELL OF LATENT CREATIVITY.

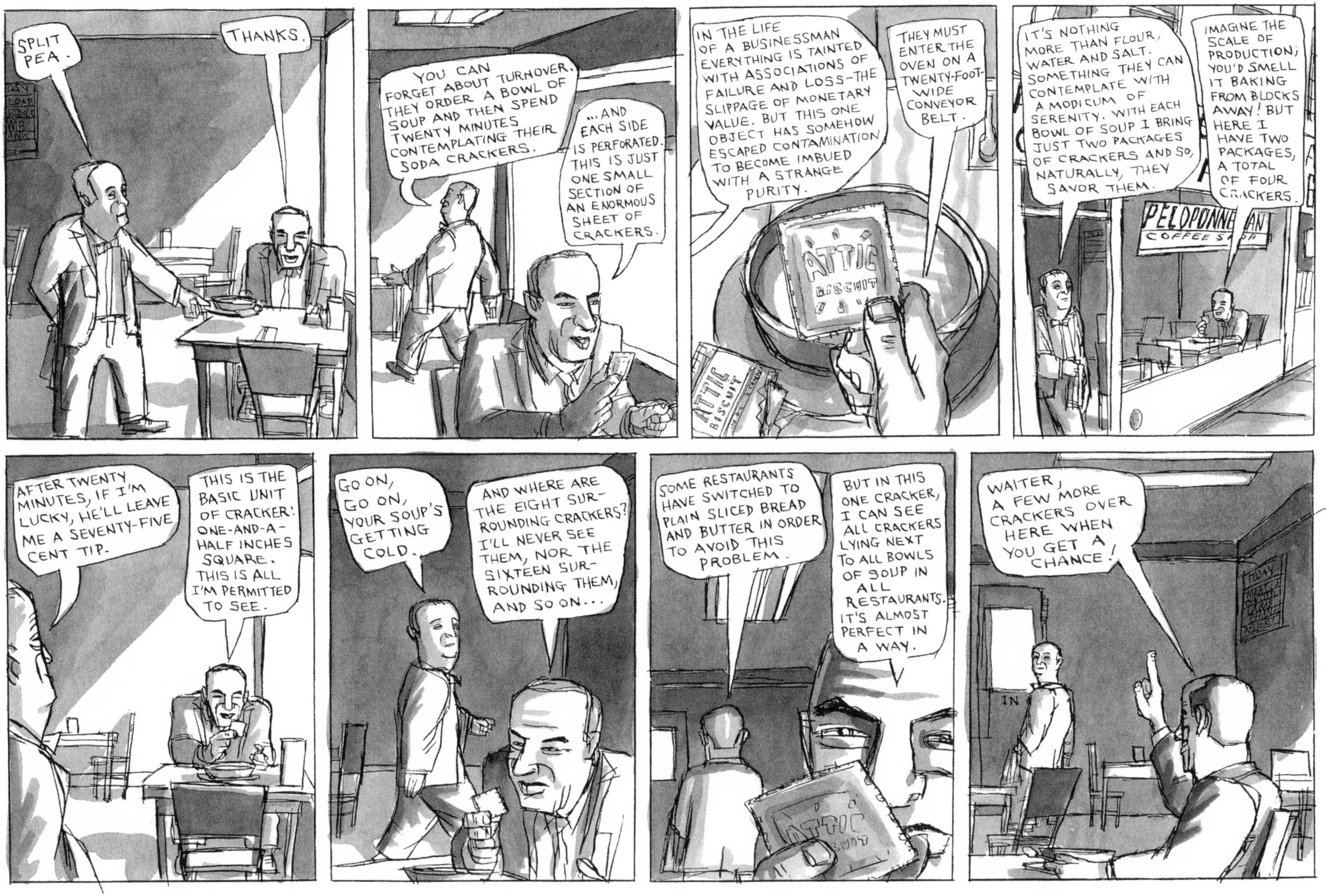

SPLIT PEA.
THANKS.
YOU CAN FORGET ABOUT TURNOVER. THEY ORDER A BOWL OF SOUP AND THEN SPEND TWENTY MINUTES CONTEMPLATING THEIR SODA CRACKERS.
...AND EACH SIDE IS PERFORATED. THIS IS JUST ONE SMALL SECTION OF AN ENORMOUS SHEET OF CRACKERS.
IN THE LIFE OF A BUSINESSMAN EVERYTHING IS TAINTED WITH ASSOCIATIONS OF FAILURE AND LOSS—THE SLIPPAGE OF MONETARY VALUE. BUT THIS ONE OBJECT HAS SOMEHOW ESCAPED CONTAMINATION TO BECOME IMBUED WITH A STRANGE PURITY.
THEY MUST ENTER THE OVEN ON A TWENTY-FOOT-WIDE CONVEYOR BELT.
ATTIC BISCUIT
IT'S NOTHING MORE THAN FLOUR, WATER AND SALT. SOMETHING THEY CAN CONTEMPLATE WITH A MODICUM OF SERENITY. WITH EACH BOWL OF SOUP I BRING JUST TWO PACKAGES OF CRACKERS AND SO, NATURALLY, THEY SAVOR THEM.
IMAGINE THE SCALE OF PRODUCTION; YOU'D SMELL IT BAKING FROM BLOCKS AWAY! BUT HERE I HAVE TWO PACKAGES, A TOTAL OF FOUR CRACKERS.
COFFEE S
AFTER TWENTY MINUTES, IF I'M LUCKY, HE'LL LEAVE ME A SEVENTY-FIVE CENT TIP.
THIS IS THE BASIC UNIT OF CRACKER: ONE-AND-A-HALF INCHES SQUARE. THIS IS ALL I'M PERMITTED TO SEE.
GO ON, GO ON, YOUR SOUP'S GETTING COLD.
AND WHERE ARE THE EIGHT SURROUNDING CRACKERS? I'LL NEVER SEE THEM, NOR THE SIXTEEN SURROUNDING THEM, AND SO ON...
SOME RESTAURANTS HAVE SWITCHED TO PLAIN SLICED BREAD AND BUTTER IN ORDER TO AVOID THIS PROBLEM.
BUT IN THIS ONE CRACKER, I CAN SEE ALL CRACKERS LYING NEXT TO ALL BOWLS OF SOUP IN ALL RESTAURANTS. IT'S ALMOST PERFECT IN A WAY.
WAITER, A FEW MORE CRACKERS OVER HERE WHEN YOU GET A CHANCE!
IN

IT WAS ONCE ESTIMATED THAT HIS VOICE WAS HEARD, EACH DAY, BY AT LEAST TWO HUNDRED AND FIFTY THOUSAND PEOPLE.

PASSENGERS FOR THE 4:57 TRAIN, "THE BANQUET REPEATER" TO LAKE HEFSOLL, MAKING STOPS AT PAJAMA VALLEY, CAL O'MINE AND SITZTIL JUNCTION...

CROWDS WOULD GATHER AND THEN DISPERSE EACH TIME HE SPOKE.

PLEASE BE ADVISED THAT YOUR TRAIN IS NOW BOARDING ON TRACK SIX.

INDIVIDUALS WOULD FORSAKE THEIR OWN WRISTWATCHES AND RUN FOR THEIR LIVES UPON HIS SAY-SO.

AH-HEM.

AND EVEN WHEN HE HAD NOTHING TO SAY, THOUSANDS COCKED THEIR EARS IN ANTICIPATION.

WOULD MRS. FRANCINE LOCHIA PLEASE MEET HER PARTY AT THE INFORMATION CRIB ON THE MAIN CONCOURSE.

AT SIX, EACH NIGHT, HE WOULD LEAVE HIS AIR-CONDITIONED BOOTH AND BEGIN THE SLOW ADJUSTMENT TO PRIVATE LIFE.

EMPLOYEES ONLY

WHAT ARE YOU IN THE MOOD FOR: EEL SHANK AT THE ELEVATOR BAR, OR AMERICAN-STYLE CHOP SUEY AT WOMEN'S COLLEGE?

HOW LONG HAVE YOU BEEN TOGETHER WITH THIS DOCTOR? AND SHE STILL REFUSES TO GIVE YOU A CERTIFICATE OF POOR HEALTH?

WHAT DO YOU THINK, DELICIOUS?

THEY SPEND OUR TAX DOLLARS KEEPING TRACK OF VALISES AT ALL THE MAJOR AIRPORTS! WOULD YOU CARE IF EVERY LAST PERSON AT THIS BAR EMIGRATED TONIGHT TO SOME ISLAND IN THE PACIFIC OCEAN?

WHAT ARE YOU DRINKING?

"WHAT IS THE USE OF SPEAKING," HE THOUGHT, "WHEN FEWER THAN SIX HUNDRED PEOPLE ARE LISTENING?"

WHERE TO?

FROM THE VANTAGE POINT OF A CASH REGISTER, LEOPOLD LAYETTE SURVEYS THE ACTIVITY IN HIS STORE.

SOME CUSTOMERS CONFUSE THEIR LOVE FOR MY MERCHANDISE WITH THEIR FEELINGS TOWARD ME.

WHY NOT TAKE THE AFTERNOON OFF? THERE'S A 4:20 SHOWING OF "NOTHING CAN HAPPEN HERE" AT THE VILLATRAUM CINEMA.

CASH OR CHARGE?

CASH.

THEY GRAVITATE TOWARD THIS PINK SUN-DRESS. I SHOULD REORDER. O.K., O.K., I'LL BE THERE.

THE WOMAN RUSHES HOME TO CHANGE INTO HER NEW DRESS

IN MOST MODERN MANUFACTURING PROCESSES THAT IT IS UNAVOIDABLE THAT SOME SMALL PORTION OF MATERIAL IS CAST OFF AS WASTE.

WHILE MR. LAYETTE BREAKS IN A PART-TIME CASHIER.

HOLES ARE PUNCHED, CARDBOARD EDGES GRIPPED AND ODD SHAPES CUT FROM STANDARD ROLLS OF PLASTIC SHEETING. YOU GET IT?

AT 5:30, THE WOMAN'S HUSBAND COMES HOME TO AN EMPTY APARTMENT.

YOO-HOO, IT'S ME.

IF THESE SCRAPS HAVE NO RESALE VALUE THEY'RE LEFT TO CLING TO THE FINISHED PRODUCT.

EXIT

A PETAL OF CRIMSON PLASTIC, STAMPED TO FORM THE HANDLE OF A SHOPPING BAG, FALLS TO THE BEDROOM FLOOR.

ROSETTA?

EVERYONE'S EXPERIENCED THAT SINKING SENSATION IN THE SOLAR PLEXUS. IT USUALLY HITS IN THE LATE AFTERNOON — THAT'S WHEN WE FEEL THE PHYSICAL PASSAGE OF TIME MOST ACUTELY. WHO KNOWS WHY? BLOOD SUGAR, CIRCADIAN RHYTHMS, BIRTH TRAUMA...

IT'S ALMOST 4:30.

BUT SOME UNFORTUNATE INDIVIDUALS BEGIN, FROM AN EARLY AGE, TO ASSOCIATE THE DAILY ONSET OF THIS MELANCHOLY DISCOMFORT WITH THE LAST SCHEDULED PICK-UP OF MAIL IN THEIR NEIGHBORHOOD.

THE COINCIDENCE IS UNDENIABLE.

AND FOR THEM, THIS DELICIOUS ACHE IS PERFECTLY EMBODIED IN THE FIGURE OF THE MAILMAN WITH HIS LEATHER-REINFORCED SACK, CHAIN OF KEYS AND AIR OF UTTER INDIFFERENCE — TYPICAL OF A FEDERAL EMPLOYEE.

THEY CONSTRUCT AN ENTIRE LIFESTYLE BASED UPON THE PICK-UP TIMES POSTED ON THE INNER LID OF THEIR CORNER MAILBOX. YOU'VE SEEN THEM HANGING AROUND, AS THOUGH WAITING TO MAIL A LETTER.

SOME ARE SHY AND PREFER TO WATCH FROM A DISTANCE AS HE CROUCHES DOWN, UNLOCKS THE BOX WITHOUT LOOKING, AND THEN SWEEPS OUT ITS CONTENTS, CAREFUL NOT TO MISS A SINGLE BUSINESS-REPLY POSTCARD.

OTHERS ARE BOLD ENOUGH TO STRIKE UP A CONVERSATION. THROUGH SMALL TALK THEY HOPE TO EFFECT A MOMENTARY PAUSE IN THIS RELENTLESS ACTIVITY.

IS THERE REALLY ANY DIFFERENCE BETWEEN BOOK-RATE AND FOURTH-CLASS MAIL?

SOME WILL GO SO FAR AS TO INVITE THE MAILMAN INTO A NEARBY BAR FOR A DRINK, WHICH MAY LEAD TO DINNER OR WHO KNOWS WHAT.

ANOTHER "SPECIAL DELIVERY" ON THE ROCKS FOR MY FRIEND HERE.

ANYTHING TO PREVENT THE MAILMAN FROM COMPLETING HIS APPOINTED ROUNDS AND THUS PROLONG THIS EXCRUCIATING PLEASURE.

NEXT PICK-UP'S AT 6 A.M.

THESE SMALL ADS APPEAR EACH WEEK IN THE BUSINESS SECTION OF THE SUNDAY PAPER.

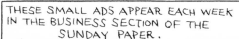

FOR TWENTY-FIVE DOLLARS A MONTH, ONE CAN RENT THE USE OF A PRESTIGIOUS MID-TOWN ADDRESS— A COMPLETE MAIL-DROP FACILITY AND 24-HOUR TELEPHONE ANSWERING SERVICE.

THE VIRILE-HINGE BUILDING, 2500 GERMINAL AVE., SUITE 2116.

THE ILLUSION OF A CORPORATE OFFICE IN A CHOICE LOCATION MASKS THE REALITY OF A BUSINESS RUN FROM A PHONE BOOTH, OR, THE KITCHEN TABLE OF A BASEMENT APARTMENT ON BISCUIT BOULEVARD.

SNIFF, SNIFF, DIRTY LINEN.

THESE "PRESTIGE ADDRESS" BUSINESSES ARE THEMSELVES LOCATED IN THE LEAST DESIRABLE, WINDOWLESS SPACES WITHIN THESE DISTINGUISHED BUILDINGS.

A ROOM FILLED TO CAPACITY WITH TELEPHONE ANSWERING EQUIPMENT, DUSTY MAILBOXES AND A STAFF OF CHAIN-SMOKING WOMEN WHO MANUALLY FORWARD THE MAIL.

DON'T FORGE

AMONG THE BUSINESSMEN WHO'VE USED THESE SERVICES FOR DECADES THERE HAS ARISEN A CLEAR SOCIAL AND ECONOMIC HIERARCHY.

I TOOK THE PLUNGE. FOR TEN DOLLARS MORE A MONTH I'M NOW AT THE SEWERDONA BUILDING.

CONGRATULATIONS, IT'S A WONDERFUL MOVE.

IN THEIR MINDS, THERE IS A WIDE, GRADED SPECTRUM OF DIFFERENCE BETWEEN THE VARIOUS ADDRESSES AVAILABLE FOR RENT.

1400 GRAYBALD AVENUE. A NICE EVEN NUMBER, SOUNDS HONEST, RELIABLE. PEOPLE ENJOY WRITING IT ON ENVELOPES.

THE ASSIGNED "SUITE" NUMBER REVEALS THE COMPLEX HISTORY OF EACH BUSINESS AND DESCRIBES THE POSITION OF ITS MAILBOX IN RELATION TO THE HUNDREDS OF OTHER MAIL-BOXES AT THAT LOCATION.

HE'S A FOUR-DIGIT OPERATION, BEEN AROUND FOR NO MORE THAN SIX MONTHS. I'M ON THE THIRD TIER, SIXTH FROM THE LEFT, ABOVE JOHNSON'S GIVE-YOURSELF-A-TROPHY CO. AND NEXT DOOR TO THE ILLOBAT CORPORATION OF AMERICA.

SOME RENTERS MANAGE TO LEARN THE NAME OF AN EMPLOYEE ON THE STAFF AND TURN THIS BIT OF CONFIDENTIAL KNOWLEDGE TO THEIR ADVANTAGE OVER THE YEARS.

LISTEN, SYLVIA, MY DEAR, IF ANYTHING COMES FROM THE PETA-NEUSTRAL COMPANY, THROW IT RIGHT IN THE GARBAGE, DON'T EVEN PUT IT IN MY BOX. REMEMBER, I'M GOOD TO YOU—VAL MOURICE CORPORATION, SUITE 817.

A BUOYANT FIGURE, WITH A RENTED VIDEOTAPE TUCKED UNDER ITS ARM, GLIDES GENTLY DOWN THE STREET.

"THE ONLY DIAL-TONE" IN TOWN, STARRING EDGAR WALLET AND ALMA CALVES.

PASTA

NOW, AT LAST, FREED FROM ALL CONSTRAINTS OF PUBLIC DECORUM, HE ANTICIPATES THE PLEASURE OF VIEWING THIS FILM IN THE PRIVACY OF HIS OWN HOME.

A COPY OF A FILM WHICH LAST PLAYED THE LOCAL THEATERS IN 1958.

2 GOOSANDER
3 LUGGAGE RAQUE
4 NEFRO-TITI

GIFTS

AT THE ENTRANCE TO HIS BUILDING HE IS NOT SUBJECTED TO THE SCRUTINY OF A CALLOUS TICKET-TAKER.

GOOD EVENING ELIJAH.

ALMA CALVES IS MY FAVORITE TOO.

THERE ARE NO UNIFORMED USHERS PROWLING THE FOYER OF HIS APARTMENT.

IN WHICH ROOM SHALL I WATCH?

THE CUES FOR LAUGHTER AND SOBS PROVIDED BY AN AVERAGE AUDIENCE ARE WHOLLY UNNECESSARY.

THIS WAS ONCE CONSIDERED A COMEDY.

DON'T WORRY, MY DEAR, IT'S NOTHING — A LITTLE PSYCHOLOGICAL ROPE BURN.

THE FILM WILL BEGIN AND END WITHIN THE CONFINES OF HIS LIVING ROOM.

IN TEN MINUTES, THE SCREEN WILL SEEM TO EXPAND TO FILL MY FIELD OF VISION.

TURN OVER ANY PIECE OF TRASH IN THE STREET AND WHAT'LL YOU FIND?

MUMTAZ CORP.

AS THE POWERFUL NARCOTIC OF A MEDIOCRE BLACK-AND-WHITE MOVIE BEGINS TO COURSE THROUGH HIS VEINS,

WHO IS THIS FELLOW IN THE BURNOOSE?

ECCH! IT'S FEEDING TIME AT THE PHONE COMPANY.

HE REALIZES THAT HE WILL NOT BE AWAKENED AT THE FILM'S CONCLUSION TO TAKE A BRISK WALK HOME THROUGH THE COOL NIGHT AIR.

I CAN REMAIN HERE UNTIL THE TAPE ENDS AND THEN REWINDS AUTOMATICALLY.

IT'S THERE FOR EVERYONE TO HEAR— YOU, ME, THE BLIND DR. MUMTAZ, MURIEL THE WINDOW DRESSER —EVERYONE!

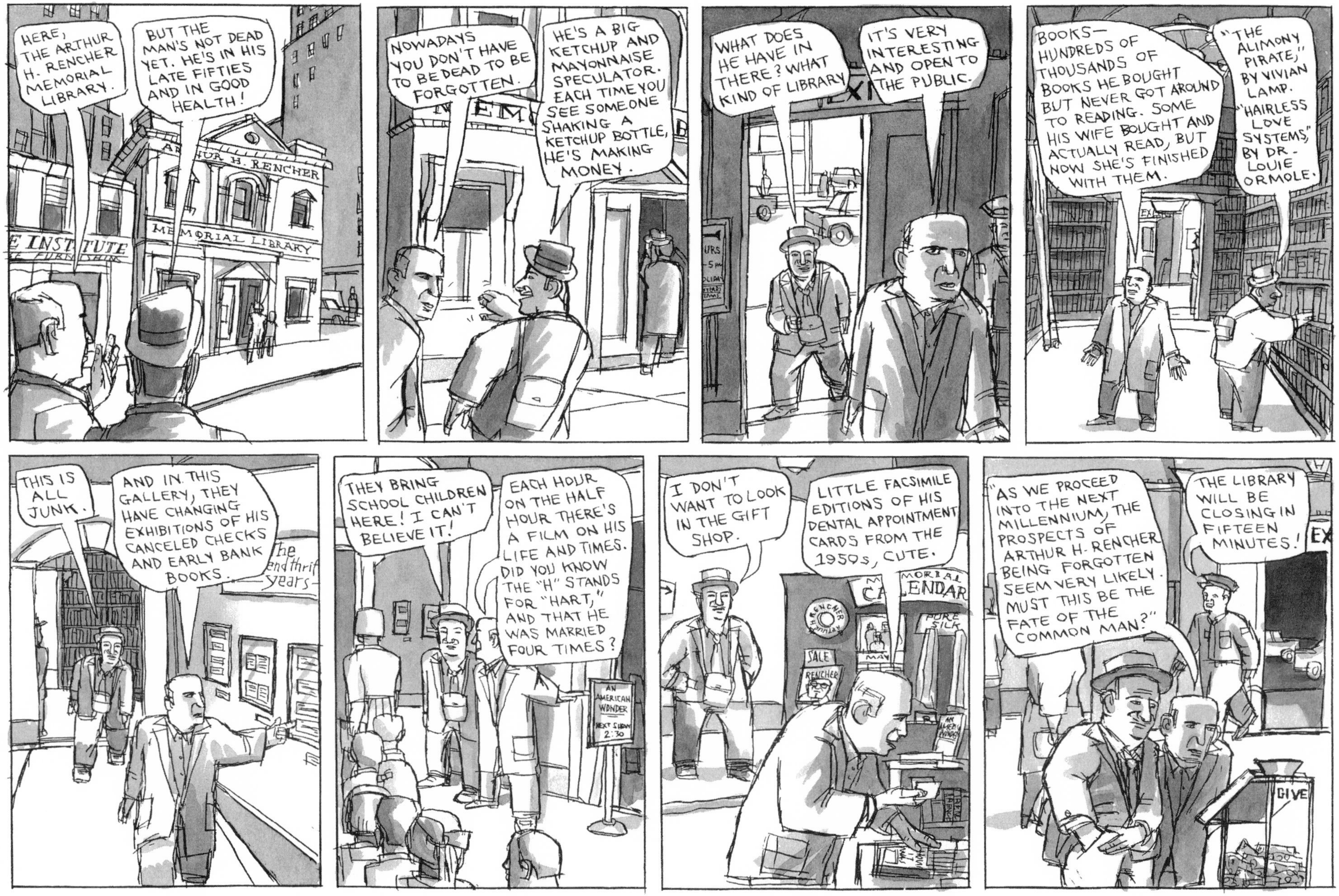
HERE, THE ARTHUR H. RENCHER MEMORIAL LIBRARY.
BUT THE MAN'S NOT DEAD YET. HE'S IN HIS LATE FIFTIES AND IN GOOD HEALTH!
MEMORIAL LIBRARY
NOWADAYS YOU DON'T HAVE TO BE DEAD TO BE FORGOTTEN.
HE'S A BIG KETCHUP AND MAYONNAISE SPECULATOR. EACH TIME YOU SEE SOMEONE SHAKING A KETCHUP BOTTLE, HE'S MAKING MONEY.
WHAT DOES HE HAVE IN THERE? WHAT KIND OF LIBRARY
IT'S VERY INTERESTING AND OPEN TO THE PUBLIC.
BOOKS— HUNDREDS OF THOUSANDS OF BOOKS HE BOUGHT BUT NEVER GOT AROUND TO READING. SOME HIS WIFE BOUGHT AND ACTUALLY READ, BUT NOW SHE'S FINISHED WITH THEM.
"THE ALIMONY PIRATE," BY VIVIAN LAMP. "HAIRLESS LOVE SYSTEMS," BY DR. LOUIE ORMOLE.
THIS IS ALL JUNK.
AND IN THIS GALLERY, THEY HAVE CHANGING EXHIBITIONS OF HIS CANCELED CHECKS AND EARLY BANK BOOKS.
THEY BRING SCHOOL CHILDREN HERE! I CAN'T BELIEVE IT!
EACH HOUR ON THE HALF HOUR THERE'S A FILM ON HIS LIFE AND TIMES. DID YOU KNOW THE "H" STANDS FOR "HART," AND THAT HE WAS MARRIED FOUR TIMES?
AN AMERICAN WONDER
NEXT SHOW 2:30
I DON'T WANT TO LOOK IN THE GIFT SHOP.
LITTLE FACSIMILE EDITIONS OF HIS DENTAL APPOINTMENT CARDS FROM THE 1950s, CUTE.
CALENDAR
PURE SILK
SALE
RENCHER
"AS WE PROCEED INTO THE NEXT MILLENNIUM, THE PROSPECTS OF ARTHUR H. RENCHER BEING FORGOTTEN SEEM VERY LIKELY. MUST THIS BE THE FATE OF THE COMMON MAN?"
THE LIBRARY WILL BE CLOSING IN FIFTEEN MINUTES!
GIVE

MR. KNIPL ENCOUNTERS ANOTHER UNFAMILIAR NAME EMBROIDERED ON THE CROWN OF A STRANGER'S CAP.

"RUMEN-8" A RAP GROUP? AN AUTOMOTIVE PRODUCT? I'M ALWAYS TEMPTED TO ASK.

DON'T BOTHER, I CAN GUARANTEE YOU THAT HE DOESN'T KNOW HIMSELF WHAT IT MEANS. YOU CAN TELL BY THE EXPRESSION ON HIS FACE. LOOK AT HIS FINGERNAILS —HE'S A CITY BOY.

OUT WEST, YOU'LL SEE THAT NAME IN TWENTY-FOOT-HIGH LETTERS PAINTED ON THE SIDE OF BARNS AND STENCILED ONTO HUNDRED-GALLON DRUMS.

IT'S A SYNTHETIC CUD MIX: GREEN CELLULOSE FIBER, ARTIFICIAL CLOVER EXTRACT AND CHLOROPHYLL JUICE CONCENTRATE BLENDED WITH A MILD EMETIC. THE COWS DON'T KNOW THE DIFFERENCE.

LAST YEAR, ONE OF THEIR SALESMEN TRIED TO SINGLEHANDEDLY CRACK THE RESTAURANT SUPPLY MARKET IN THIS CITY. HE BROUGHT FOUR DOZEN CAPS WITH HIM TO USE AS PROMOTIONAL GIVE-AWAYS.

IT'S A WHOLESOME SALAD ADDITIVE, OR PERFECT AS A GARNISH FOR THE MAIN COURSE.

$2.95 lb.

HE GOT MIXED UP WITH A LOCAL SALAD BAR SYNDICATE AND THAT WAS THE LAST ANYONE HEARD OF HIM. IT WAS IN ALL THE PAPERS.

YOU CAN CHEW IT FOR SEVERAL HOURS AND THEN IT REPEATS ON YOU ALL EVENING.

WHATEVER THEY FOUND IN HIS HOTEL ROOM WAS SOLD AT AUCTION THIS SPRING.

WHAT DO I HEAR FOR LOT 17: FOUR DOZEN COTTON BASEBALL-STYLE PROMOTIONAL CAPS?

THE CAPS PROBABLY ENDED UP IN A JOB-LOT STORE ON PLAYTZER AVENUE WHERE THIS FELLOW'S TEENAGE SON PICKED ONE UP FOR 79 CENTS AND THEN GOT TIRED OF WEARING IT.

I HAVE NO IDEA.

MR. KNIPL WATCHES AS HIS FRIEND REMOVES THE COTTON FROM A BOTTLE OF ASPIRIN.

WHAT DID I DO? WHAT DID I DO TO DESERVE THIS?

IT PREVENTS THE TABLETS FROM BREAKING.

EACH TIME I OPEN A BOTTLE AND PERFORM THIS SMALL MANUAL TASK, I'M OVERWHELMED BY AN INEXPLICABLE FEELING OF GUILT AND SADNESS. TEN YEARS FROM NOW, AS MY HEALTH DETERIORATES, THERE'LL BE DOZENS OF OTHER BOTTLES OF MEDICINE TO OPEN—EACH WITH A BALL OF COTTON STUFFED DOWN ITS THROAT.

TAKE A LOOK!

DOWNSTAIRS, IN THE STREET, A MAN SELLS SHIRTS OUT OF A CARDBOARD BOX.

FIRST QUALITY MEN'S SHIRTS, 100% COTTON, TWO FOR $14.00!

"MADE IN FALOTUNIA." WHO KNOWS WHERE THAT IS? WHO KNOWS WHAT GOES ON THERE? HE BOUGHT THEM FOR LESS THAN SEVEN. THE PEOPLE WHO SOLD THEM TO HIM PROBABLY PAID A DOLLAR IN MATERIAL AND LABOR—IF THAT.

WHEN THESE GO, THERE ARE NO MORE.

AND THE COTTON IT'S MADE OF—WHERE DOES THAT COME FROM? IS IT PICKED BY MACHINE OR DO THEY STILL RELY ON CHEAP HUMAN LABOR? WHAT COULD THEY POSSIBLY PAY?

HMM? TWO FOR $14.00? NOT BAD.

TEN THOUSAND MILES AWAY, IN A CHEMICAL PLANT ON THE ISLAND OF TINIMAR, THE BODY OF A UNION ORGANIZER IS WRAPPED IN A BALE OF CLOTH.

100% POLYESTER.

HE WAS AN EXPERT ON THE HISTORY OF SLAVE LABOR.

WAIT A MINUTE, WAIT A MINUTE. THIS SHIRT IS ONLY 50% COTTON, THE REST IS SYNTHETIC.

AND THAT'S WHAT THEY SAY—PROBABLY MORE LIKE 70/30.

NAH, THIS FEELS TOO SOFT TO BE COTTON.

HERE, PLEASE, GIVE ME A HAND WITH THESE NEW VITAMINS.

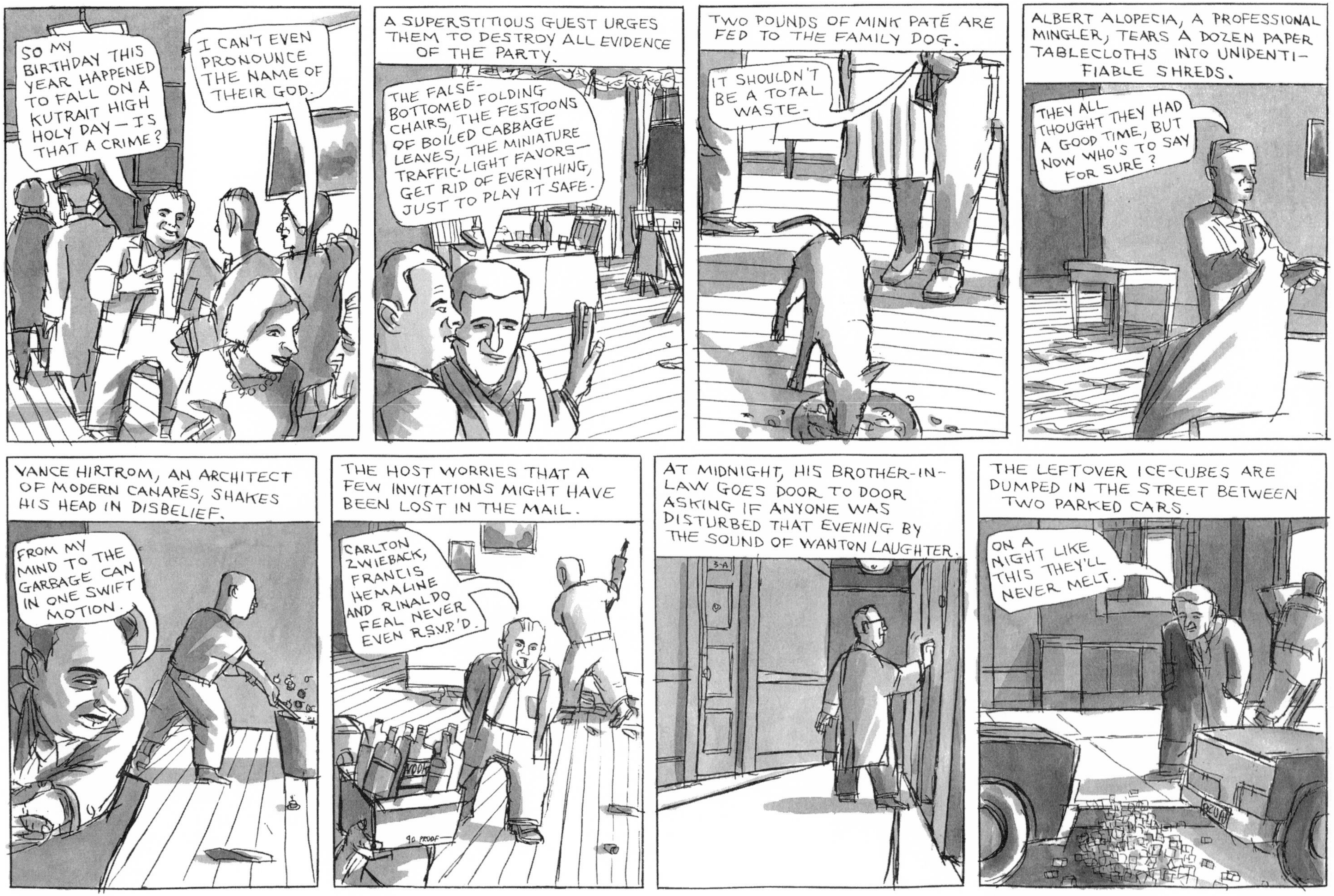
SO MY BIRTHDAY THIS YEAR HAPPENED TO FALL ON A KUTRAIT HIGH HOLY DAY—IS THAT A CRIME?
I CAN'T EVEN PRONOUNCE THE NAME OF THEIR GOD.
A SUPERSTITIOUS GUEST URGES THEM TO DESTROY ALL EVIDENCE OF THE PARTY.
THE FALSE-BOTTOMED FOLDING CHAIRS, THE FESTOONS OF BOILED CABBAGE LEAVES, THE MINIATURE TRAFFIC-LIGHT FAVORS—GET RID OF EVERYTHING, JUST TO PLAY IT SAFE.
TWO POUNDS OF MINK PATÉ ARE FED TO THE FAMILY DOG.
IT SHOULDN'T BE A TOTAL WASTE.
ALBERT ALOPECIA, A PROFESSIONAL MINGLER, TEARS A DOZEN PAPER TABLECLOTHS INTO UNIDENTIFIABLE SHREDS.
THEY ALL THOUGHT THEY HAD A GOOD TIME, BUT NOW WHO'S TO SAY FOR SURE?
VANCE HIRTROM, AN ARCHITECT OF MODERN CANAPÉS, SHAKES HIS HEAD IN DISBELIEF.
FROM MY MIND TO THE GARBAGE CAN IN ONE SWIFT MOTION.
THE HOST WORRIES THAT A FEW INVITATIONS MIGHT HAVE BEEN LOST IN THE MAIL.
CARLTON ZWIEBACK, FRANCIS HEMALINE AND RINALDO FEAL NEVER EVEN R.S.V.P.'D.
90 PROOF
AT MIDNIGHT, HIS BROTHER-IN-LAW GOES DOOR TO DOOR ASKING IF ANYONE WAS DISTURBED THAT EVENING BY THE SOUND OF WANTON LAUGHTER.
3-A
THE LEFTOVER ICE-CUBES ARE DUMPED IN THE STREET BETWEEN TWO PARKED CARS.
ON A NIGHT LIKE THIS THEY'LL NEVER MELT.

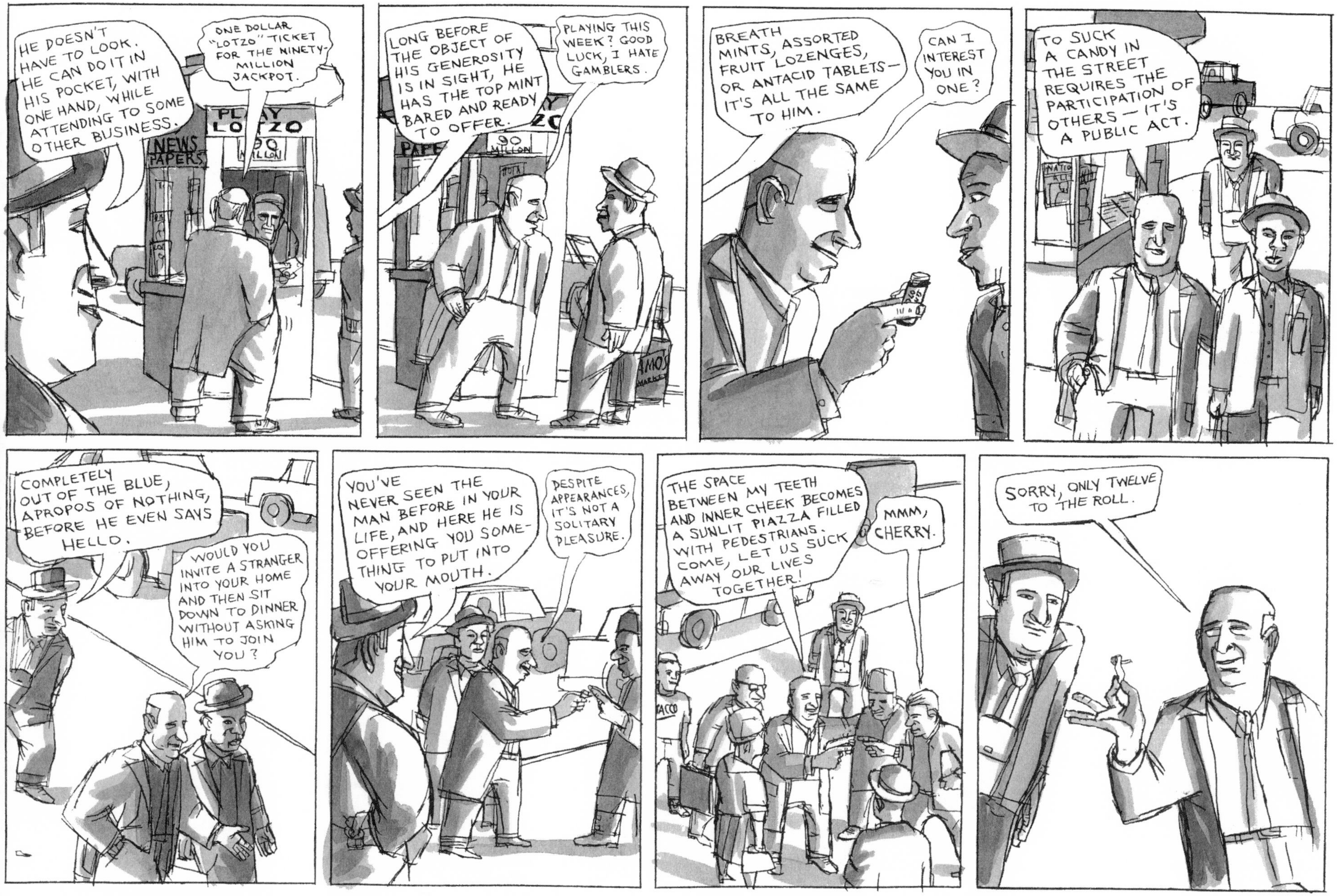
HE DOESN'T HAVE TO LOOK. HE CAN DO IT IN HIS POCKET, WITH ONE HAND, WHILE ATTENDING TO SOME OTHER BUSINESS.
ONE DOLLAR "LOTZO" TICKET FOR THE NINETY-MILLION JACKPOT.
PLAY LOTZO
NEWS PAPERS
90 MILLION
LONG BEFORE THE OBJECT OF HIS GENEROSITY IS IN SIGHT, HE HAS THE TOP MINT BARED AND READY TO OFFER.
PLAYING THIS WEEK? GOOD LUCK, I HATE GAMBLERS.
BREATH MINTS, ASSORTED FRUIT LOZENGES, OR ANTACID TABLETS— IT'S ALL THE SAME TO HIM.
CAN I INTEREST YOU IN ONE?
TO SUCK A CANDY IN THE STREET REQUIRES THE PARTICIPATION OF OTHERS — IT'S A PUBLIC ACT.
COMPLETELY OUT OF THE BLUE, APROPOS OF NOTHING, BEFORE HE EVEN SAYS HELLO.
WOULD YOU INVITE A STRANGER INTO YOUR HOME AND THEN SIT DOWN TO DINNER WITHOUT ASKING HIM TO JOIN YOU?
YOU'VE NEVER SEEN THE MAN BEFORE IN YOUR LIFE, AND HERE HE IS OFFERING YOU SOMETHING TO PUT INTO YOUR MOUTH.
DESPITE APPEARANCES, IT'S NOT A SOLITARY PLEASURE.
THE SPACE BETWEEN MY TEETH AND INNER CHEEK BECOMES A SUNLIT PIAZZA FILLED WITH PEDESTRIANS. COME, LET US SUCK AWAY OUR LIVES TOGETHER!
MMM, CHERRY.
SORRY, ONLY TWELVE TO THE ROLL.

SEAT 11 ROW S SECTION 5

FOYER HALL
Gymnarchus Ave. at 11th St.

Johnson's "Ripsatik Potsyfilia"

APR. 13 2000

THURS. EVE. 8:00 P.M.

ORCHESTRA CIRCLE
Est. Price
Federal Tax
City Tax
$35.00

NO REFUND

GOOD ONLY
THURS. EVE. 8:00 P.M.
APRIL
13
2000

FOYER HALL

Orchestra Circle $35.00

SECTION 5 ROW S SEAT 11

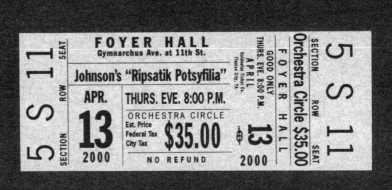

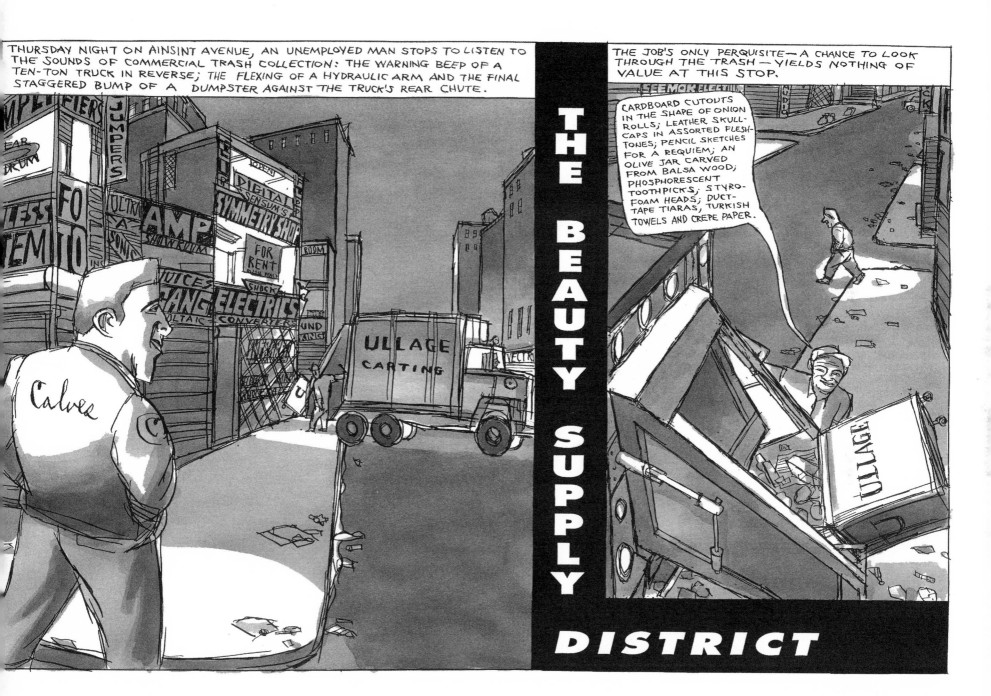

THURSDAY NIGHT ON AINSINT AVENUE, AN UNEMPLOYED MAN STOPS TO LISTEN TO THE SOUNDS OF COMMERCIAL TRASH COLLECTION: THE WARNING BEEP OF A TEN-TON TRUCK IN REVERSE; THE FLEXING OF A HYDRAULIC ARM AND THE FINAL STAGGERED BUMP OF A DUMPSTER AGAINST THE TRUCK'S REAR CHUTE.

THE JOB'S ONLY PERQUISITE—A CHANCE TO LOOK THROUGH THE TRASH—YIELDS NOTHING OF VALUE AT THIS STOP.

CARDBOARD CUTOUTS IN THE SHAPE OF ONION ROLLS; LEATHER SKULL-CAPS IN ASSORTED FLESH-TONES; PENCIL SKETCHES FOR A REQUIEM; AN OLIVE JAR CARVED FROM BALSA WOOD; PHOSPHORESCENT TOOTHPICKS; STYRO-FOAM HEADS; DUCT-TAPE TIARAS, TURKISH TOWELS AND CREPE PAPER.

THE BEAUTY SUPPLY DISTRICT

TAKING THE MOST DIRECT ROUTE BACK TO THE INCINERATOR PLANT...

THE GARBAGE TRUCK, BEARING AN EVENING'S FULL LOAD, PASSES FOYER HALL.

BUILT IN 1895, THE CELEBRATED HALL WAS NOT DESIGNED WITH ACOUSTIC PERFECTION IN MIND.

ITS FUNCTION WAS PURELY SOCIAL: A MEETING PLACE AND BREEDING GROUND FOR ITS WEALTHY PATRONS AND THEIR CHILDREN — THAT MUSIC WOULD BE PLAYED WAS INCIDENTAL.

THE LONG NARROW LOBBY WITH ITS SLOPING FLOOR ENCOURAGED PHYSICAL INTIMACY.

UPSTAIRS THERE ARE SEVERAL PRIVATE "PRACTICE ROOMS."

THE CHANDELIERS CAST A FLATTERING LIGHT; THE MIRRORS WERE FITTED WITH OPTICAL REDUCING GLASS.

ONCE THE CONCERT BEGAN, THE AIR-VENTS FROM OUTSIDE COULD BE TIGHTLY CLOSED.

THIS DOOR LEADS TO A PRIVATE BANQUET ROOM WHERE DRINKS ARE SERVED ALL NIGHT.

THE SEATS WERE OF A PLUSH VELVETEEN IN DARK MAROON — A COLOR CHOSEN FOR ITS SOPORIFIC QUALITIES.

ONE HUNDRED AND FIVE YEARS LATER, IN A LUXURY HIGH-RISE ON ROMAN BOULEVARD,

I APOLOGIZE.

CAESAR KOUROS, AN IMPORTER OF FANCY OLIVES, SHAVES HIS FACE IN RECKLESS HASTE.

TONIGHT'S CONCERT COMPLETELY SLIPPED MY MIND.

THAT'S WHY WE SUBSCRIBE FOR THE SEASON.

HIS WIFE, VESTA, WAITS, READY TO GO, DRESSED IN THE LATEST STYLE: A 1960s FEMALE CAFETERIA-WORKER'S UNIFORM RECAST IN SILK.

WITHOUT MAKING A MONETARY COMMITMENT FAR IN ADVANCE, PEOPLE WOULD FORGET ABOUT ALL MUSIC, ART AND POETRY.

IS THAT WHAT YOU'RE WEARING?

BEFORE LEAVING, HE PUTS A TEN-OUNCE JAR OF PITTED OLIVES INTO HIS COAT POCKET.

WE'LL HAVE DINNER WITH KONRAD AND POLLY AFTERWARDS AT PICKABACK'S— THAT PLACE YOU LIKE.

IN A FURNISHED ROOM NEAR FOYER HALL, AN IMPASSIONED MAN STRUGGLES WITH HIS TELEPHONE.

HELLO, IT'S YOUR DEAR FRIEND, LIONEL PALPUS, SPEAKING. BY SHEER LUCK, A PAIR OF TICKETS CAME INTO MY POSSESSION LATE THIS AFTERNOON. IT'S DIFFICULT MUSIC AND SO I THOUGHT OF YOU.

IN A LOW-RENT OFFICE BUILDING ON ROSSEL AVENUE, THE REAL-ESTATE PHOTOGRAPHER, JULIUS KNIPL, CANNOT MAKE UP HIS MIND.

A FREE TICKET? THE CREMOLORA? A WORLD PREMIERE? FROM EIGHT TO TEN?

ALDO SINO, DIRECTOR OF "THE CONCERT THEATER PARTY GUILD," SITS ALONE IN HIS OFFICE.

I GUARANTEED THEM WALL-TO-WALL BODIES TONIGHT AT FOYER HALL AND STILL HAVE A HUNDRED AND FIFTY EMPTY SEATS.

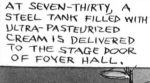

I CAN IMAGINE AT THE ZOO, RIGHT NOW, WANDERING IN THE MONKEY HOUSE, SOME TOURIST OF MODEST MEANS WHO'D JUMP AT THE CHANCE TO HEAR A WORLD-CLASS CONCERT FOR FREE... AND YET THESE TICKETS GO UNCLAIMED.

AT SEVEN-THIRTY, A STEEL TANK FILLED WITH ULTRA-PASTEURIZED CREAM IS DELIVERED TO THE STAGE DOOR OF FOYER HALL.

THE MANNERCHOIR COFFEE SHOP JUST ACROSS THE STREET, DOES A BRISK PRE-CONCERT BUSINESS.

AH, KNIPL! SO YOU WERE JUST PLAYING HARD TO GET!

LIONEL PALPUS, THE WELL-KNOWN ART ENTHUSIAST, FLITS FROM TABLE TO TABLE.

BELIEVE ME, IT'LL DO YOU GOOD —AN AEROBIC WORKOUT FOR THE SOUL.

I WOULD NEVER HAVE THOUGHT OF COMING.

AND HERE'S THE SCULPTOR MANNY BRELLELAH AND HIS LATEST COMPANION WHOSE NAME I WON'T REMEMBER.

LOOK WHAT THE WAITER BROUGHT FOR DESSERT!

PLEASE, DON'T TEMPT ME. MY UPCOMING SHOW CONSISTS OF SCULPTURAL VARIATIONS UPON THE FORM OF A COMMON BOX OF PACKAGED DONUTS: THE SEE-THROUGH WINDOW, THE FLAPS, ETC.

IN THE MIDST OF ALL THIS GAIETY, LET'S NOT FORGET THAT WE'RE HERE FOR A SERIOUS PURPOSE: TO WITNESS THE LONG-OVERDUE WORLD PREMIERE OF AN EARLY COMPOSITION BY COLZA JOHNSON.

SAVE YOUR APPLAUSE FOR THE CONCERT HALL.

AT A QUARTER TO EIGHT, THE CHANDELIERS IN FOYER HALL BEGIN TO TREMBLE IN ANTICIPATION OF THE EVENING'S PERFORMANCE.

TWENTY YEARS AGO THERE WAS NO AUDIENCE FOR SUCH MUSIC; THE CREMOLORA WAS NOT YET PERFECTED AND TONIGHT'S PERFORMER WAS NOT YET BORN.

ON STAGE, A GROUP OF SERIOUS YOUNG MEN BALANCE A HUNDRED AND THIRTY-SIX SHALLOW BOWLS OF HEAVY CREAM UPON AN INTRICATE FRAMEWORK OF WIRE AND STRING.

A DELICATE LEATHER TONGUE, HELD IN CHECK BY A SPRING MECHANISM, CAN BE PULLED ACROSS THE SURFACE OF THE CREAM AT AN ANGLE AND VELOCITY CHOSEN BY THE PERFORMER.

THE "LICK" OF THE TONGUE DIS-PLACES A SMALL QUANTITY OF CREAM WHICH, FALLING IN A STEADY STREAM UPON A TAUT INTESTINAL MEMBRANE, SUSPENDED BELOW, PRODUCES A TONE OF EXQUISITE PURITY.

IT'S ALL DONE BY RADIO CONTROL FROM THE PERFORMER'S BEDROOM AT HOME.

THE CREMOLORA HAS SUPERSEDED BOTH THE VIOLIN AND THE MODERN ELECTRIC KRY-BABY.

TONIGHT, AT LAST, WE HEAR COLZA JOHNSON'S 1980 "RIPSATIK POTSYFILIA."

A SLUGGISH STREAM OF CABS AND LIMOUSINES CLOGS THE STREET IN FRONT OF FOYER HALL.

THERE THEY ARE! HELLO, POLLY!

KONRAD MANNUH, THE DONUT TYCOON, LEANS HEAVILY AGAINST A SHUTTERED TICKET WINDOW.

MY GOD, YOU LOOK LIKE YOU JUST CRAWLED OUT OF A LION'S CAGE.

I'M A SICK MAN.

LIONEL PALPUS RUSHES ABOUT THE LOBBY CONGRATULATING HIS FRIENDS AND ACQUAINTANCES FOR BEING PRESENT ON THIS NIGHT OF RARE ARTISTIC BEAUTY.

FORGET ABOUT THE WAR IN GRACCHUS MINOR, THE FAMINE IN PEESHOOT— PLEASE— JUST FOR THE NEXT TWO HOURS.

POLLY, VESTA, HOLD ON TO YOUR COATS; THE AIR CONDITIONING'S TURNED WAY UP TONIGHT TO STOP THE CREAM FROM GOING BAD.

HOW EXCITING FOR ALL OF US TO BE HERE!

WHERE ARE YOU SITTING?

WHO IS THAT LITTLE HUNCHBACK KISSING MY WIFE?

LIONEL PALPUS— HE'S A REGULAR ON THE MUSEUM AND LIBRARY FREE-LECTURE CIRCUIT. POLLY CALLS HIM THE LAST TRUE ENTHUSIAST. THEY'RE ALL SOUL MATES.

WHAT DOES HE DO FOR A LIVING?

OUR WIVES TAKE HIM OUT FOR LUNCH, AND HE WORKS PART-TIME IN THE CONCERT HALL "CARPETING" BUSINESS.

A MAN IN A PAINT-SPLATTERED SUIT PULLS MANNY BRELLELAH ASIDE.

I SAW IT WITH MY OWN EYES: THE CONTENTS OF SENSUM'S SYMMETRY SHOP PILED LIKE JUNK IN A DUMPSTER WAITING FOR PICKUP!

OH?

OUTSIDE, ALDO SINO TRIES HALF-HEARTEDLY TO DISPOSE OF THE LAST HUNDRED AND FIFTY TICKETS.

A THIRD-EMPTY HOUSE DOESN'T HELP THE ACOUSTICS. MUST BE SOMETHING BIG GOING ON TONIGHT THAT I DON'T KNOW ABOUT.

NO THANKS.

 AND YOU SAY THIS DISEASE RUNS IN THE FAMILY?

YES, AT THE AGE OF SIXTY-EIGHT MY FATHER WAS SUDDENLY STRICKEN: HE BECAME MOROSE, WEARY, SICK OF LIFE.

 A FRIEND OF HIS RECOMMENDED A SURE CURE:

HAVE THE PACKAGING FOR YOUR WHOLE LINE OF IMPORTED OLIVES REDESIGNED—TOP TO BOTTOM. THE TASTE OF AN OLIVE IS INFLUENCED BY THE SHAPE OF THE JAR FROM WHICH IT IS PLUCKED.

HE GAVE HIM THE ADDRESS OF A CLUTTERED LOFT ON AINSINT AVENUE. I REMEMBER GOING ALONG FOR THE RIDE.

PA, WHY RELY ON YOUR OWN EYES? THESE PEOPLE OFFER UNBIASED JUDGEMENTS BASED UPON EXACT MEASUREMENTS—THEY HAVE THE EQUIPMENT!

THE BEAUTY SUPPLY DISTRICT WAS THEN IN ITS HEYDAY. FOR SHOW, EACH BUSINESS ALIGNED ITSELF WITH A DIFFERENT AESTHETIC THEORY OR SCHOOL OF THOUGHT.

 WHAT'S WRONG WITH THIS JAR? LOOKS FINE TO ME.

PLEASE, SEE WHAT YOU CAN DO.

DOWNSTAIRS, IN A DIRTY CHIAROSCURO MAINTENANCE GARAGE, TWO MEN ARGUED OVER THE TRANSITION FROM HIGHLIGHT TO SHADOW ON A CAN OF TOMATO PASTE.

 IN THE WINDOW OF A SUPERMARKET AT DUSK IT WILL BE PERFECT.

YES, PERFECTLY ILLEGIBLE.

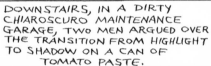

ACROSS THE WAY, A PROPORTIONS SURVEYOR CUT A LEMON MERINGUE PIE INTO EIGHT EQUAL SLICES.

AND FROM A BASEMENT WORKSHOP CAME THE HIGHPITCHED SCREAM OF A TWO-DIMENSIONAL ALUMINUM CONTOUR EXTRUDER.

 THE HUMAN MIND WILL FILL IN THE MISSING ARC IN AN OTHERWISE PERFECT CIRCLE. WE PROJECT THE SYMMETRY OF OUR OWN BODY ONTO THE EXTERNAL WORLD, BUT IN THIS CASE... I DON'T KNOW. COME BACK TOMORROW AFTER FOUR.

FOR HIM, IT WAS A MAJOR ALTERATION.

 WE INCREASED THE HEIGHT BY THREE-SIXTEENTHS OF AN INCH AND TOOK A THIRTY-SECOND OFF THE DIAMETER—NOT BAD.

IT CHANGED MY FATHER'S WHOLE OUTLOOK ON LIFE. FOR THE NEXT TEN YEARS—RIGHT UP UNTIL HE DIED—THE OLIVE BUSINESS KEPT HIM BUSY.

 MAYBE WE SHOULD GO WITH A SPANISH-GREEN LID? I'LL ASK SENSUM.

SOMETIMES WE'D HIT THE EARLY EVENING "RUSH HOUR"!

A QUARTER TO FIVE ON A THURSDAY IN MID-OCTOBER?!

POETS, PAINTERS, COMPOSERS, INTERIOR DECORATORS, HAIRDRESSERS AND BUSINESSMEN, LIKE MY FATHER, ALL CLAMORED FOR SERVICE.

NO ONE WANTS TO LEAVE THEIR COZY STUDIO AFTER A HARD DAY'S AVOIDANCE OF WORK, BUT WE ALL KNOW WHEN SOMETHING'S MISSING.

SORRY, NO REFUNDS.

SENSUM'S A RELIABLE SOURCE FOR SUCH LAST MINUTE REVISIONS, FINAL TOUCHES AND INSPIRED IMPROVISATIONS —DECISIONS YOU CAN BE PROUD TO PUT YOUR NAME ON. IS THAT A BALSA WOOD MODEL OF AN OLIVE JAR YOU'RE HOLDING?

STILL, CREDIT MUST BE GIVEN WHERE CREDIT IS DUE.

DOES THE NOVELIST WHO WORKS AT NIGHT THANK THE ELECTRIC COMPANY FOR HIS SUCCESS? ONE'S INSPIRATION IS MORE OFTEN THAN NOT PURCHASED—EITHER HERE, DIRECTLY, OR THROUGH THE RENT ON A SUMMER COTTAGE WITH A VIEW. I HAD THE TRAIN RUNNING IN THE OTHER DIRECTION!

A HUNDRED YEARS FROM NOW, ART HISTORIANS WILL REFER TO MY BANK STATEMENT TO UNDERSTAND WHAT I ATE, DRANK, SAW AND FELT ON A DAILY BASIS. SENSUM'S CHARGE FOR SERVICES RENDERED WILL BLEND RIGHT IN.

A BOY, MY AGE, MADE RUSH DELIVERIES.

THIS SIDE UP! 211 VALVADERE AVENUE, THEN COME RIGHT BACK!

FOR ALL THEIR BRAVADO, MOST CUSTOMERS WOULD LOOK BOTH WAYS BEFORE LEAVING THE BUILDING, AS THOUGH ASHAMED OF BEING SEEN PATRONIZING SUCH AN ESTABLISHMENT.

MY FATHER, ON THE OTHER HAND, BASKED IN THE RESTORATIVE POWERS OF ARTHUR SENSUM.

COME, LET'S GO FOR A HOT DRINK ON THE CORNER!

SO YOU'RE GENETICALLY PREDISPOSED.

IT HITS ME ONCE EVERY FOUR OR FIVE YEARS. I LOOK AT THESE JARS MORE THAN MOST PEOPLE AND SO, NATURALLY, I'M THE FIRST TO BECOME JADED: SICK AND TIRED OF LOOKING AT A PARTICULAR LINE.

I KNOW IT ALL BY HEART: THE SHAPE OF THE GLASS, THE SIZE OF THE LID, THE ANGLE OF THE LABEL. I CAN'T BEAR TO LOOK, BECAUSE THERE'S NOTHING MORE TO SEE.

MY SALESMEN CAN NEVER UNDERSTAND.

IT'S A PERFECTLY GOOD JAR— OUR BIGGEST SELLER; BEEN ON SUPERMARKET MARKET SHELVES FOR THE PAST FIVE YEARS. ITS SHAPE SAYS "OLIVES" MORE ELOQUENTLY THAN ANY LABEL.

AND SO, I WOULD TAKE A RIDE OVER TO AINSINT AVENUE— GET SOME FRESH AIR—

AINSINT AVENUE? BETWEEN ODYL AND LASSY STREETS THERE'S A GOOD ROUNEZIAN RESTAURANT, A SURGICAL SUPPLY STORE, A LIQUOR STORE...

TO THE SAME PLACE MY FATHER WENT: SENSUM'S SYMMETRY SHOP— SMACK IN THE MIDDLE OF THE BEAUTY SUPPLY DISTRICT.

I'D UNWRAP THE BOTTLE; HE'D ASK ME HOW MY FATHER WAS DOING;

MY FATHER DIED TEN YEARS AGO.

I'M VERY SORRY... HE WAS A GOOD CUSTOMER.

HE'D CONGRATULATE ME FOR HAVING THE GOOD SENSE TO CONTINUE THE FAMILY BUSINESS,

YOU CAN'T HAVE A RECEPTION OR COCKTAIL PARTY WITHOUT THEM. THEY WORK UP YOUR APPETITE FOR EVERYTHING ELSE.

AND THEN TELL ME OF THE FAILURES AND TRIUMPHS OF HIS OWN SON, RANDALL.

HIS FIRST YEAR IN COLLEGE, TO MAKE ME HAPPY, HE TOOK AN INTRODUCTORY COURSE IN AESTHETICS.

THE CLASS MET AT NIGHT IN THE ANNEX OF THE PHILOSOPHY BUILDING.

TONIGHT, WE TAKE A LOOK AT CURCULIO'S THEORY OF THE "VERACIOUS PEEK."

AS A GRADUATE STUDENT IN THE 1950s, CLAUDE CURCULIO SPENT HIS DAYS WANDERING THE GALLERIES OF THE TENFOYLE MUSEUM OF ART.

AT NOON, MENTALLY EXHAUSTED FROM HOURS OF LOOKING AT PAINTING, SCULPTURE AND OTHER VISITORS, HE WOULD STOP TO HAVE LUNCH IN THE MUSEUM'S BASEMENT CAFETERIA.

HIS PROFESSORS WARNED HIM AGAINST THIS PRACTICE.

ONE SHOULD BREAK THE SPELL OF BRUSHSTROKE AND CHISEL; RESTORE A SENSE OF AESTHETIC DISTANCE BY HAVING LUNCH OUTSIDE IN THE NEIGHBORHOOD — ANYWHERE BUT HERE.

CURCULIO IGNORED HIS PROFESSORS' ADVICE AND ATE HIS LUNCH EACH DAY IN THE MUSEUM'S BASEMENT CAFETERIA.

STILL IN THE THRALL OF SOME WELL-KNOW EUROPEAN PAINTING, HE WOULD DESCEND VIA THE STAIRS TO THE BASEMENT LEVEL.

A DREARY HALLWAY, DECORATED WITH POSTERS ANNOUNCING EXHIBITIONS THAT HAD COME AND GONE, LED INTO THE LUNCHROOM.

IN THOSE DAYS, THE CAFETERIA WAS A HOMELY ESTABLISHMENT CATERING TO OFF-DUTY GUARDS, PICTURE HANGERS AND ART STUDENTS ACCUSTOMED TO INSTITUTIONAL FOOD.

HE WOULD CHOOSE THE SAME MEAL EVERY DAY — AN ASSORTMENT OF THREE COLD SALADS, A BUTTERED ROLL, PIE AND COFFEE — AND SIT AT THE FIRST CLEAN TABLE HE COULD FIND.

IN THE MOMENT AFTER TAKING HIS SEAT, BUT BEFORE PUTTING THE FORK TO HIS LIPS, HE EXPERIENCED A POWERFUL RECOLLECTION OF THE LAST OBJECT THAT HE HAD LOOKED AT IN THE GALLERY.

"THE OCTOPUS AND THE OFFICE BOY" BY MELMAN RUSE.

IT WAS "AS THOUGH MY SPINE HAD BEEN PLUCKED FROM MY BODY — LEAVING BEHIND THE PERSONALITY AND BODILY APPETITES — AND PLACED IN A VASE OF COOL WATER. THE OBJECT OF CONTEMPLATION WAS NOW SEEN AS THOUGH FROM WITHIN."

"THE INTERNAL LOGIC OF THE PAINTING WAS CLEARLY REVEALED AND, LIKE THE CAFETERIA'S MENU, HUNG IN PUBLIC FOR ALL TO SEE."

IT WAS THIS PARTICULAR SUBTERRANEAN ENVIRONMENT, WITH ITS CLACKING OF DISHES, LAUGHTER OF GUARDS, SMELL OF STEAM-TABLE FOOD AND SLIGHTLY DANK, COFFEE-SOAKED FLOORS, THAT INSTEAD OF DISTRACTING HIM, PERMITTED HIM TO ENTER INTO A UNIQUE RELATIONSHIP WITH THE OBJECT OF HIS CHOICE.

"PUDDING SHAPE #6" BY SIMON TROTYL.

IT WAS, HE PROCLAIMED, "THE PERFECT POINT FROM WHICH TO MEDIATE THE LONGSTANDING HOSTILITY BETWEEN SUBJECT AND OBJECT — A POINT SITUATED DIRECTLY BETWEEN THE APPETITIVE URGE TO CONSUME A WORK OF ART AND THE DISINTERESTED GAZE OF THE CAFETERIA PATRON CHOOSING HIS LUNCH." ONLY AT THIS MOMENT CAN WE ENJOY WHAT HE CALLED THE "VERACIOUS PEEK."

HE TAUGHT HIMSELF TO SIT AT HOME AND CONSTRUCT A MENTAL MODEL OF THAT BASEMENT CAFETERIA FROM WHICH TO VIEW A DIFFERENT ART OBJECT EACH DAY.

DE FUCA'S "STEPMOTHER!!"

HE WENT ON TO EXPERIMENT WITH THE CONTEMPLATION OF OBJECTS FROM THE NATURAL WORLD:

A STEWED PRUNE, A FALLEN STRAND OF BLACK HAIR FROM THE HEAD OF A FOOD PREPARER, A PIECE OF SHREDDED CABBAGE, A BEET-JUICE-STAINED FINGERNAIL...

NEXT WEEK, WE'LL EXAMINE CONTEMPORARY RESPONSES TO CURCULIO'S THEORY: FROM THOSE WHO SEE IT AS A PATHETIC FALLACY BASED ON A DEWY-EYED READING OF MARX, TO...

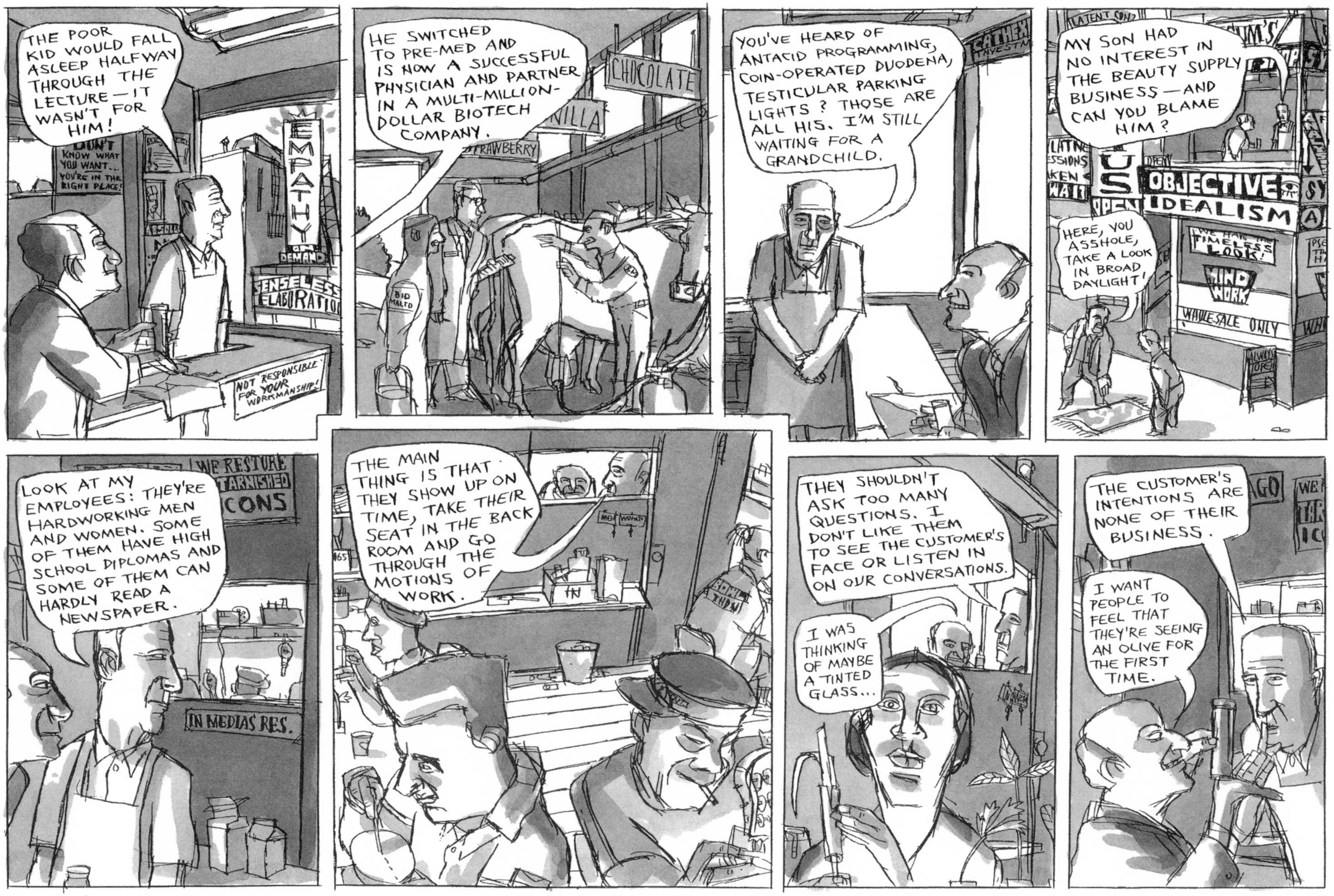

THE POOR KID WOULD FALL ASLEEP HALFWAY THROUGH THE LECTURE—IT WASN'T FOR HIM!
YOU'RE IN THE RIGHT PLACE!
EMPATHY
DEMAND
NOT RESPONSIBLE FOR YOUR WORKMANSHIP!
HE SWITCHED TO PRE-MED AND IS NOW A SUCCESSFUL PHYSICIAN AND PARTNER IN A MULTI-MILLION-DOLLAR BIOTECH COMPANY.
CHOCOLATE
YOU'VE HEARD OF ANTACID PROGRAMMING, COIN-OPERATED DUODENA, TESTICULAR PARKING LIGHTS? THOSE ARE ALL HIS. I'M STILL WAITING FOR A GRANDCHILD.
MY SON HAD NO INTEREST IN THE BEAUTY SUPPLY BUSINESS—AND CAN YOU BLAME HIM?
OBJECTIVE IDEALISM
HERE, YOU ASSHOLE, TAKE A LOOK IN BROAD DAYLIGHT!
MIND WORK
WHOLESALE ONLY
LOOK AT MY EMPLOYEES: THEY'RE HARDWORKING MEN AND WOMEN. SOME OF THEM HAVE HIGH SCHOOL DIPLOMAS AND SOME OF THEM CAN HARDLY READ A NEWSPAPER.
WE RESTORE TARNISHED ICONS
IN MEDIAS RES.
THE MAIN THING IS THAT THEY SHOW UP ON TIME, TAKE THEIR SEAT IN THE BACK ROOM AND GO THROUGH THE MOTIONS OF WORK.
THEY SHOULDN'T ASK TOO MANY QUESTIONS. I DON'T LIKE THEM TO SEE THE CUSTOMER'S FACE OR LISTEN IN ON OUR CONVERSATIONS.
I WAS THINKING OF MAYBE A TINTED GLASS...
THE CUSTOMER'S INTENTIONS ARE NONE OF THEIR BUSINESS.
I WANT PEOPLE TO FEEL THAT THEY'RE SEEING AN OLIVE FOR THE FIRST TIME.

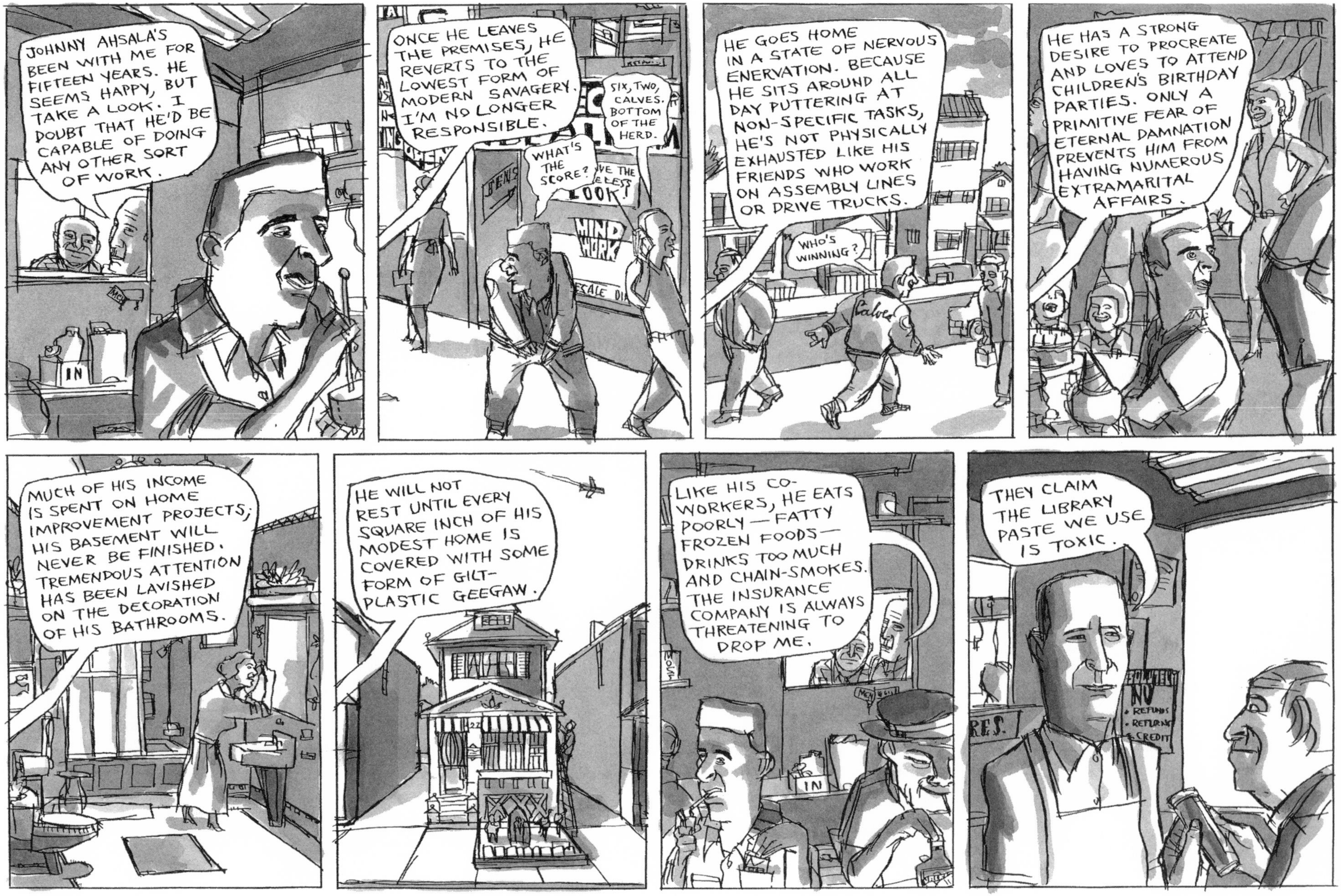
JOHNNY AHSALA'S BEEN WITH ME FOR FIFTEEN YEARS. HE SEEMS HAPPY, BUT TAKE A LOOK. I DOUBT THAT HE'D BE CAPABLE OF DOING ANY OTHER SORT OF WORK.
ONCE HE LEAVES THE PREMISES, HE REVERTS TO THE LOWEST FORM OF MODERN SAVAGERY. I'M NO LONGER RESPONSIBLE.
SIX, TWO, CALVES. BOTTOM OF THE HERD.
WHAT'S THE SCORE?
HE GOES HOME IN A STATE OF NERVOUS ENERVATION. BECAUSE HE SITS AROUND ALL DAY PUTTERING AT NON-SPECIFIC TASKS, HE'S NOT PHYSICALLY EXHAUSTED LIKE HIS FRIENDS WHO WORK ON ASSEMBLY LINES OR DRIVE TRUCKS.
WHO'S WINNING?
HE HAS A STRONG DESIRE TO PROCREATE AND LOVES TO ATTEND CHILDREN'S BIRTHDAY PARTIES. ONLY A PRIMITIVE FEAR OF ETERNAL DAMNATION PREVENTS HIM FROM HAVING NUMEROUS EXTRAMARITAL AFFAIRS.
MUCH OF HIS INCOME IS SPENT ON HOME IMPROVEMENT PROJECTS; HIS BASEMENT WILL NEVER BE FINISHED. TREMENDOUS ATTENTION HAS BEEN LAVISHED ON THE DECORATION OF HIS BATHROOMS.
HE WILL NOT REST UNTIL EVERY SQUARE INCH OF HIS MODEST HOME IS COVERED WITH SOME FORM OF GILT-PLASTIC GEEGAW.
LIKE HIS CO-WORKERS, HE EATS POORLY — FATTY FROZEN FOODS — DRINKS TOO MUCH AND CHAIN-SMOKES. THE INSURANCE COMPANY IS ALWAYS THREATENING TO DROP ME.
THEY CLAIM THE LIBRARY PASTE WE USE IS TOXIC.

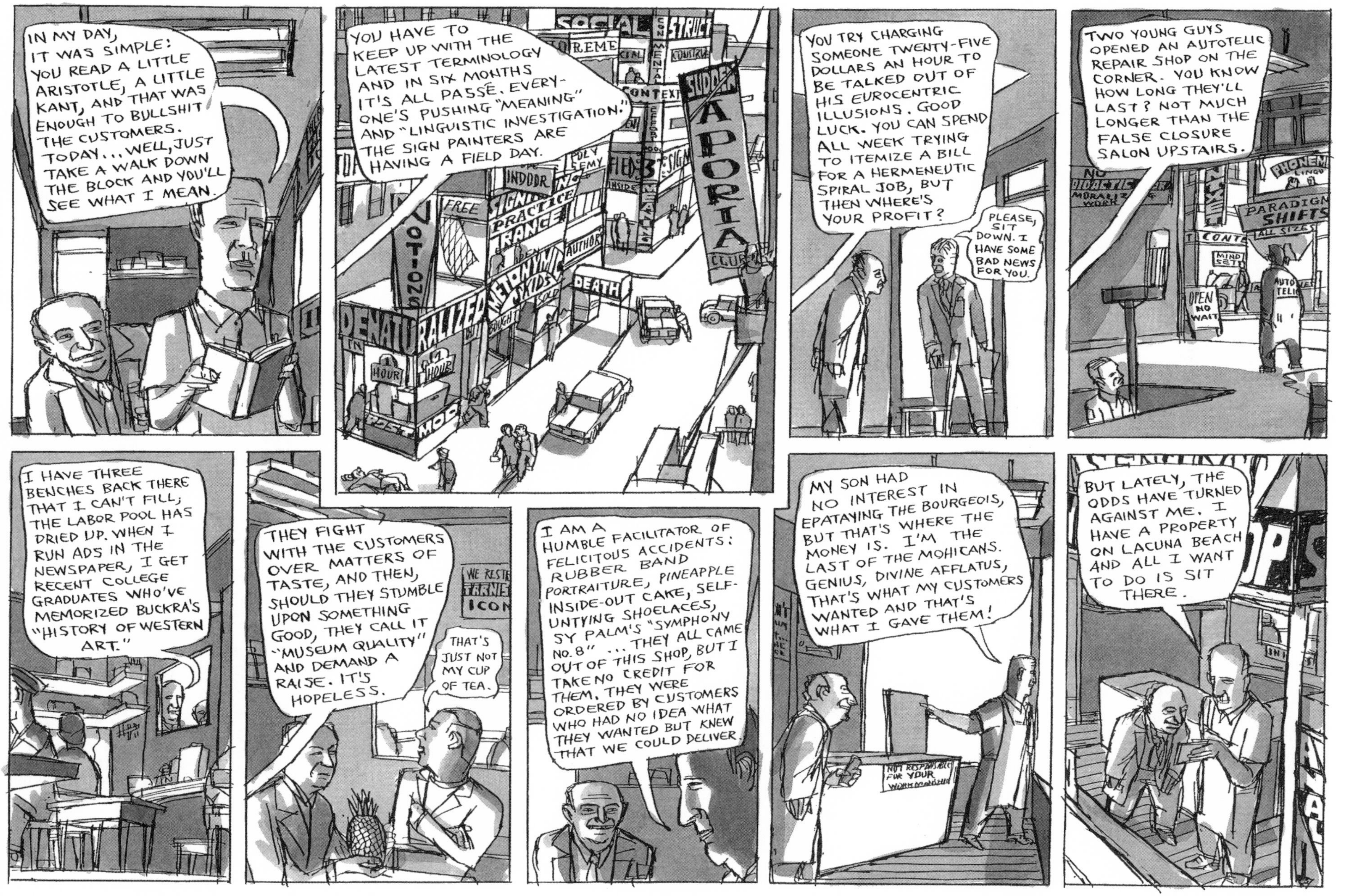
IN MY DAY, IT WAS SIMPLE: YOU READ A LITTLE ARISTOTLE, A LITTLE KANT, AND THAT WAS ENOUGH TO BULLSHIT THE CUSTOMERS. TODAY... WELL, JUST TAKE A WALK DOWN THE BLOCK AND YOU'LL SEE WHAT I MEAN.
YOU HAVE TO KEEP UP WITH THE LATEST TERMINOLOGY AND IN SIX MONTHS IT'S ALL PASSÉ. EVERYONE'S PUSHING "MEANING" AND "LINGUISTIC INVESTIGATION." THE SIGN PAINTERS ARE HAVING A FIELD DAY.
SOCIAL
CONSTRUCT
CONTEXT
SUDDEN
APORIA
CLUB
NOTIONS
DENATURALIZED
METONYMY
DEATH
YOU TRY CHARGING SOMEONE TWENTY-FIVE DOLLARS AN HOUR TO BE TALKED OUT OF HIS EUROCENTRIC ILLUSIONS. GOOD LUCK. YOU CAN SPEND ALL WEEK TRYING TO ITEMIZE A BILL FOR A HERMENEUTIC SPIRAL JOB, BUT THEN WHERE'S YOUR PROFIT?
PLEASE, SIT DOWN. I HAVE SOME BAD NEWS FOR YOU.
TWO YOUNG GUYS OPENED AN AUTOTELIC REPAIR SHOP ON THE CORNER. YOU KNOW HOW LONG THEY'LL LAST? NOT MUCH LONGER THAN THE FALSE CLOSURE SALON UPSTAIRS.
PARADIGM SHIFTS
ALL SIZES
OPEN NO WAIT
I HAVE THREE BENCHES BACK THERE THAT I CAN'T FILL; THE LABOR POOL HAS DRIED UP. WHEN I RUN ADS IN THE NEWSPAPER, I GET RECENT COLLEGE GRADUATES WHO'VE MEMORIZED BUCKRA'S "HISTORY OF WESTERN ART."
THEY FIGHT WITH THE CUSTOMERS OVER MATTERS OF TASTE, AND THEN, SHOULD THEY STUMBLE UPON SOMETHING GOOD, THEY CALL IT "MUSEUM QUALITY" AND DEMAND A RAISE. IT'S HOPELESS.
THAT'S JUST NOT MY CUP OF TEA.
I AM A HUMBLE FACILITATOR OF FELICITOUS ACCIDENTS: RUBBER BAND PORTRAITURE, PINEAPPLE INSIDE-OUT CAKE, SELF-UNTYING SHOELACES, SY PALM'S "SYMPHONY NO. 8" ... THEY ALL CAME OUT OF THIS SHOP, BUT I TAKE NO CREDIT FOR THEM. THEY WERE ORDERED BY CUSTOMERS WHO HAD NO IDEA WHAT THEY WANTED BUT KNEW THAT WE COULD DELIVER.
MY SON HAD NO INTEREST IN EPATAYING THE BOURGEOIS, BUT THAT'S WHERE THE MONEY IS. I'M THE LAST OF THE MOHICANS. GENIUS, DIVINE AFFLATUS, THAT'S WHAT MY CUSTOMERS WANTED AND THAT'S WHAT I GAVE THEM!
NOT RESPONSIBLE FOR YOUR
BUT LATELY, THE ODDS HAVE TURNED AGAINST ME. I HAVE A PROPERTY ON LACUNA BEACH AND ALL I WANT TO DO IS SIT THERE.

YESTERDAY, WHILE SITTING IN MY BOOTH AT THE HORS D'OEUVRE AND DAINTY FOODS SHOW, I BEGAN TO FEEL IT AGAIN: AN IRKSOME FATIGUE AT THE VERY SIGHT OF MY OWN JARS OF PITTED OLIVES.

I HAVEN'T SEEN A PIMIENTO SINCE 1972.

SO THIS MORNING, I PACKED A FEW SAMPLES INTO A BOX AND TOOK A CAB OVER TO SENSUM'S SYMMETRY SHOP...

AND WHAT DO I FIND? A HANDWRITTEN NOTE TAPED TO THE DOOR:

"TO ALL OF MY DEVOTED CUSTOMERS: THE TIME HAS COME TO CLOSE OUR DOORS FOR GOOD. THANK YOU FOR YOUR MANY YEARS OF KIND PATRONAGE..." AND SO ON AND SO FORTH.

I WANDER OUT INTO THE STREET THINKING: "NO PROBLEM, I CAN ASK AROUND AND FIND ANOTHER SYMMETRY SHOP IN THE NEIGHBORHOOD."

EXCUSE ME.

HE LOOKS AT ME LIKE I'M CRAZY...

ASYMMETRY SHOP?

AND THEN IT DAWNS ON ME. A FEW VACANT LOFTS WITH THE OLD SIGNS ARE LEFT—I SEE ONE LITTLE CORNER STAND SELLING HOT FRANKFURT SCHOOL AURAS—BUT OTHERWISE THE STREET'S COMPLETELY TAKEN OVER BY ELECTRONICS WHOLESALERS.

TONIGHT WE SPEAK OF THE BEAUTY SUPPLY DISTRICT IN THE PAST TENSE.

THESE PLACES COME AND GO. I CAN GIVE YOU THE NUMBER OF THE FELLOW WHO REVAMPED OUR MINI-DONUT BOX LAST YEAR. I ASSUME HE'S STILL IN BUSINESS.

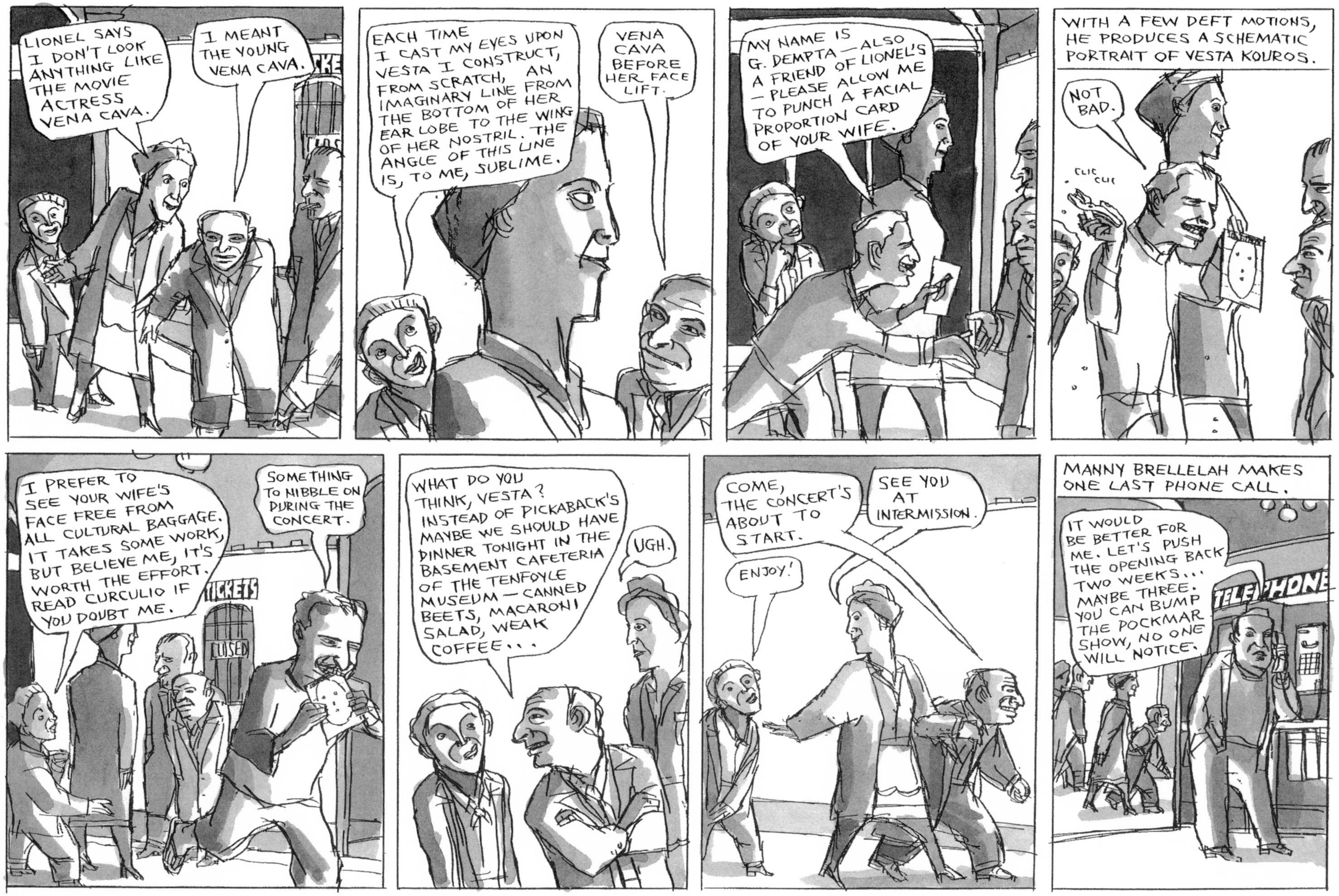
LIONEL SAYS I DON'T LOOK ANYTHING LIKE THE MOVIE ACTRESS VENA CAVA.
I MEANT THE YOUNG VENA CAVA.
EACH TIME I CAST MY EYES UPON VESTA I CONSTRUCT, FROM SCRATCH, AN IMAGINARY LINE FROM THE BOTTOM OF HER EAR LOBE TO THE WING OF HER NOSTRIL. THE ANGLE OF THIS LINE IS, TO ME, SUBLIME.
VENA CAVA BEFORE HER FACE LIFT.
MY NAME IS G. DEMPTA—ALSO A FRIEND OF LIONEL'S —PLEASE ALLOW ME TO PUNCH A FACIAL PROPORTION CARD OF YOUR WIFE.
WITH A FEW DEFT MOTIONS, HE PRODUCES A SCHEMATIC PORTRAIT OF VESTA KOUROS.
NOT BAD.
CLIC CLIC
I PREFER TO SEE YOUR WIFE'S FACE FREE FROM ALL CULTURAL BAGGAGE. IT TAKES SOME WORK, BUT BELIEVE ME, IT'S WORTH THE EFFORT. READ CURCULIO IF YOU DOUBT ME.
SOMETHING TO NIBBLE ON DURING THE CONCERT.
TICKETS
CLOSED
WHAT DO YOU THINK, VESTA? INSTEAD OF PICKABACK'S MAYBE WE SHOULD HAVE DINNER TONIGHT IN THE BASEMENT CAFETERIA OF THE TENFOYLE MUSEUM—CANNED BEETS, MACARONI SALAD, WEAK COFFEE...
UGH.
COME, THE CONCERT'S ABOUT TO START.
SEE YOU AT INTERMISSION.
ENJOY!
MANNY BRELLELAH MAKES ONE LAST PHONE CALL.
IT WOULD BE BETTER FOR ME. LET'S PUSH THE OPENING BACK TWO WEEKS... MAYBE THREE. YOU CAN BUMP THE POCKMAR SHOW, NO ONE WILL NOTICE.
TELEPHONE

THE LIGHTS DIM UPON A ONE-THIRD EMPTY HALL.

SO THEY ALL MEET FOR LUNCH ON WEDNESDAYS.

THE PERFORMER, VIA RADIO CONTROL FROM THE COMFORT OF HIS BEDROOM, RAISES THE "TONGUE" TO BEGIN THE FIRST MOVEMENT.

VESTA WOULD INSIST ON PICKING UP THE CHECK.

SUNK INTO HIS REGULAR SEAT, CAESAR KOUROS IMAGINES THE WORST.

AFTERWARDS THE TWO OF THEM GO BACK TO HIS DIRTY LITTLE APARTMENT TO LOOK THROUGH ART BOOKS.

LIONEL, WHAT DO YOU THINK OF MY HUSBAND'S NEW OLIVE JAR?

AND THEN HIS POWERS OF INVENTION FAIL HIM.

SHE'D TAKE HER SHOES OFF ... BUT WHERE ARE HER TOES?

PLEASE, VESTA, LET'S NOT MIX ART WITH COMMERCE.

THE SCULPTOR MANNY BRELLELAH QUIETLY EATS A DONUT.

IT WAS EVERY ARTIST'S SECRET DREAM: TO BE ABLE TO GO OUT, LIKE AN ORDINARY SHOPPER, AND PICK UP HIS OWN WORK— NO DIFFERENT THAN A CARTON OF MILK— FINISHED, READY TO HANG, WITHOUT THE DISCOMFORT OF CREATION.

I'D SUGGEST A BASIC THEME AND SENSUM WOULD PRODUCE TWO DOZEN VARIATIONS UPON IT, READY TO BE CAST IN BRONZE, I WAS PREOCCUPIED WITH THE TYPEFACE FOR MY INVITATION, THE ANGLE OF THE TRACK LIGHTING, THE CHOICE OF WINE FOR THE OPENING...

MANNUI MINIS

KONRAD MANNUH SHIFTS HIS HEAVY FRAME TO A NEW POSITION.

THIS SEAT WAS NOT MEANT TO ACCOMMODATE A TWENTY-FIRST CENTURY MAN.

SNIFF. WHAT SORT OF BORE BRINGS CHOCOLATE DONUTS TO A CONCERT?

LIONEL PALPUS SITS BELOW A BRIGHTLY LIT EXIT SIGN— A VACANT EXPRESSION ON HIS FACE.

EXIT

THE FUR COAT OF A WOMAN SEATED IN FRONT OF MR. KNIPL BEGINS TO SHED.

COUGH—PALPUS WASN'T KIDDING; THESE REALLY ARE FORTY-DOLLAR —COUGH— SEATS.

HE OPENS HIS PROGRAM TO A FULL-PAGE ADVERTISEMENT FOR AN EXPENSIVE LEATHER POCKET-BOOK AND IS OVERWHELMED BY THE SMELL OF PERFUME.

AH, SNIFF, SNIFF... "PALINODE NO. 6."

A BEADED PURSE FALLS TO THE FLOOR.

"COMPOSED MORE THAN FIFTEEN YEARS AGO ..."

BRANCE

HE SHIFTS HIS WEIGHT FORWARD AND THE SEAT MOVES WITH HIM...

"UNDER THE INFLUENCE OF SIAMESE CATER-WAULING AND THE DRONE OF RADIO-CONTROLLED MODEL AIRPLANES ..."

TO DROP INTO POSITION JUST BELOW THE FALSE CUSHION OF THE SEAT BEFORE HIM.

"THE 'POTSYFILIA' RECEIVES ITS FIRST PUBLIC PERFORMANCE THIS EVENING IN FOYER HALL."

LIONEL PALPUS HAD TOLD HIM OF THESE "LAP SEATS" SPECIALLY DESIGNED FOR THE CONVENIENCE OF THE HALL'S ORIGINAL BENEFACTORS.

IN THOSE DAYS, THE WEALTHY WERE NOT USED TO REINING IN THEIR PASSIONS —EVEN WHEN IN PUBLIC.

SHE'S NO MORE THAN AN INCH ABOVE MY LAP. I CAN FEEL IT WHEN SHE MOVES.

HE FURTIVELY STUDIES THE PEOPLE SEATED TO EITHER SIDE...

A YOUNG GIRL —HER NIECE?— AND A MALE STRANGER WITH THINNING HAIR.

THEN COVERS HIS FACE WITH THE PROGRAM AND SURRENDERS TO THE SMELL OF PERFUME, THE WARMTH OF THE WOMAN'S BODY AND THE DULCET TONES OF THE CREMOLORA.

TWENTY ROWS BACK, CAESAR KOUROS TOYS WITH HIS JAR OF OLIVES.

IF I'VE LOST INTEREST, CAN THE PUBLIC BE FAR BEHIND?

THE JAR SUDDENLY SLIPS FROM HIS SWEATY HANDS...

CAESAR, SHH.

KLINK

AND ROLLS THE LENGTH OF THE CONCERT HALL.

SHH.

SHH.

RIKITADIKITARIKITADIKITA

MR. KNIPL'S REVERIE IS CUT SHORT BY THE LOUD BANG OF A GLASS JAR AGAINST THE FOOT OF HIS SEAT.

SHH!

KNOK

THIRTY SECONDS LATER, THE END OF THE FIRST PART OF JOHNSON'S "RIPSATIK POTSYFILIA" IS GREETED WITH POLITE APPLAUSE,

THE HOUSE LIGHTS COME UP, SIGNALING INTERMISSION.

"KOUROS BRAND, EXTRA-LARGE PITTED OLIVES."

THE SEAT OF THE WOMAN'S DRESS IS SOAKED IN WHAT MR. KNIPL ASSUMES TO BE HIS OWN SEMINAL FLUID.

AH, DR. SENSUM, I DIDN'T KNOW THAT YOU WERE A CONTEMPORARY MUSIC AFICIONADO.

I'M NOT — COLZA JOHNSON IS AN OLD FAMILY FRIEND.

"AH, FOR FIFTEEN MINUTES THE AUDIENCE IS RETURNED TO THE WORLD OF PHYSICAL NECESSITY AND IDLE CHATTER. I BASK IN THE JOYOUS DISCHARGE OF THESE LOWLY HUMAN NEEDS. NO ARTIFICE, NO TRAINING, NO FORMAL RIGOR—IT'S WORTH THE PRICE OF ADMISSION."

"CHEER UP, CAESAR."

THE COMPOSER, COLZA JOHNSON, STATIONS HIMSELF IN THE MEN'S ROOM.

"NOT FIVE MINUTES HAVE ELAPSED AND ALREADY MY MELODIES ARE BASTARDIZED THROUGH SLOPPY WHISTLING!"

"COLZA!"

"CONGRATULATIONS! IT'S ME, RANDALL—ARTHUR SENSUM'S SON—FROM THE SYMMETRY SHOP ON AINSINT AVENUE. DAD'S RETIRED; I WENT INTO MEDICINE... AND YOU'RE DOING WELL: QUARTER-PAGE AD IN THE NEWSPAPER—I COULDN'T MISS IT."

"I'M SORRY. YOU MUST BE CONFUSING ME WITH SOMEONE ELSE."

"AS A KID I HELPED OUT WITH DELIVERIES—YOU WERE A REGULAR! LOTS OF MUSICIANS CAME BY WHEN THEY WERE STUCK, BUT YOU WERE A FAVORITE OF MY FATHER'S. HE NEVER CHARGED YOU A RUSH-FEE FOR THOSE DISSONANT CHORDS IN THE "RIPSATIK POTSYFILIA." THEY SOUNDED GREAT TONIGHT."

"AS FAR AS I KNOW, AINSINT AVENUE IS AN ELECTRONICS WHOLESALE DISTRICT."

A LONG LINE FORMS OUTSIDE OF THE LADIES' ROOM.

"IF ANY OF YOU WOULD CARE TO EXPEDITE THINGS, I HAVE A PERFECTLY GOOD TOILET IN MY APARTMENT JUST ACROSS THE STREET."

AT INTERMISSION, THE VALUE OF ALDO SINO'S UNSOLD TICKETS SUDDENLY INCREASES THREEFOLD.

"THAT'LL BE ONE HUNDRED AND TWENTY-FIVE DOLLARS, EACH."

"WE'RE COLLECTORS WHO RELISH THE IDEA OF AN UNUSED TICKET, AN OPPORTUNITY FOREVER MISSED, PROOF OF AN EMPTY SEAT TO HISTORY. WE CAN'T GET ENOUGH OF THEM."

"FOR INSPIRATION I TAKE BRISK WALKS AND SMOKE HASHISH. NO ARTIST WORTH HIS SALT WOULD PATRONIZE A SYMMETRY SHOP. THE DISCOURSE ON ART TAKES PLACE IN UNIVERSITY LECTURE HALLS, BRIGHT, WELL-VENTILATED STUDIOS AND MUSEUM CAFETERIAS—NOT IN THE FOUL SECOND-STORY, WHILE-U-WAIT, PAY-AS-YOU-GO WHOREHOUSES THAT YOU REFER TO. WITHOUT A PROLONGED RELATIONSHIP OF LOVE AND MUTUAL RESPECT BETWEEN THE ARTIST AND HIS MUSE, ALL THAT CAN RESULT IS A MALFORMED, CRETINOUS OFFSPRING."

"JULIUS! GLAD YOU CAME?"

"THE TACTLESS MORON! HIS FATHER WOULD HAVE KNOWN BETTER THAN TO SHOW UP AT A CUSTOMER'S WORLD PREMIERE."

MANNY BRELLELAH AND HIS COMPANION LEAVE THE HALL.

I CAN'T CONCENTRATE. LET'S GO SOMEWHERE FOR DESSERT.

TAXI!

TO THE TENFOYLE MUSEUM — AND STEP ON IT. THEY CLOSE AT NINE.

THE DRIVER TAKES A SHORTCUT ACROSS AINSINT AVENUE.

THE CLOSING OF SENSUM'S SYMMETRY SHOP MARKS THE END OF A SMOOTH WORKING RELATIONSHIP BETWEEN THE ARTIST AND HIS SUPPLIER OF INSPIRATION. THE FABRIC OF SOCIETY HAS BEEN RENT ASUNDER; I FEEL THE GUST OF A PHILISTINE'S BREATH UPON MY HIND-QUARTERS.

THE BEAUTY SUPPLY DISTRICT WAS NOT DRIVEN OUT BY HIGH RENTS TO RELOCATE IN SOME SUBURBAN STRIP MALL WHERE IT CAN CONTINUE TO FUNCTION VIA MAIL ORDER.

IT DEVELOPED ON AINSINT AVENUE FOR A REASON: THAT NON-RENEWABLE NATURAL RESOURCE — LUCK — WAS ONCE FOUND THERE IN ABUNDANCE AND HAS NOW BEEN EXHAUSTED.

I'M SURE THAT IN SOME OTHER PART OF THE WORLD THERE IS ANOTHER BEAUTY SUPPLY DISTRICT STILL THRIVING AS OURS ONCE DID. I IMAGINE IT RUNS TWENTY-FOUR HOURS A DAY ON DOG-POWER AND SEAWEED...

IN A FEW MONTHS' TIME WE'D ACCOMMODATE OURSELVES TO THEIR STRANGELY BEAUTIFUL PRODUCTS. PERHAPS ONE ITEM WILL CATCH THE EYE OF AN ENTER-PRISING YOUNG IMPORTER. WHO KNOWS?

GO ON, HAVE ANYTHING YOU LIKE.

POUND CAKE, CHERRY PIE, TAPIOCA PUDDING...

OVER COFFEE, MANNY BRELLELAH BEGINS TO SKETCH UNCONSCIOUSLY, ON A PAPER NAPKIN, THE FORM OF HIS NEXT SCULPTURE.

HMM, NOT BAD.

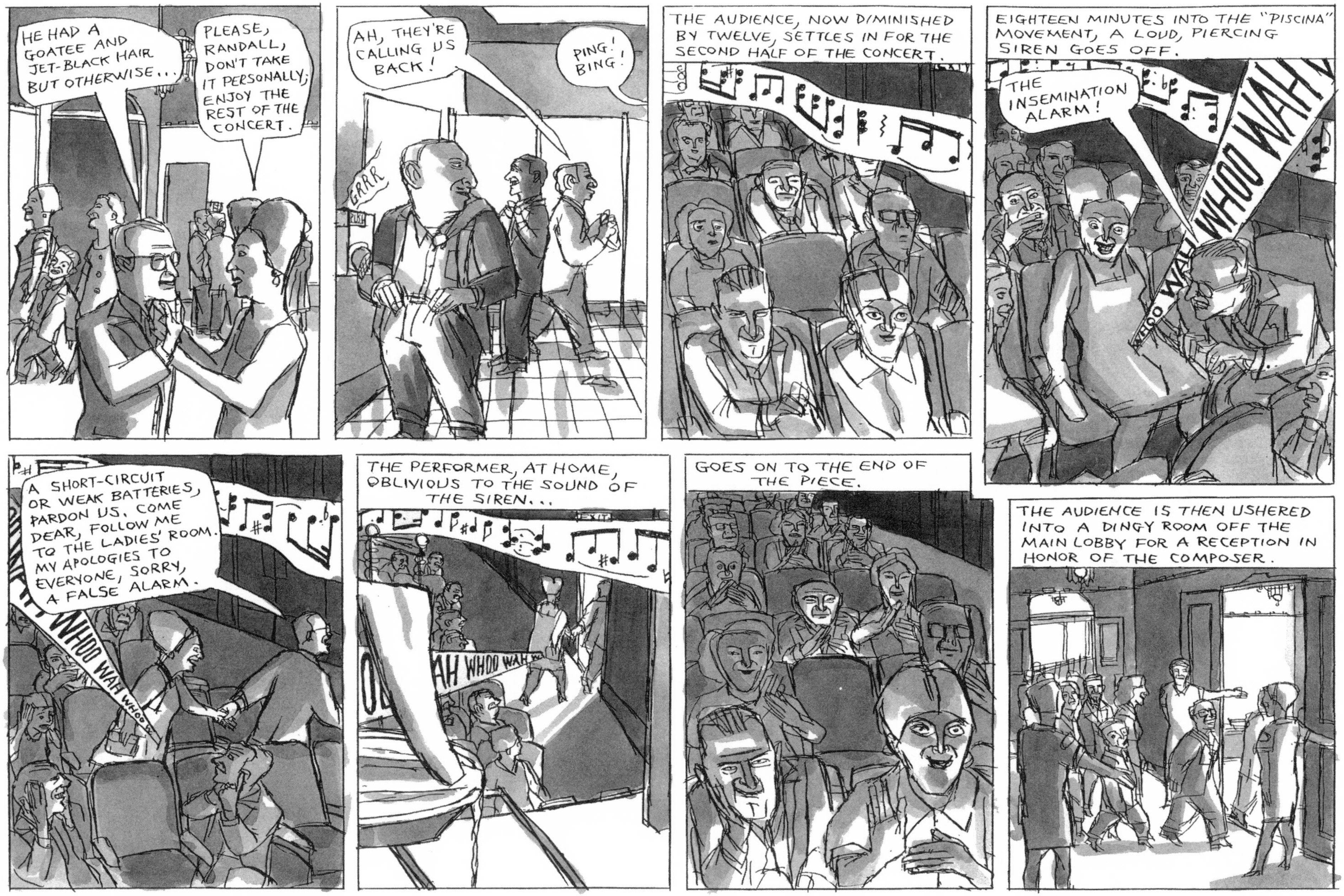
HE HAD A GOATEE AND JET-BLACK HAIR BUT OTHERWISE...
PLEASE, RANDALL, DON'T TAKE IT PERSONALLY; ENJOY THE REST OF THE CONCERT.
GRRR
AH, THEY'RE CALLING US BACK!
PING! BING!
THE AUDIENCE, NOW DIMINISHED BY TWELVE, SETTLES IN FOR THE SECOND HALF OF THE CONCERT.
EIGHTEEN MINUTES INTO THE "PISCINA" MOVEMENT, A LOUD, PIERCING SIREN GOES OFF.
THE INSEMINATION ALARM!
WHOO WAH
A SHORT-CIRCUIT OR WEAK BATTERIES, PARDON US. COME DEAR, FOLLOW ME TO THE LADIES' ROOM. MY APOLOGIES TO EVERYONE, SORRY, A FALSE ALARM.
THE PERFORMER, AT HOME, OBLIVIOUS TO THE SOUND OF THE SIREN...
EXIT
GOES ON TO THE END OF THE PIECE.
THE AUDIENCE IS THEN USHERED INTO A DINGY ROOM OFF THE MAIN LOBBY FOR A RECEPTION IN HONOR OF THE COMPOSER.

A NICE SPREAD: CHEESE, SALAMI, CRACKERS, MUSTARD ...COULD USE SOME OLIVES.

WHY SHOULD A SIREN IN THE MIDDLE OF A QUIET PASSAGE BOTHER ME?

PALPUS KNOWS OF A LATE-NIGHT SUPERMARKET...

EXCUSE ME, I'LL BE RIGHT BACK.

OLIVES?

JUST AROUND THE CORNER.

HUMANITY FOODS

OPEN 24

IN THE BLINDING GLARE OF ARTIFICIAL DAYLIGHT, HE FINDS HIS WAY TO THE CONDIMENTS AISLE...

PICKLES

AND IS IMMEDIATELY DRAWN TO A PARTICULAR JAR OF OLIVES.

"ENTASIS BRAND."

HE LOOKS AT THE SMALL WHITE STICKER ON ITS LID, RETURNS IT TO THE SHELF, AND BEGINS TO COMPARE PRICES.

"INVIVO BRAND," 6 OZ. FOR $1.29; "REALIA BROS.," 7½ OZ. FOR $1.79...

HE MAKES A FINAL CHOICE...

"KOUROS BRAND," 7 OZ. FOR 89¢.

RELISH PICKLES

AND RUSHES TO THE CASHIER.

ITEMS OR LESS

EXIT

AFTER FIFTEEN YEARS AT SENSUM'S SYMMETRY SHOP, JOHNNY AHSALA HAD A HARD TIME FINDING WORK.

HE'S INCAPABLE OF FOLLOWING SIMPLE DIRECTIONS.

NO, NO, A 7½!

IN THE WEEK FOLLOWING HIS LAY-OFF, HE WENT THROUGH A SUCCESSION OF LOW-PAYING, MENIAL JOBS.

YOU CAN'T BE A DATA STORAGE BACK-UP BOY IF YOU REFUSE TO REPEAT YOURSELF.

HIS HOME IMPROVEMENT PROJECTS WERE ABANDONED FOR LACK OF FUNDS.

WHAT ARE WE GOING TO DO ABOUT THE ELECTRIC TOOTH-PASTE DISPENSER IN THE SECOND-FLOOR GUEST BATHROOM?

LIKE A BRUTE NEEDING TO EXPEND ITS EXCESS ENERGY, HE'D WALK THE STREETS AT NIGHT.

SHOULD HE COME ACROSS A MAN OR WOMAN WHOSE COAT LAPELS HE DIDN'T LIKE, OR WHOSE HAIRCUT DIDN'T FIT THEIR FACE...

HE WOULD SET UPON THEM WITH A SAVAGE FURY:

TEARING LIMBS FROM THEIR SOCKETS;

MASHING CRANIUMS WITH HIS BARE FISTS.

CAESAR KOUROS RETURNS TO THE RECEPTION...

TRY THE GOOSE LIVER PATÉ.

IMAGINE A BAKERY WITHOUT FLOUR; A LIQUOR STORE WITHOUT ALCOHOL.

AND MAKES HIMSELF A CANAPÉ.

HMM!

CAESAR, DON'T SPOIL YOUR APPETITE.

AS EACH SHOP CLOSED, THE GROWING NUMBER OF DESPERATE CUSTOMERS OVERWHELMED THE SHOPS STILL IN BUSINESS.

LIKE A BURNING BUILDING, IN WHICH EACH FLOOR GIVES WAY UNDER THE COMBINED WEIGHT OF THE FLOORS ABOVE, THE WHOLE DISTRICT COLLAPSED WITHIN A MONTH.

QUITE A CATASTROPHE. WHO WANTS TO SIT IN A CONCERT HALL ON SUCH A NIGHT?

YOU HEARD THE ALARM.

BUT IS IT POSSIBLE! THROUGH A FUR COAT, FOUR LAYERS OF CLOTHING AND A HEAVILY UPHOLSTERED SEAT?

PALPUS, HE WOULD KNOW THE ANSWER.

WHERE'S LIONEL? WE HAVE TO GO TO THE BATHROOM!

THE PERFORMER — A YOUNG MAN IN PAJAMAS — FINALLY ARRIVES BY CAB AND IS GIVEN A ROUND OF APPLAUSE.

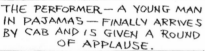

A NICE SPREAD: CHEESE, SALAMI, CRACKERS, MUSTARD...

...COULD USE SOME OLIVES.